IMPLANT

For Victor, my link to the past, and who is more than a great friend

Affectionately,

Don

A novel

by

Donald R. Klein, M.D.

Implant

Copyright © 1999 by Donald R. Klein, M.D.

All rights reserved. No part of this book may be reproduced or utilized in any form or by any means, electronic or mechanical, including photocopying, recording or by any information storage and retrieval system, without permission in writing from the Publisher. Inquiries should be addressed to

Harker-Schumann-New York
137 Running Water Street
Georgetown, TX 78628

Library of Congress Catalog Card Number 99-60121

ISBN 0-9669773-4-3

Printed in the United States of America
at Morgan Printing in Austin, Texas

This work is dedicated to the two million women with breast implants who have survived the social and political pressures of the silicone controversy and who have held steadfastly to their convictions that the improvement of the quality of life is an honorable goal.

> *I am convinced that the desire to formulate truths is a virulent disease.*
> — William James (1842-1910)
> American psychologist and philosopher

Chapter 1

The deep velvet black was turning into dark gray. First his left index finger stirred ever so slightly. Then the right hand twitched. Then increasing movements of limbs, all involuntary and disconnected. Lighter gray. Flashes of white light. The eyelids separated into narrow slits. The earliest signs of consciousness were returning, but not with much gratitude. He felt as though he were riding on the crest of an enormous wave with accelerating swiftness, uncontrollably hurled onto a jagged and rocky shore. Then the unbearable ringing in his ears was coupled with a relentless pounding, pounding at his temples. He was alive. His eyes opened wider. He began to focus.

Awareness. He found himself prone and surprised that waves were not splashing about him. He was dry or almost. He could feel that his head was turned on his left ear. Even through the ringing and pounding he was aware of a wetness about his face. Unsteadily he raised his left hand to touch it. Slowly he moved the hand toward his barely focusing eyes. Red. Yes, definitely blood. He had to move. He had to get up. Cautiously on all fours, he raised his aching body. Standing was not possible. Finally, with all the effort he could draw from somewhere deep within himself, he lifted his head and clumsily flopped into an awkward sitting position, supporting his entire mass on his buttocks, left heel and right elbow. As his vision cleared he could focus on individual objects, but nothing looked familiar.

At the same time he was becoming aware of pain, total body pain. He knew he was injured and bleeding. Where was he? He tried to think. Too painful. He saw a door and crawled toward it slowly, inch by inch. Thankfully it was slightly ajar. A bathroom. A toilet. The sight of the latter stimulated severe nausea. He couldn't make it to the bowl before vomiting and retching consumed him. Again darkness enveloped him. He found himself reaching from the bathroom floor to the sink above. He pulled himself up. At last he could stand! Painfully he raised his head and looked into the mirror. He saw the image of a man he did not recognize. He moved this way and that. It was real. Ghastly! Panic! He felt his legs giving way. He grasped the sink bowl for support and tried to think. Nothing, absolutely nothing! Again the mirror. Something had to come. Staring back at him was a face covered with blood and a mess of dark hair matted with drying clots. Still no recognition.

Instinctively he turned on the water and gingerly began to splash his face and dab at it. Panic and pain obliterated logic. He gave up on the mirror and turned to lean on the doorjamb. He looked about and saw a bed in the room from which he had come. He staggered to it and fell upon it. A little more comfortable. He knew he had overdone it and had to get into a horizontal position. Maybe he would die here. He didn't care. He prayed for the previous oblivion. It came, and as it approached he wondered briefly if it was unconsciousness, sleep, death. It didn't matter if only he got relief from the worst feeling he had ever known.

Chapter 2

Marcus Hamilton was born in 1952 in Cleveland, Ohio, the only son of Elizabeth and James Hamilton. His grandfather had been a country doctor in the Midwest and was beloved by his patients. During those hard days of the Big Depression, when the Melton Steel Plant closed, the old Doc was often paid in chickens or eggs or pies or not at all. It really didn't matter. They were his flock and his responsibility. Doc's two sons were Daniel and James, who were expected to follow their father's path. They were coached and included in all household medical conversations from early childhood. While Danny, the older, was always more interested in baseball, girls and anything he could get away with, James was curious, fascinated and always asking questions. He knew all about Jimmy Elder's appendix, Mrs. Lathem's heart flutters and Miss Sally's hypochondria. His father said that Miss Sally needed more horseback riding... whatever that meant. James accepted these discussions as natural. He absorbed them and they became part of him.

There was no question that James would have a medical career. His school grades were at the top of the class and Harvard was the only option. He was accepted into medical school there and did well. It was expected. It was also expected that James would go into practice with his father and eventually take over, but that was not to be. While at Harvard his older brother, Danny, had already graduated law school and was earning a more than decent income by having joined the prestigious Boston law firm of Peterson, Briggs, Cohen and Day. The family had long ago given up on a medical career for Danny. After all, he was doing well and the world seemed to need lawyers too.

Although James knew he was the favorite son, he envied Danny and his easy success. It was tough being the favorite. He remembered the Depression years all too well and longed for fancy cars, girls, clothes and a better life than he had known. He met Elizabeth Fairbanks at a Radcliff mixer. She was pretty, witty and the only daughter of Thomas Fairbanks, the CEO of The Ohio Union Bank and Trust Co. in Columbus. Through Elizabeth and the Fairbanks family he became familiar with finance, theater, country clubs. He absorbed these like a sponge.

The wedding was planned for June just after James's graduation from Harvard. It was more than a Columbus wedding. It was the event of the year. The Hamiltons felt out of place at first but the Fairbanks family doted over them and never left them alone for a moment. This was not so much out of kindness as it was to ensure that the new country cousins would not be an embarrassment at such a socially prominent occasion. The Hamiltons were completely surprised when they were invited to stay in Columbus for a few days to unwind after the wedding while the young couple honeymooned in Barbados. Naturally Tom Fairbanks paid for the honeymoon. The Hamiltons accepted the invitation reluctantly, but it was the right thing to do.

Implant

During the visit, Tom suggested that he and Doc go to the Club, have a drink and a nice talk. Tom wore white slacks and a silk sport shirt. Doc felt foolish in his dark suit, white shirt and tie. The entire scene was foreign to him. He may as well have been on another planet. They ordered and Tom began, "I'm so pleased that Jim has decided to remain in Columbus and accept the offer at Ohio State for his cardiology residency. As I'm sure you know, it's the best program in the state. With Willis Casper, it would have to be. I have a surprise for you, Doc. Willis will be joining us for lunch. I knew you would be pleased to meet your son's new mentor." It was a done deal. Doc Hamilton was smart enough to realize that. James had been a good boy, graduated Harvard, married well and it was his life after all. Secretly he was crushed. Now at the frontier of retirement he longed to work with his son, to break him in and to have him take over the country practice. He wanted desperately to be his son's mentor but he never said a word. He was cordial to Willis Casper. Reserved but cordial. He would never do anything to jeopardize his son's future.

James and Elizabeth, following the cardiology residency, made their home in Cleveland after Willis Casper pushed a few buttons for his friend, Tom. He had a huge line of credit at the Ohio Union Bank. But in all fairness he also did it for James, who showed every sign of becoming a star in the field. James was offered an assistant professorship at Cleveland Memorial, which he happily and gratefully accepted. After a year Marcus was born.

Under the nurturing wings of loving parents, Marcus went to private school, was introduced to symphony, theater, museums and a good dose of interscholastic sports. Beneath it all was the absolute expectation of a medical career. Marc went through his teenage rebellion by knowing how to push all the right buttons. He threatened to go into business, which didn't seem to bother

Elizabeth at all. When that didn't elicit a significant response, he told his father he wanted to be a lawyer like his Uncle Danny. That sent a chill down James's spine. When Marc really wanted to get to them, he said he wasn't going to go to college at all and wanted to become a citizen of the world, whatever the hell that meant.

There were some heated arguments and he certainly got his parents' attention. Of course that was what the kid wanted. Nevertheless, medicine was in his blood, in his genes, an indivisible part of him. There were a few indiscretions with girls, nothing serious, thank God. Then there were a few drinking sprees with a group of "bad friends," as Elizabeth called them. Finally things seemed to settle down. He went to Ohio State University, did reasonably well and was accepted into medical school there, much to the relief of his parents. Internship followed at Cleveland General Hospital. He didn't even apply to Memorial where his father was still actively practicing. He felt strongly independent and knew that at Memorial it would be impossible not to be identified as the son of Dr. James Hamilton.

He performed his duties well but had a fiery temper and wouldn't take any crap off of any nurses, senior residents or staff men. He made more than a few enemies along the way. On his surgery rotation he was assigned to scrub for the first time in his life with Richard Welch, the notorious plastic surgeon known as the SOB of Cleveland General. He knew the assignment was no accident.

Welch was already scrubbing when Marc approached and introduced himself as the intern assigned for the day. Welch was short and round. His fat face looked overstuffed with very few lines although he was over sixty years old. His small piercing eyes and thin lips were menacing. Marc wondered if that frozen face could ever smile. Welch began, "You're unshaven and look like shit!"

"Dr. Welch, if you'll pay less attention to my appearance and more to your miserable personality, we may get through this scrub!" Welch glowered at Marc over his half glasses, but there was absolute silence. Once in the operating room, Welch let Marc have it! Everything he did was wrong and of course that was expected, but to the horror of the o.r. personnel, Marc didn't let a single sarcastic comment from Welch pass without a zinging retort. "You've got a big enough mouth! Why don't you use it to teach me?" The supervisor nearly passed out. The resident kicked Marc under the table. He got the message. This time he had gone too far. He began to tremble. Welch ever observant, noticed and said, "What's the matter, kid? Surgery too much for you?" No smart answer this time. Marc was convinced that his brief medical career was over before it had barely begun. Perhaps a talk with Uncle Danny about law school would now be a serious consideration

The case was finally over. He had no idea what it had been all about. For God's sake, he was stationed to retract something under the arm of the scrub nurse! He couldn't even see the surgical field. Still on stage, Marc stormed out walking rapidly toward the doctors' lounge, partly angry but mostly terrified. Here it came! Welch was fast on his heels catching up with him. "Hamilton, wait!" Walking papers for sure! Then the unbelievable happened. Welch caught up with Marc, put his arm around him and said, "Have you ever given any thought to plastic surgery? I wish you'd consider it for your free rotation. Come on my service. I'll teach you a few tricks." Marc's mouth opened in disbelief. He wondered if the prerequisite to becoming a plastic surgeon was first to be a real class sonofabitch. "Think about it," said Welch over his shoulder as he walked away. Marc did and in later years he came to realize that this incredible moment with Welch was actually the origin of his career.

Chapter 3

It was early October in 1989 in Paris. The leaves were gone and so were the tourists. A damp, chilling wind penetrated the city. The clouds were heavy and ominous, and it looked and smelled like rain. It was 5:15 and already dark. Ashley Barton sat at the bar at La Coupole slowly sipping her glass of Montrachet. She sat with her back to the restaurant, gazing expectantly out the large picture window. She was not aware of being hungrily observed by the men at the bar, as well as by the envious women. Her honey blond hair, shoulder length, framed an oval face with soft, transparent skin and amazingly balanced features. The prominent cheek bones complemented her deep green eyes, which sparkled even in the low, dim lighting of the bar. Her nose had the slightest hint of an upward tilt. Her lips were generous, full, and sensuous. She was a natural beauty at thirty-two and could easily pass for twenty-five.

She wore a long-sleeved navy blue blouse, open at the neck, with brass buttons down the front. The blouse was fitted just enough to reveal her lovely breast contours and just enough to make any man dream and wonder. Her sheath skirt was tan and simple. With her legs crossed, the short slit at the bottom lead the eyes to slender, shapely calves and delicate ankles. Three-inch plain brown leather pumps completed the picture. She wore no jewelry, as if she instinctively knew it could only detract from her quiet elegance. On the stool beside her she had placed her navy cashmere coat and small navy handbag.

She glanced at her leather-band watch. It was past six o'clock. He was over an hour late. That wasn't at all like Marc. She was getting worried. They had agreed to meet here after he made a few finishing touches on his presentation to the Aesthetic Plastic Surgery Society of France. She had gone to the Louvre and then took a taxi to Montparnasse to meet him at exactly five o'clock, the agreed upon time. He was punctual to a fault. With everything that had been going on during the past week, events that occurred in rapid succession, she was more than worried. She was frightened.

Ashley found the public telephone and rang the room. Ten rings. No answer. Maybe he was having trouble finding a taxi during rush hour. She didn't want to miss him, so she decided to wait. She was churning inside. She ordered another Montrachet. Perhaps it would calm her. He would walk in any moment all apologetic with explanations. At least she prayed so.

Chapter 4
1979

Marc was glad he had made the decision to go to Cleveland General. It had one of the few rotating internships remaining. He had three months of internal medicine experience, three months of obstetrics and gynecology, three months of general surgery and finally three months elective. This was prior to his commitment to a residency program. It was a tough year, but one that seemed to make sense to him. Fresh out of medical school he simply didn't know what he wanted.

The new concept was to begin the first year of residency immediately, as green as a sapling. He didn't feel that he could make such an important decision without knowing more about what was available and hopefully finding where he belonged. He knew that he was surgically oriented, but that was as far as it went. There was something about the instant result, the immediate gratification of fixing it now, that attracted him. The thought of pills and injections and waiting for an uncertain outcome didn't suit his needs. It was the drama of the operating theater, the lights, the smells, working with his hands that turned him on. Being constantly on guard, ever watchful and living closer to the edge was more than what he wanted. It was what he needed.

He took his elective three months in plastic and reconstructive surgery. Dr. Richard Welch kept his word. They worked together every day. The two of them were almost a comical sight in the operating room. Welch was short, round faced and had an enormous paunch. It was just short of a miracle that his arms could reach the surgical site. His thick stubby fingers belied their sensitivity and agility. At six feet two Marc towered over him. Even through his scrubs a lean and muscular form was evident. His long arms led to strong and yet delicate fingers. Although his face was mostly concealed by cap and mask, the strong jaw line was unmistakable. His full brows accentuated large, alert hazel eyes, always intent and always seeking and absorbing. At the end of a case when he shed the cap and mask there was a face, not actually handsome but very attractive. At least this was the composite opinion of the o.r. nurses, especially when his tousled light brown hair fell carelessly upon his forehead.

Welch discussed each new case and made him observe and study the shape and form. He tought Marc to see with new eyes. He grilled him mercilessly in surgical anatomy and pounded into him the importance of the nerve supply and vascular structures that had to be saved to preserve normal function. "Dr. Hamilton, stop! Put the retractor down. Look at that neck defect. How do we close it? Think, damn it, think! Which is the best option? Use your imagination, man. We'll stand here all day until I get the right answer." Welch made Marc encircle the hand bearing the instrument so he could feel every subtle, delicate movement. He was the best teacher Marc would ever have. The long hard days at Memorial mellowed Marc. He learned to control his temper. He learned respect for his teacher. He engrossed himself in plastic surgery and studied and learned.

There had developed between them a father-son type of relationship. This was out of character for Welch, who had divorced two wives and virtually deserted six kids. Perhaps in his declining years he had a need to pass on his vast knowledge. Perhaps it was his way of achieving a measure of academic, if not genetic, immortality. He didn't want all those years of precious experience to be lost. Undoubtedly this was egotistical. However that was Richard Welch, and it wasn't all bad.

Dr. Marcus Hamilton was now certain of his goal, and that was to become a plastic surgeon. It would take a lot more formal training, and he wondered about his chances of getting into a good teaching program. Despite Welch's excellence, Cleveland General did not have a formal plastic surgery residency. There simply wasn't enough teaching material to satisfy Board requirements. Marc knew he would have to leave.

One morning over coffee in the doctors' lounge Welch asked Marc about his plans for the future. Marc told him about the three applications he had made for general surgery residency programs, a prerequisite for plastic surgery, and that he was waiting to hear about acceptances. "Wrong," said Welch. With that he drew an envelope from his pocket and handed it to Marc. "Two weeks from tomorrow you have an appointment with Allen Greenberg at Texas University Hospital."

"You mean the chief of plastic there?"

"You got it."

"But I need my general surgery first, don't I?"

"I've told him about you and he wants to meet you. If he likes what he sees and hears, he'll set up the general surgery and have a place waiting for you, if you don't fuck up. Hamilton, please don't fuck it up!"

"Dr. Welch, I don't know what to say! That's a real plum! I..."

"Just get your ass to Houston. I've already set up your leave with administration here. I'll see you when you get back, and don't disappoint me or I'll have your nuts."

"I, I... Thanks." He took the envelope and turned his face toward the window.

When Marc arrived at Houston International Airport, he took a taxi directly to Texas University Hospital. It was going to be tight, and he told the cab driver to step on it. It was already 2:05. His appointment with Dr. Greenberg was for 2:45. The fact that the plane was late made no difference. At least he had learned this much about plastic surgery. Excuses were universally unacceptable. He was determined not to be late.

At 2:35 the cab pulled up to the main entrance. He ran to the reception desk in the lobby and asked for directions to the department of plastic and reconstructive surgery. The white-haired woman volunteer said, "Fourth floor. Take the second bank of elevators on the left. Go down the corridor in front of you and turn right. It's just there. You can't miss it." She smiled politely. The Texas accent was unmistakable.

Marc found the office of the Chairman of the Department of Plastic and Reconstructive Surgery. He entered and was greeted by an attractive young woman who eyed him from head to toe. Although this made him very nervous, he remained in complete control. He had thought he was dressed well for the occasion. He prayed that his fly was zipped but he didn't dare check. He quickly glanced at his watch. 2:47. The young woman asked, "Dr. Hamilton?" No smile.

"Yes Ma'am."

"Professor Greenberg is expecting you. Let me introduce you." She knocked on the mahogany door to the right and preceded Marc into a lavishly decorated room, oriental in style and impeccable in taste. "Professor Greenberg, this is Dr. Marcus Hamilton." Greenberg looked at his watch and then looked up.

"How do you do?" Marc noted his firm handshake. "Please take this chair," he said, gesturing toward a high-backed chair beside him.

"It's a pleasure to meet you, sir. It's kind of you to take the time to see me," said Marc. Greenberg was much younger than he had expected. He was in his late forties and graying at the temples and not at all handsome. His nose was too long but in proportion to the elongated face. Even through the loose white clinical coat he wore, he appeared to be thin and wiry. Deep forehead furrows gave the appearance of constant worry. His eyes were large and brown and his gaze seemed to miss nothing. So this was the newest star on the plastic surgical horizon. Marc knew that he had gained his reputation during his residency by doing most of the research on silicone breast implants in the late 1950s. His work was legendary and was directly responsible for the development of the breast prothesis currently in use.

"I trust you had a good flight. How is Richard? I haven't seen him since the last national meeting when he spoke so highly of you." Somewhat embarrassed, Marc said, "He's very well, sir, and sends his best regards."

"I understand you're interested in our plastic surgery program."

"Yes, sir, I am."

"Dr. Welch says you have good hands. Do you?"

"Well, I try, sir."

"Don't be modest, Dr. Hamilton. Tell me whether or not you're good. Please don't waste my time."

"I think I'm good, but I need training."

"Good, an honest answer, and training is what you can get here. I can't make you any promises. You'll have to prove yourself in general surgery and then we'll see. It will be tough, I assure you. I'll expect you to assist in surgery every free moment you have. In addition you'll have to put long hours into the clinics and into significant research projects. Of course this is during your general surgery training. At this institution we expect you to be published several times before you finish the entire program."

"Yes, sir, I understand." He was burning for the opportunity.

"While you are here, let's see if we can track down Gallsworthy. I think he's in the clinic today." Marc knew that Charles Gallsworthy was the head of general surgery at the university. That was the beginning, and everything hinged on him.

They found Gallsworthy teaching his residents in the clinic. Greenberg introduced Marc to him and then excused himself to return to his office. Before departing he shook hands with Marc and asked to be remembered to Richard Welch.

Gallsworthy was about five foot ten, medium build, about fifty with balding red hair and a smile that wasn't a smile at all. It was a cynical grin. He looked bored and promised to be boring. "So you're Welch's fair haired boy! Well, come join us for rounds, if you care to," said Gallsworthy in not a very cordial manner. There were five residents attentively following the chief and hanging on his every word. A short dark-haired young man fell a little behind to introduce himself to the newcomer. He whispered, "Hamilton, I'm Dave Stein, first year. Don't let the schmuck intimidate you. It's just his way of being sweet. Are you going to be part of this team?"

"Don't know but I hope so."

When rounds were over, Gallsworthy turned to Marc and said in a very matter-of-fact and seemingly uninterested manner, "We'll let you know in a few weeks." Marc's heart sank. This did not sound promising, but it was his cue to leave. He shook hands with Gallsworthy and thanked him. He nodded a curt goodbye to Dave, who nodded back with a concealed thumbs up sign. He took a cab back to the airport. On the flight home he really didn't know what to think. He had arrived with hope and was leaving with anxiety. He had no idea of where he stood or what his chances were. Maybe he should call Uncle Danny.

When he returned to Cleveland General, he told Dr. Welch about the Houston experience. "You gave it your best shot, didn't you?" said Welch. That didn't help much. Marc wanted that residency more than he had ever wanted anything in his whole life. He had to get it. He had to! He had always seemed to have a fairly tight control over the way things went for him. He couldn't just let things happen. He had the urgent need to make things happen. It was this compulsiveness and determined ego that were his blessing as well as his curse. It was precisely this that made the days following Houston unbearable. He felt impotent. He was completely at the mercy of others, absolute strangers. Why should they care about him? They had plenty of choices for residents in general surgery. So he could go somewhere else! Yes, of course, somewhere else! After all, he hadn't planned on Texas University Hospital anyway. That was Welch's brilliant idea, the sonofabitch! He had gotten his hopes up for nothing.

The ensuing days were torture. He went through them hoping, sometimes praying, an experience fairly uncommon to Marcus Hamilton. Mostly he tried to convince himself that he really didn't give a shit. He worked with Welch but they barely spoke. Welch didn't press him. Finally, nearly three weeks later, he received a registered letter at Memorial from the department of general surgery, University Hospital, Houston, Texas. He went into the men's room, locked himself into a cubicle and tore it open:

> Dear Dr. Hamilton,
>
> It is with much pleasure that I inform you of your approval by the Hospital Board of Regents as a first-year resident in the Department of General Surgery at The Texas University Hospital at Houston. Should you decide to accept the appointment, we would appreciate a confirmation to that effect at your earliest convenience. You may contact me at the Office of Administration any day, Monday through Friday, between 9:00 AM and 4:00 PM. Your presence at the hospital would be required on Tuesday, July 2nd, at 2:00 PM for orientation and a conference with Dr. Charles Galsworthy.
>
> I shall be pleased to assist you with off campus housing through a referral service. If I can assist you in any other manner, please do not hesitate to call upon me.
>
> Very truly yours,
>
> Margaret Green
> Administrative Secretary
> Department of General Surgery
>
> cc: Dr. Charles Galsworthy/ mg

He got it! And the old sonofabitch had gotten it for him!

It was Friday morning and it was to be the last time Marcus Hamilton would ever scrub with Richard Welch. Neither one tried to think about that. A few days before, Marc had mentioned his acceptance to Welch. The older man acknowledged with a simple nod. Nothing more. Had he secretly known about it all along? While they were dressing in the locker room Welch said, "I expect you to write to me once in a while." That was the closest thing to emotion that he could allow himself. Understanding this, Marc nodded affirmatively, put on his clinical coat and left the room without another word. Words were not necessary. They understood one another.

Marc was excited and busy making the arrangements for the move to Houston. His parents had prepared a farewell dinner for him and a few close friends on Saturday night. When Elizabeth had him alone for a moment after the guests had left she asked, "Marc, how much money will you be earning in Houston?"

"About $18,000 a year, Mom."

"Not very generous, are they!"

"Now, Mom, it's a teaching institution, and I do get meals and laundry free."

"Where will you live?"

"I'm not sure yet, but they will help me make arrangements. Please stop worrying. It'll be fine."

"Marc, now, if you need a little extra, you know Dad and I will be happy to..."

"I promise to let you know," he said with a reassuring smile.

On Sunday he took the early morning flight to Houston. He was at the hospital early for the orientation on Tuesday morning. Dr. Gallsworthy explained the routine and his expectations of the new house staff in terrifying terms with threats of banishment to Children's Hospital or worse for any noncompliance. Marc and the others took it as mostly BS, which is what it was. They knew it was expected to be said. There were certain rules in medical training and one of them was to get tough with the new kids on the block. It usually wasn't taken too seriously.

Afterward a group of these young men and women went to the cafeteria for coffee. Marc was engulfed in conversation with a few of them at a long table. Introductions were made and there was much groaning about the expected grueling routine. This, too, was usual. He looked up and saw a familiar face trying to get his attention. It was Dave Stein, the resident he had met and the only friendly face he had seen on his first visit to the surgery clinic a few weeks ago. He excused himself and went over to Dave who extended a hand and gave him a sincere smile. "Hamilton, congratulations. I was happy to learn you'll be on my service. Are you situated... a... have a place to live?"

"No, not yet. I'm staying at the Green Gables Motel until I find something," said Marc.

"Man, this is your lucky day. Billy Burns was rooming with me. He got into a hotshot trauma group in Dallas so I'm single again. Frankly I could use the help sharing the expenses. Look, how about grabbing a bite with me tonight? We could talk about the program and you could take a look at the flat. No strings attached, honest."

"Why not?" said Marc.

It was a small two bedroom apartment just two blocks from the hospital and it became Marc's home for the next three years. Dave wised him up and broke him into the University Hospital routine. They supported each other through rough times, as when Dave broke up with Sharon and when James Hamilton died of a sudden stroke. Dave even went with Marc to the funeral in Cleveland. They became best friends, and the friendship would last throughout their lives.

* * * * *

Dave Stein was born in 1951, the only son of Hilda and Sandor Stein, survivors of the Holocaust. Hilda, who was from Miscolc, the second largest city in Hungary, had been taken to Auschwitz when the Nazis rounded up the Jews for deportation in 1943. She, along with her father, mother and two sisters had been crammed into cattle cars for the three-day journey without food or water. The sickly and the elderly didn't survive the trip. Hilda could never forget the stench of death on that ghastly train to hell. She was young and strong, and somehow she made it to the death camp only to see her parents and sisters given the thumb sign to the left, to the gas chambers. She thought she would lose her mind in the early days of incarceration. Many did. Many succumbed later to the starvation, cruelty and disease and became part of a mound of human carcasses that commemorated the ultimate inhumanity of man.

Despite the smoke of the ovens and the constant presence of death about her, Hilda survived. She survived because she knew only one law, and that was survival at any cost. As would an animal, she killed for a piece of bread. She would take an extra crumb from the dead. She was subjected to the lowest forms of degradation and accepted it to survive.

It was a frigid day in December of 1944 when an SS officer came into her stalag and asked if anyone played the violin. Hilda stepped forward and was instructed to follow the officer. Thank God, she had studied violin as a child and prayed she could still play. It had been a lifetime ago. She was taken to the archway that led to the gas chambers. Across the arch was written "Arbeit

Macht Frei" and in front of the arch was a string ensemble. She learned that she was to replace the violinist who had died the night before. The duty of the musicians was to play classical chamber music to pacify and delude the condemned into believing that they were simply going into showers. She played as the parade of the living-dead passed before her. She played and never gave them a glance. She knew their fate and still she played. She would survive!

It was here that Hilda met Sandor Stein, the cellist. In the moments when the SS guards turned away she learned that he was from Budapest and that he had played in the famous Budapest Symphony Orchestra. They saw each other every day. Because of their special work they had extra rations, and while wolfing down the crusts of bread they spoke in hushed tones of friends they knew in common, of good times before the war, of their country that had betrayed them. It was this friendship that sustained them, and that friendship became a bond. If they survived, they would marry and make a new life for themselves in America.

At last in 1945 the allied forces liberated the death camps. The war was over. The two living skeletons, Hilda and Sandor, were taken to a hospital along with a handful of other survivors. After six months of care they were well enough to be discharged. Where should they go? Where did they belong? Go back to that God-forsaken Hungary? No way! In the post-war confusion national borders became indistinct. If one was clever and very lucky, under the cover of night he might pass into a land were he could find temporary safety. Hilda and Sandor were caught twice and forced to turn back, but with the third attempt they found themselves in Austria. From there they made it to Paris where they were married. Then with false papers they managed to escape to Venezuela. Sandor got a job driving a taxi in Caracas and Hilda took in sewing. They applied for a visa to the United States and finally, in 1949, their prayers were answered.

They were grateful to have found an affordable two bedroom flat on Nelson Avenue in the Bronx, even though it was a five-story walkup. They set up housekeeping with the money they had managed to save in Caracas. It was tough. A new country. A new language. New customs. No work and no friends. But they were survivors, and this was America! Sandor finally learned enough English to drive a taxi and Hilda made a few dresses for herself. Her bold mode of advertising worked, and she was the envy of the neighborhood in her frilly frocks. It didn't take long. Orders for dresses came in faster than she could sew them. Owning a dress by Hilda became a status symbol in the neighborhood. After two years of saving every dime they opened a shop off the Grand Concourse. *Fashions by Hilda* became known throughout the Bronx for its unique designs and fine quality.

Even with this measure of success the Steins were cautious, bordering on paranoid. Although they could now afford to move to a better neighborhood, they didn't dare leave the security of their Nelson Avenue flat. Would they be safe here? Could they trust that neighbor? Could it happen again here? The scars of Auschwitz would remain forever. The people in the neighborhood tried to understand, but they finally wrote them off as unfriendly. It was into this uncertain environment that David Aaron Stein was born. His parents glowed with happiness. "He's going to be a professor," said Hilda.

"No, he will be a famous doctor like my uncle Ference," said the happy father.

"Very well, Sandor, a famous doctor." And so young David's future had been decided.

Growing up in the Bronx was hard enough, but contending with over protective parents was nearly impossible. "Davey, don't play with those rough boys... Davey, you'll break your neck... Davey, don't stay out after dark... Davey, don't make us worry." Somehow the boy understood and at the same time realized that he was starved for independence. The fights with his parents and his violent teenage rebellion were as predictable as day following night. He did well in school when he wanted to do well. He stayed out late, regularly got into fights, had some minor brushes with the police and drove his parents nuts.

"But, Mom, this isn't the Old Country. Everybody does that! I'm going out with the guys and I don't know when I'll be home... Pop, you can hit me but you can't stop me!" Young Dave was a survivor too. The few happy childhood memories he would recall in later years were those of music in his home. There was always music, and it seemed to be the only thread that tied the small family together. He loved to hear his parents play the violin and cello. It was like medicine for his soul.

Who knows what would have happened to Dave if not for the young couple who moved into 5A? Myron and Deborah Berkowitz were newlyweds and taught psychology at City College in Manhattan. One evening when Davey was fifteen, he saw them sitting on the stoop getting a breath of air and having a cigarette. "Hey, you guys got an extra smoke for me?"

"Sure, if your mom says it's okay," said Myron.

"Hey, man, I'm no baby. I can smoke if I want to."

"Yep. I guess you're right but I'm not the one whose going to give you a cigarette without your mother's permission."

"Hey, what do you think I am, some little queer?"

"No. I think you're a young man trying to be a grownup."

"So, what's wrong with that?"

"Nothing," said Deborah. "I have an idea. How about a glass of lemonade?"

"And then a smoke?"

"Well, let's start with the lemonade. Come on up. We're on five," she said.

"Hey, me too. I'm in 5D... Okay."

"I've seen you in the building," said Myron. "What's your name?"

"Why? You gonna tell my folks?"

"Friends don't snitch," said Myron.

Perhaps it was chance or fate, but the real education of Davey Stein began here. The Berkowitzes gradually gained his confidence and he became a frequent visitor in 5A. Slowly and in small increments a new world began to open for him. He joined Myron and Deborah for Sunday outings to the art museum or Shakespearean plays at the park, but only with his parents' permission. He did this reluctantly at first but soon he began to look forward to the events. He could discuss anything with his new friends. No subject was off limits, including sex. The Berkowitzes recognized his intellect and took pride in seeing their young pupil and friend bloom into a caring and sensitive young man.

The Steins were comfortable with the friendship and all was well until that particular Sunday in June of 1967. Myron suggested an outing to the newly opened Holocaust Museum and, as usual, asked for the Steins' permission for Dave to go along. Dave was present when Myron hit the brick wall. "No, I won't allow it," said Sandor.

"He should never know from that!" shouted Hilda.

"But, Mrs. Stein, it's history. How can you keep it from him?" asked the shocked Myron.

"No! Absolutely no! He should never see that. He should never know!" repeated Sandor.

"But Mr. Stein... Mrs. Stein... if you'll excuse me, that's a very narrow..." Sandor became enraged. "Young man, you don't know! You weren't there! And no is no! That's it. End of discussion!"

"Mom! Pop! I want to go!"

"Never! End of discussion!" said Sandor, his face crimson with anger. "And I'll thank you not to put such ideas into this boy's head."

"Mr. Stein, I never meant to..."

"Sha! End!" He left the room and slammed the door behind him.

"I'm so sorry, Mrs. Stein. I didn't understand. Please excuse me."

"It's all right. Enough now. Myron, would you... have a piece of strudel?"

"Thank you. Perhaps another time. I guess I'd best be getting along." Dave was embarrassed at his parents' volatile reaction to what seemed to be a simple request. Myron turned to him and said, "Sorry, Dave. I guess your parents know best."

"No! You know best, Myron. You know best." The boys eyes were filled with tears. It wasn't so much because of the canceled excursion as because he looked up to Myron who had been cut off at the legs by his stupid, backward European parents. Too much had been made of the incident. The sixteen year old was too stubborn to let it go. A few days later he went alone to the museum.

Although his parents never spoke of it, Dave knew about the holocaust. After all it was common knowledge but he didn't know the details, the horror his parents had lived through, until that moment. The gas chambers. The furnaces. The bodies. Yes, his parents wanted to protect him and perhaps that was naive, even wrong, but what kind of love would ever again shield him from such evil? His parents lived it! They had survived it and didn't want him to know their pain. That was love! Now he understood. Now he was ashamed of his attitude. Now he learned respect for his European parents. They had earned it. And how they had earned it! Dave never spoke of it again, not even with Myron. The boy grew about ten feet taller that summer.

The Berkowitzes had been a stabilizing and growing influence upon Dave. His grades were near the top of his class, much to the surprise of his supervisor and teachers. Fashions by Hilda had become a huge success and the Steins opened their second shop in Queens on Francis Lewis Boulevard near the Eastern Long Island Expressway. Sandor joined Hilda in the shops and became the bookkeeper and financial advisor. They had set aside enough for Dave to attend college and to go on to medical school. Medicine had been drummed into his head from the time he was a toddler. There was something about the idea that intrigued him, but what did he know about medicine? Nothing at all!

Dave knew he had to get away. He applied only to schools that were out of town. Finally he was accepted into Cornell as a pre-med student. The Steins knew their son and knew that his leaving was inevitable. At the same time they were grateful that he was heading for a medical career. They had a small party for him on the Sunday prior to his departure. Naturally the Berkowitzes were invited, as well as several of Dave's closest friends.

Dave had invited Sharon Gardner, the girl he had taken to the Senior Prom. She was small, had a fine figure, a lovely face framed with fiery red curls, dark blue eyes and a million dollar smile. She was also a Gentile. His parents tried to discourage the relationship but treaded softly. They knew their son, and they knew that pushing him too hard would encourage the friendship. Anyway it had been only one date and Dave would be leaving soon. What they didn't know was that Dave and Sharon had been seeing each other for months and Sharon was going to go to

Julliard to study voice. They would be able to be together often. Ithaca and Rochester were less than one hundred miles apart. Dave had explained the situation to Sharon and she understood his parents' coolness. Try as they would, they couldn't get themselves to dislike her, but she was a Gentile.

The days at Cornell were wonderful days. He filled his head with worldly knowledge and was now certain of shooting for a medical career. For once his parents had been right. Dave and Sharon spent most weekends together. They were deeply in love. The relationship continued even when Dave was accepted to medical school in Houston. Sharon moved there with the understanding that marriage was imminent. She got a job teaching music in an elementary school. Dave wanted to keep the status quo and managed to do that through the next four years of medical school.

However Sharon was getting restless and hungered for more of Dave's attention. He had never been able to get himself to make a firm commitment to marriage. He rationalized that funds were tight, but he knew that they could get by with the addition of Sharon's salary to his. In fact, he needed her financial support for the lean years ahead. Then he thought about the religious differences, but that had not been a problem in the past. He knew he loved her, but he simply couldn't marry. Not now. Was it his own insecurity? Was it immaturity? He didn't have an answer to those. He tried to be there for her. He tried with all his heart, but there was always another exam or late rounds on the wards or hours of study at the library. When he spent more time with Sharon, he felt guilty about neglecting his studies. And conversely, when he shortchanged her he felt terrible. Damn that Jewish guilt!

Although Sharon understood this, her impatience with him grew daily. After all, she had an eight-year investment in the relationship. When Dave got the general surgery residency with Dr. Gallsworthy at the Texas University Hospital, he leased a large apartment and planned on Sharon moving in with him. He was telling her about the apartment over a cup of coffee when she became furious at being taken for granted and let him know it.

"I think we'd better cool this down, Dave."

"Why, Baby? We love each other."

"Look, Dave, its been eight years. I'm not getting any younger and I still don't have a commitment from you."

"You know I'm serious. You know that I want to marry you, don't you?"

"No. I thought that before but I don't know that now. I love you..." Tears were rolling down her cheeks. "But how long do you expect me to wait for you? Dave, I have to back off for a while and get a different perspective." He tried to put his arm about her to console her but she stopped him. She meant it! She turned away and walked out of the coffee shop. Dave followed.

"When will I see you?"

"I don't know," she said. "I've taken an apartment closer to town. I need some time and space, Dave."

"Please don't do this, Sharon. I need you."

"I'm sorry Dave." She kissed his cheek gently, got into her red convertible wiped away her tears with the back of her hand and drove off leaving the bewildered Dave just standing there.

During the next year they saw each other less frequently. He found out that she had been dating other guys, but he wouldn't give up. "Sharon, come on back. We'll get married... whatever you want."

"Dave, I'm sorry. Its too late. It's gone. I'm really sorry."

He nearly went out of his mind. He cut clinics. He was late for scrubs. His career was on the line. This was the time that Marc Hamilton came into the picture as his roommate. It was

Implant

Marc who stood by his friend and made him realize the futility of grieving over a lost cause. "It's over, Dave, so shape up and fly right!" He and Marc had become very close. There was virtually nothing that one didn't know about the other. Marc was there for him when he needed to talk. When he was depressed, Marc pulled him out of his funk. In time Dave began to date and his life assumed some kind of order out of the months of chaos.

Sometimes Dave and Marc double dated. They respected each other's privacy when it came to girls in the apartment. "All clear" was the phone signal to return. It was Dave who introduced Marla Brashear to Marc. She was the cute charge nurse on the surgical ward on 6 West. Marla was five-three, large breasted and slim everywhere else. Her dark brown hair matched bright eyes of the same color. Her smile and demeanor said, "I love fun and I'm game for anything." She had been after Dave for an introduction to Marc for a couple of weeks. He hadn't done it just to tease her. It started with a movie. Then next time it was dinner. Although they saw each other every day at the hospital, it took two months before they made it to the bedroom.

She was a pro. She had played it exactly right with Marc. Not too soon but soon enough to keep his desire fueled. Marla was wonderful. She was everything Marc thought she would be. She knew exactly where and how to touch him. She was an expert and knew how to drive him to the absolute brink of passion until the hunger to enter her was the most overwhelming, delicious sexual experience he had ever known. No other woman he had ever been with was as exciting as Marla. She was unselfish, completely giving and had fallen hopelessly in love with Marc. They were together constantly. Although she didn't share the same love for the arts as Marc did, she went with him to the symphony and on Sundays, off duty, went with him to the latest exhibit at the art museum. He understood and loved her all the more for trying to learn to share these things with him. She preferred movies and picnics and bike rides. These were fine with him too. They seemed to complement one another. At the hospital they were regarded as a definite couple. So it was no surprise to anyone when Marc and Marla announced their engagement. At the end of his third year of general surgery residency they had a small quiet wedding at the Houston Arboretum. Mother Elizabeth came and so did Uncle Danny. Of course Dave was best man.

Marla was born in Buffalo, Texas, a small town not far from Houston. Her father deserted the family when she was an infant and her mother died of breast cancer when Marla was only fourteen. She had a younger sister, Billie, and the two of them were brought up by a caring aunt who did what she could for her young nieces. Billie was the proud maid of honor and Aunt Mary wept copious tears of joy. The honeymoon was a fast weekend at the Shamrock Hilton. They both had to be on duty Monday. Someday they would have a real honeymoon.

Dave was single again. He had no trouble finding another roommate, but no one could ever live up to Marc. Dave missed his friend, but such was life. The young couple moved into Marla's neat little apartment. They used Marla's salary for their maintenance and at Marla's insistence saved Marc's salary in a bank account, all except for a new Mustang convertible bought on time. Although Mother Elizabeth was always offering help, Marc wanted to be independent and always gently refused. However on their first anniversary Elizabeth sent a check for $1,000, which they gratefully accepted and put into a few shares of Houston Power and Light. It was a happy time for making plans, talking about their future, and dreaming about wonderful days to come. They were together, invulnerable and in love.

Implant

Every afternoon following his surgical chores Marc made his presence known to Professor Allen Greenberg. The professor was cordial and often invited him to scrub in on a case. Marc was proving himself. He attended the plastic surgery clinics and made rounds with Greenberg whenever possible. Greenberg had asked Marc to do some research for him on the rate of scar tissue formation following augmentation mammaplasties. Marc spent hours studying, reading and writing his findings. Marla was lonely much of this time and she let Marc know in no uncertain terms about the lack of attention she was receiving. It was their first big fight. He apologized and said he would try to do better. She was sorry and said she understood and tried to keep her mind off of it with work and household chores.

When the research was complete, Marc wrote it up in the form of a formal paper and presented it to Allen Greenberg. He didn't hear about it for several months and nearly forgot about the whole thing. One afternoon Dr. Greenberg's secretary tracked him down and said that the chief wanted to see him at his office at 5:00 PM. Marc arrived and Greenberg was smiling. "A nice piece of research, Hamilton. I've presented it to the Journal and it will be published in the January issue. Would you please go over the galley proofs so I can get it in on time?"

"Of course, sir." Marc took the proofs and looked at the author line. "By Marcus Hamilton, M.D. and Allen Greenberg, M.D."

"Dr. Greenberg..."

"You did the work. Your name comes first. How do you feel about your first publication?"

"Great! I don't know what to say. Thanks."

"You're okay, Hamilton. Welch said you were and he was right. I think you can count on the plastic surgery residency. There's an opening next year, that is if you still want it. I'd be pleased to have you on my service."

"Professor, you've got to be joking! Do I want it!"

"Well, do a good job finishing up with Gallsworthy. I don't need any flack from him and neither do you."

Surely he had a charmed life. It was all falling into place. He was invincible. He was indestructible. He was dog tired and wanted to run home with the news to Marla and go to sleep.

* * * * *

When he arrived home the table was set for dinner. Marla was preparing the last artistic touches to the meatloaf. He looked so tired but she could see his excitement.

"Hi, Honey," she said, turning her chin upward for a peck. "You have something good to tell me!"

"Dr. Greenberg called me to his office this afternoon and guess what! The research paper is going to be published... and with my name as the first author. Can you believe it? And there's more, much more!" She stopped and was smiling with her mouth half open with expectation. "And Greenberg wants me. He really wants me for the residency for next year. He told me to count on it. Can you believe it? I almost fell on my ass."

"Oh, Babe," she said. "It's really happening. You've worked so hard for it. No one could deserve it more. I'm so happy for you."

"For us, Honey. For us!" Her smile blunted just slightly.

"Yes, of course. It's wonderful. I'm so proud of you. Dinner's ready. Better wash up and come to the table."

Even through his excitement he sensed that something was wrong. But he was too tired to let it penetrate. He sat down to dinner still talking excitedly. "And he said he had plans for me. Probably more research on breast implants. Maybe I'll get to present a paper at the next national meeting."

"Honey, it's getting cold." He picked at it a bit.

"The meatloaf is great! Great! But I don't think I can eat. I'm too excited. I'm dead. Got to sleep. Will you forgive me?" He didn't wait for an answer. He headed for the bed and collapsed into a near coma of overwhelming fatigue. Marla took off his shoes, opened his shirt collar and loosened his belt. He didn't stir and slept deeply until morning.

It was Marla's day off duty. After Marc left she thought for a long time. Hesitantly she picked up the phone and called Dave Stein. She hoped he was still at home. "Dave this is Marla."

"Hi stranger. What's going on? How is the great Dr. Wellby?"

"Dave, I've got to see you." Her voice cracked slightly. He could hear the urgency.

"What's wrong, Marla?"

"Everything," and she began to sob. "I've got to see you today. Please, Dave, please."

"Sure, Marla. I'll get Gary Gold to cover for me. Lunch at the hospital?"

"No, not near the hospital."

"Do you know Randy's coffee shop near the Galleria?"

"Yes. Fine. When?"

"How about I meet you there at 12:30?"

"I'll be there."

"Marla, are you okay?"

"I'll be okay. See you there and thanks, thanks, Dave."

They sat in a booth and ordered coffee. Dave had never seen Marla look so distraught and he was worried for his friend. "Out with it," he said gently. She took a sip of the strong black brew for support. "What do you mean? Is he beating you, cheating on you?" He knew that was impossible for Marc. He was simply trying to draw her out.

"Of course not. He's the same gentle Marc."

"Well then?"

"We hardly see each other. Between surgery and research projects he hardly knows that I exist. He's too tired to eat. He's too tired for sex. He lives for his work. I thought it would be different. I love him so much but I can't reach him."

"Marla, for God's sake, you're married to a surgery resident. You're a nurse. You knew what to expect."

"I guess I was secretly hoping he wouldn't go on into a plastic program and would just go into a general surgery practice. I knew he'd be busy but we could have had some kind of life. Two more years of residency and all that research and soon I won't be in the picture at all. I barely am now."

"You mean Greenberg gave him the residency? But that's great!"

"Dave, I was deserted by my father. My mother died when I was fourteen. I just can't handle being deserted any more. I guess it's selfish but I can't deal with it. I don't see any light at the end of the tunnel. I love him. I need him and I can't seem to reach him. I know he loves me. Maybe I expect too much. When I give, I give all I have. Maybe I need too much, but I know I need much more than Marc will ever be able to give me." Now the tears were flowing freely and Dave gave her his handkerchief.

"Marla, you can't change him. You know that he's been living for this moment. You're talking about his life, his soul."

"I know. I know! I'm happy for him but I'm dying inside, each day a little more. Dave, I just want to run to some safe protected harbor. I don't know what to do. I want Marc and I want all of him. I can't share him with Greenberg, research, plastic surgery. I guess what I need is an 8:00 to 5:00 guy and I know I'll never find another man like Marc. I need someone who can be there for me. Just me. Tell me what to do, Dave. I'm being so unfair to him. Tell me what to do."

Implant

"You know I can't, Hon. I'm too close to both of you. Have you spoken with Marc?"

"I'm not going to burst his bubble. I'm mixed up but I know it can't work out for me. I had to talk to someone. I'm sorry to lay this on you but thanks for listening."

"What will you do"?

"Leave, when I get the courage, I guess. Maybe I'm making the biggest mistake of my life but I can't change my needs either, and I can't go on with this vacant space inside of me."

They finished the rest of their coffee in silence. Marla left first and gave Dave a grateful hug. Dave looked at his watch. He had to get back to the hospital. He felt sick. He ached for his dearest friends.

Chapter 5

He began to stir as his eyelids separated. He was in the uncharted state between sleep and wakefulness. He must have had a nightmare. Fighting and blood. Then a hot arrow shot through his skull, temple to temple, and the pain lunged him into a state of awareness. He remembered a bed and the need to sleep. It had been light then. He glanced across the room to a curtained window. The darkness and distant flashing red sign confirmed that it was night. He wondered how long he had slept. Even through the increasing awareness of his pain the urgent human need for orientation was primary and prompted thinking.

The first thought was of an unfamiliar bloody face. It was no nightmare. That was terrifyingly real. He had seen blood many times before. He knew that it had been many times before. It wasn't the blood. It was the face of a stranger, his face that was terrifying. Pain, bed, night, blood and his face. All were disconnected but at least he could think. Cautiously he sat on the edge of the bed cradling his head in his cupped hands. He felt the matted hair. Slowly he stood up, afraid to leave the bed. He was unsteady and very shaky on his feet. He must have lost a lot of blood. A shower seemed very important and he knew where the bathroom was without thinking. Good! He could walk to the bathroom in a weaving path, but at least he could walk. He had to pass the mirror but intentionally didn't look. He needed no confirmation of the image it would reflect. He turned on the shower and let it run while he stripped off his stiff, blood-soaked clothes. He was certain that he had lost at least a liter of blood. He stepped in, adjusted the temperature, set a gentle spray and sat on the floor of the shower. He leaned into the flow. It was comforting and it relaxed him. After a long while, still sitting, he took the bar of soap just at the right above his head and began to wash, starting with the hair and face and then the rest. He saw the pink water swirling down the drain and didn't stop until it was clear.

    He pulled himself up by the metal hand grip. The shower had helped. The overall pain was subsiding. He stepped out, still supported by the shower wall, and sat on the covered toilet seat. He reached for a towel on the rack above him and began to dry himself. The mirror was there! Should he? He had to look. It was a stranger, but he began to accept with less anxiety the fact that it was *his* face. Cleansing now allowed him to study it. It was swollen with dark purple bruises under both eyes. There was a trickle of blood tracking down the left side of his forehead. He followed it into the hair and searched for the laceration. He found the rent which was wide and gapping, at least ten centimeters long and down to the bone. It had to be repaired. The swollen and cut lower lip, a through and through cut, explained the burning sensation.

    Slowly he left the bathroom, naked, and found a closet. The clothes were carelessly arranged and some lay on the floor. It was clear that the garments belonged to a man... and a woman. He reached with trembling hands for a jacket, slacks and shoes. He laid them on a chair in front of the window and switched on the lamp beside the chair. As he turned he saw that the room was in complete disarray with papers strewn over the floor. The sofa cushions were overturned and torn and chest drawers had been pulled out and their contents dumped. He saw the dried blood on the shag carpet a few feet from the door.

It was now apparent to him that this was a hotel room. Perhaps it was his... and some woman's as well. In the mess on the floor he saw bras and panties mingled with shorts, shirts and socks. Someone must have tried to rob him. Pretty obvious. He was feeling better but waves of lightheadedness would overtake him. He had to get out of here and get medical attention. He reached for one of the shirts by his feet and began to dress. It was no surprise that it fit. While dressing by the chair, he looked out the window onto an unfamiliar street scene. Rain fell in oblique sheets making the street, several floors below, reflect the lights of car traffic and flashing neon signs.

As he started for the door he noticed a wallet lying on the floor among the papers which partially concealed it. He bent down to pick it up in the midst of the mess and immediately regretted having done so. Darkness began to obscure his vision. Finally when it subsided he counted about $400 dollars in US currency and about 1,800 French Francs. He noticed several credit cards with the name *Marcus Hamilton, M.D.* Next he found a Texas driver's license with the same name and a birth date, Sept. 14, 1952. So he was Marcus Hamilton, 37 years old and in France. Why? And why had the robbers left the money? His vision was still fuzzy but clearing. He noticed a blue folded brochure and on the front cover was printed:

Implant

AESTHETIC PLASTIC SURGERY SOCIETY
of FRANCE
Annual Meeting October 4, 1989
Paris, France

As he opened it, with some difficulty he could read the scientific program. "October 4, 8:30 AM. Breast Augmentation Panel: Moderator, Marc Hamilton M.D., Houston Texas." It nearly jumped at him and he had to read it several times. Plastic surgery and breast augmentation. He knew those things and yet they seemed to be distant and in another time. It hurt to think about it so he let it go. He took the wallet and pocketed the brochure.

Getting off the floor was tough, but his balance was now improving. He made it to the door, opened it and stepped out into the crimson carpeted corridor. He had enough cognizance not to take the elevator. Surely it would open onto a lobby. He knew he looked like shit and didn't want to be seen. Someone might call the police and he really didn't want that. He was probably mixed up in something sinister. He needed attention fast... medical and not police. He found a rear stairway and started his descent step by step and all the while he clutched the hand rail. He thought he had counted four flights when he exited through the door and found himself in the chilling rain of the night.

He noticed the lighted signpost marked Rue St. Jacque. He hugged the hotel wall and tumbled along the street for several minutes until he saw a taxi. He hailed it, and as the taxi approached him it accelerated and sped away. He knew he looked like hell but the bastard could have stopped! Another cab. This time he raised his hand to hail it while turning his face away from the street. It stopped. He opened the door and got in. It was too late for the driver to run. "Monsieur!" exclaimed the driver in terror when he saw his face.

"Do you speak English?" asked Marc.

"Oui, Monsieur, but..."

"Please take me to the nearest hospital."

"Oui!" The cab driver just wanted to get rid of this fare he was suckered into taking. He was afraid of getting involved in something terrible. With his record he couldn't afford another police encounter. His license was already on the line and he was on probation. A scene with a passenger was the last thing he wanted. His only choice was to comply and dump the creep at the nearest hospital. They drove fast down the Rue St. Jacque. Marc was drifting in and out, sometimes a little more alert and sometimes not at all. Finally they drove up to the emergency entrance of what Marc knew to be a hospital.

"How much?"

"It's okay," said the driver just wanting to dump him fast. Marc gave him 100 Francs anyway. He really didn't know how much that was and he didn't care. The driver took the money and helped him out of the taxi. He nodded briefly, got back behind the wheel and sped off with screeching tires. Marc was alone in the driveway entrance of the emergency room. It was still cold. The wind and rain whipped about him. Only a few more steps to help. He stumbled through the entrance and collapsed in the hallway.

Chapter 6

It was now after seven o'clock. Ashley had been waiting for Marc to arrive for over two hours. She was starting to get strange looks from people at the bar and she couldn't stay any longer. She asked for the check, paid and went out into the small entry way of La Coupole. It had begun to rain heavily. Ashley put on her coat and turned up the collar. It wasn't much protection from the harsh wind and driving rain. She decided to wait until there was a lull before braving the elements to find a taxi. She was in France and didn't speak the language. Ashley silently cursed herself for not having studied French in school. At least she should have taken a fast course for tourists, just enough to learn a few necessary words to be able to get by in an emergency.

Something was seriously wrong. Marc would never let her wait like this without a phone call or a message. She knew him too well for that to be logical. The more she thought about it, the more frightened she became. From the time of the last trip to Seattle nothing had gone right. They had been living in a state of panic ever since the bizarre encounter at the deli. Marc was constantly on edge, irritable and difficult. It was planning the trip to Paris that had made life bearable for both of them. Ashley saw it as a refuge, at least a temporary one, and Marc looked forward to the meeting.

This trip, besides being a scientific meeting where Marc was moderating the most important panel of the entire congress, was also to be a celebration. Marla had agreed to the divorce. Since Ashley had gone through a divorce several years ago she understood what Marc had been going through. The initial despair, the guilt, the uncertainty and Marla's feelings all weighed heavily upon him. Then the pressures from the FDA and the curious calls from Alcott Labs had become so stressful for Marc that she was genuinely worried about how he could bear up under it all. He was one of the most stable men she had ever known, but wasn't there a breaking point for everyone?

The rain had slowed to a light drizzle. She stepped to the curb and easily found a taxi. This was a popular area and taxis were always abundant, especially in such unfriendly weather. "Hotel Splendid on Rue St. Jacque," she said. The driver, accustomed to English speaking tourists, didn't reply but turned down the next street to the left, presumably toward the hotel. In less than ten minutes Ashley was at the entrance of the Hotel Splendid. She looked at the meter. It read 65. She gave the driver 75 Francs. He didn't even bother to open the door for her or to say "Merci," or anything at all.

She quickly walked to the reception desk and asked for their messages. The young clerk in a uniform that had seen better days told her in English, "There are none, Madam." Ashley immediately went toward the elevators, found one waiting and pushed 4. She rode alone. Her heart was pounding. Where was he? What had happened to him? In a few seconds she stepped out onto the floor and walked toward their room while fumbling in her purse for the key. With a trembling hand Ashley opened the door and called his name. In the same instant that she saw the mess her eyes widened when she became aware that she was standing in a huge area of dried blood on the carpet. "Oh, God! Let him be all right!" She called out again, "Marc?" She walked across the floor and then noticed the blood soaked bed. "Oh no!" she said aloud with panic seizing her. "He's dead! They've killed him!" Ashley was irrational and began to tear at the flesh on her hands, first one and then the other. She turned away from the bed and in her line of vision was the open bathroom door. Did she dare to look? What horror awaited there? Her breathing came in rapid, shallow and irregular spurts. With her last ounce of courage Ashley threw the door wide open and looked into the bathroom. She saw evidence of a shower having been taken. She tried to gain control of herself again. She swallowed, calmed down a bit and tried to think.

Could he possibly be alive? Had he showered after the attack? There was no question in her mind of a vicious attack having taken place here. She noticed that the towel on the floor had blood stains. That meant that he had probably showered after the attack. "God, let him be alive!" She had a spark of hope. Marc might still be alive! Each time she had warned him of possible harm he had just laughed it off. She knew he was worried and the careless facade was just that, an act for her benefit. Ashley had thought they would be safe in France. Obviously she had been wrong. Alcott's tentacles could reach them anywhere!

Was it really Alcott? Was it burglary? Could Marc still be alive? She had to cling to the hope that he was alive. That's all she had. Hope. It was the only thing that made rational thought possible. What should she do now? Calm down. Think. Think. Ashley looked around more carefully to see if anything was missing. Marc's presentation papers were strewn about, but all seemed to be there. She knew because she had helped him prepare them. There were no personal items missing either but they hadn't brought any significant jewelry or very much cash. They planned on using mostly credit cards. His wallet! She searched everywhere but to no avail. Would his wallet be missing if it wasn't a burglary? Perhaps she was letting her imagination run wild. And yet, all this blood for a wallet? She knew that Marc would have been too smart not to hand over the wallet if that was what they wanted. He wouldn't fight over a few lousy bucks! Maybe he had somehow escaped his attackers and taken his wallet with him. Yes, that was possible. Then if it wasn't burglary, everything had to lead back to Alcott. They must have believed that he had brought the memo to expose it at the meeting. Of course! That was what they were after. The memo! Shit! He should never have gotten into this mess anyway!

Call the police? At first that seemed to be the best course of action. No! The police would see the blood and start asking questions. She couldn't discuss the motive for the attack. She and Marc had talked about going public. It was definitely too premature and would put them in even greater danger, if that were possible. Vicky had gone over this with them and advised keeping the lid on for now. Then what should she do? What? She couldn't leave. If Marc was alive, he would try to find her. Again the thought crept back into her consciousness. What if he was dead? No, please, no!

God! She had never felt so helpless and alone. Ashley was emotionally drained. She sat down in the chair by the window to wait for something, anything, some word. She looked out into the darkness. Again there were heavy, driving sheets of rain. She saw the lights reflecting in the wet pavement below and watched and stared mesmerized for a very long time. Where was Marc? Would she ever see him again?

Chapter 7

They saw the blood-soaked form of a man staggering toward the sliding glass door of the emergency room entrance. "Catch him!" called out the heavy, middle aged nurse from behind the reception desk. The orderly with huge muscular arms reached for Marc and broke his fall an instant before his body would have met the tile floor.

"Quick! Get a gurney! He's in bad shape," he called out, while still supporting the dead weight. The nurse wheeled the gurney around and together they lifted Marc onto it. She gave the orderly instructions in rapid-fire succession.

"Get two liters of 5% glucose in lactated Ringers. Call the lab for an H. and H. Get Doctor Dumont stat! Wake him up. He's on call. I'll try to get a BP and start an IV. Get the blocks under the foot of the gurney. This man's in shock. Move, move!" This was routine for an emergency room. Fortunately the orderly was used to it and he was efficient. It had been unusually quiet all evening and now suddenly all was in motion in high gear. "Crash cart!" yelled the nurse. "Now!" She shook Marc. "Can you hear me? Can you speak?" She leaned close to his face. There was irregular shallow breathing but no response. Quickly she put a blood pressure cuff on him while another nurse appeared from somewhere and began searching for a vein. "BP 60/40, respirations 6/minute, pulse 124/minute and weak. Record," she directed another attendant holding a chart.

A young man in whites with coattails flying and a stethoscope swaying from his neck was clipping down the corridor toward the scene. He glanced at the body on the gurney and then for only an instant, at the figures on the chart. "Got the IV started?"

"Yes, Doctor," replied the nurse in charge. "I've called the lab."

"Good! Let's get him into room #2 and start nasal oxygen. Call x-ray. Keep the IV wide open." The doctor began a cursory examination. The pupils were unequally dilated. Palpation of the head and neck areas showed a wide and deep scalp laceration. Examination of the swollen, bruised face suggested right facial bone fractures. The lower lip needed repair but that was the least of the problems. This man had been beaten nearly to death. The police would have to be notified eventually, but first they had to try to stabilize him.

A sleepy attendant arrived with the portable x-ray equipment and at almost the same moment the lab technician, a frail red-headed woman, began to draw blood. The latter would show the amount of blood loss, any toxic agents or drugs and blood chemistries. These would further indicate the nature and degree of injuries. Dr. Dumont turned to the x-ray tech and said, "Raymond, a skull series, facial bones with Water's views, chest AP and laterals. His breath sounds are diminished on the right. Get all extremities and a flat plate of the abdomen." He called to the orderly and said, "Get a catheter in the bladder, in dwelling." All this had taken less than eight minutes. They were good.

There was not much more to do until lab and x-ray results could be evaluated. The orderly began to cut away his clothes which were impossible to remove otherwise. They were stiff with clotted blood and adhered to his skin. He found a wallet and blood stained brochure in the patient's pant pocket and placed the brochure, folded, into the wallet. He called, "Dr. Dumont," as he tossed over the wallet. Dumont caught it and began going through it. Very quickly he ascertained that his patient in room #2 was an American plastic surgeon, Marcus Hamilton, who was here to participate in the plastic surgery meeting being held now in Paris. The brochure indicated the man's importance as he was to moderate a panel on breast augmentation. A moderator was always selected because of particular expertise in the subject. It was obvious to Claude Dumont that there was no way Hamilton could attend the meeting let alone moderate a panel. This was curious! It was no ordinary mugging. He had his wallet. This man was in some kind of serious trouble. He wondered who would do such a thing to a visiting doctor… and why. Of course it could have been any number of reasons, a bar brawl, a political argument, a woman. Yes, probably a woman was involved. That was usually the case in his emergency room experience.

"Dr. Dumont, shall I call the authorities?" asked the head nurse attempting to follow the established protocol.

"What good would that do now? He's unconscious and can't answer any questions. Besides, the police wouldn't appreciate coming out on a night like this just to see a comatose patient. They would only have to return when he became responsive, if indeed he ever does come out of this." She looked down at her paperwork. He seemed to have convinced her. The more Dumont thought about it, the more he convinced himself that there was something important here. This was a colleague in trouble. Maybe he would regret getting involved by not calling the police but, at least for now, he was willing to take the chance. He further rationalized that he was too busy trying to save this patient to be concerned about some trivial rule.

While engrossed in these thoughts, Dumont was watching the EKG monitor. Marc had a regular sinus rhythm. His heart rate had responded to the intravenous fluids by slowing down to 98/minute. After exploring the scalp and lip wounds he clamped off the bleeders and began to suture the lacerations while waiting for the test results. He was most concerned about Marc's increasingly labored breathing. The lab results came first. The hemoglobin was down to a scary 8.2 and the hematocrit was 24.6, representing a large volume of blood loss. It was more than could be explained by the superficial wounds. "Of course!" thought Dumont. "Blood in the chest from broken ribs." He'd bet on a hemothorax. That would explain the labored respirations. Finally the x-rays arrived and confirmed the blood in the right lung. Dumont called for a chest tube and placed it posteriorly and low on the right side. He connected it to the suction apparatus to siphon off the blood and allow the lungs to expand. Slowly all vital signs were showing definite improvement.

Marc had three fractured ribs on the left side, a possible blowout fracture of the right eye socket and nasal bone fractures. The films of the limbs and abdomen were negative. It was nearly 2:00 AM when they transferred him to the intensive care unit. He was still unconscious. When Dumont was satisfied that his patient was out of imminent danger, he went to his quarters for a few minutes' sleep. He had left orders to be called the moment Marc's condition changed. Before he left he requested an immediate neurological consultation. He would wait until later in the morning to call a plastic surgeon for the facial bone injuries. The latter would mean surgery, and Marc was in no condition for that anyway.

Claude Dumont stretched out on his bed. It had been an unusually quiet night for the emergency room but the last few minutes had made up for that. He lay on his back with his hands behind his head. He couldn't sleep. He kept thinking about the American doctor. It was apparent that the man was in some kind of trouble. Who knows what? Drugs? No, there were no needle marks. Perhaps the sale of drugs? Possible but most unlikely for a respected plastic surgeon. And he must be respected otherwise how would the program chairman for something as prestigious as an international congress select him to moderate the first panel of the meeting? It was something else... something else. He was going to find out and if he could help he knew he would. He had to. Then he remembered with fondness the young French boy traveling through America. He remembered how kindly he had been treated when he was injured. He remembered the beauty of New England in the fall. The leaves... The brilliant leaves of red and gold... The scent of pine trees in the rain... These reflections always lulled him to sleep.

* * * * *

It was 1945 and the war was over. The crowd along the Champs Elysees was so thick that the people who tried to push forward toward the curb found themselves nearly immobilized. There were cheers and singing. Children were waving small French and American flags. Then the noise became louder. The crowd was mad with joy as the American troops came through the Arc de Triomphe. It was a great day in French history. It was the liberation of Paris.

Sarah Bennett was assigned by the Chicago Mirror to cover the story. She was trying to get that once-in-a-lifetime shot of the American tanks rolling through the Arc de Triomphe. Her camera was focused. She was ready to shoot and... suddenly someone grabbed her from behind, spun her around and planted a juicy kiss on her mouth.

Shit! she thought as she tried to pull away. Forget that shot! Maybe it was worth missing... The kiss was pretty damn good!

"Cheri, once more for the liberation," he said. This time the kiss was long, lingering and sweetly gentle.

"Oh what the hell! It's the liberation," she thought as she gave in. She had been only an observer and now she was a participant and loved it. When they came up for air she managed to shout, "What's your name?"

"Paul, Paul Dumont. And your name, mademoiselle?"

"Sarah Bennett. How do you do."

"Enchanté, mademoiselle. *Sarah*, it is a beautiful name. From the Bible, no?"

"Yes... Ah... oui." Her French was virtually nonexistent.

"Please, I speak English," he shouted proudly over the noise of the crowd. The tanks were just in front of them now. The people were wild. Arms reached out just to touch the outstreched hand of an American hero. A few brave girls who were lucky enough to be in front stretched their necks up for a quick kiss as the entourage slowly rolled by. Paul shouted something. Sarah shook her head and touched her ear indicating that she couldn't hear him. He grasped her hand and began to draw her backward through the crowd. She willingly followed. It was almost impossible to move. Gradually after about five minutes of pushing they had reached far enough back that the crowd had thinned out a little. The noise about them decreased in volume only to rise again a short distance away. The tanks were farther from them now. Paul shouted again.

"Come, Sarah. Two streets away. A glass of wine... only to celebrate. Bon?"

"Yes. Okay." She saw how excited and happy he was. She didn't have the heart to say no. Besides, she wanted to go. Finally they turned the corner and the row of buildings served as a sound barrier. They could talk without shouting. He saw her camera for the first time.

"What are you doing here? Taking pictures of the festivities?"

"Yes, in a way. I'm a corespondent for an American newspaper. I'm assigned to cover the liberation. Would you let me interview you?"

"It sounds delightful but first the wine." They stopped at the Café la Bonne Femme. It was quiet there. There were a few tables outside. They were the only customers. Paul pulled out the chair for her as the smiling proprietor came to them. "Vin blanc, s'il vous plait."

"Oui, monsieur, mademoiselle." Sarah, watched him as he ordered. She saw the handsome face and straight dark hair. His blue eyes stood out in strong contrast with his swarthy skin. His shirt was open at the neck revealing the thick, dark hair of his chest.

This is a hunk, she thought. "So what do you do, Paul?" she asked.

"I am a rogue of the worst kind," he said. It made her laugh. He loved the sound of it.

"No. I mean, what do you do... really?"

"I am an architect, an unemployed architect. There was no work for architects during the war. But perhaps now, with some luck..."

"Was it terrible for you during the war?" asked Sarah.

"Terrible? It was a nightmare!" The wine arrived. They toasted to the liberation. He gazed into her dark brown eyes as they sipped. He longed to stroke her long chestnut colored hair. He knew it would feel as smooth as silk. Her face was delicate with luminescent skin. And her figure! What perfection!

"Paul, would you tell me about it? Is it too painful?"

"Painful? Oui, but it must be told. We must never forget." He began.

"The Nazis came. They raped our women. They killed men and boys in the streets on the pretext that they were with the Resistance. There was little food. People became inhuman and would kill for a scrap of bread. Then there were the Jews and the Gypsies. They rounded them up and shot them on the spot. My best friend and colleague, Adam Roth, his brothers and his parents were put on a freight train and sent somewhere. Now we know it was to a death camp. There was nothing we could do. If someone tried to help them, throw them a piece of bread, they were killed. The Nazi pigs!" His eyes flashed with anger.

"And you? How did you survive?"

"One had to be very clever. They knew I was an architect of some small... how do you say... fame?"

"Yes, I understand. Please go on," she said.

"I had worked on the restoration of several very old buildings before the war. The Nazi pigs were interested in me. They wanted to preserve Paris and restore what damage they had done. One day an SS officer brought me an invitation to attend a banquet honoring Spier, Hitler's personal architect. I didn't know what to do. I secretly asked a friend who I knew was active in the Resistance. He urged me to go. It was an opportunity to get information from within. I went and met Spier and several other dignitaries. Spier liked me, perhaps more than just liked. After that, I was often invited to such functions. I kept my ears open and passed on what I learned to the Resistance. That is how I survived."

Sarah was silent for a moment. She saw his lip quiver. She didn't want to destroy his dignity. No more questions. She had heard quite enough. "Another toast," she said. "To France. To peace."

"To love," said Paul.

The courtship was brief. She continued for a time as a reporter for the *Mirror* but decided to remain in France. They were married three months later when Paul finally got back his former position doing restorations for the government. They were happy beyond belief.

Their first child, Paul, named after his father, was born in 1949 and Claude was born in 1954. In addition to their formal education Sarah made certain that they knew they were half American. She told them of the brief, but rich, history of her country and let them see the similarities of the two cultures. Both had had a revolution for freedom. Both prized liberty and equality. She told them stories of how she had grown up in America. Young Paul enjoyed listening, but to Claude the stories were exciting. He was fascinated. Someday he would see it for himself. Finally, for a graduation gift from his parents, he went with his best friend, Gilbert, on a bicycle tour of the United States.

They stored their bikes and visited New York and Washington first. The bikes were to be used for the countryside and smaller distances. Next came New England. It was spectacular. The fall colors were as wonderful as Claude had imagined from his mother's stories. It was late September when the boys rode into the town of Milbridge, Maine. The two young men were fascinated with the charming town on Route 1A. Claude had his father's eye for architecture and was completely absorbed in seeing the Victorian style of the homes. He didn't see the rock on the road. He flew over the handlebars and landed on his right arm.

His face and legs were scraped but luckily he had escaped a head injury. Gilbert went for help. He was told that the doctor's office and home were just down the road. With Gilbert's support Claude was able to hobble. The boys made it to the large Victorian house that backed up to the river. Gilbert rang the bell and a woman came to the door. She saw that Claude was injured. She was accustomed to such unannounced callers in need of her husband. "Oh, good heavens! What happened to you?" She didn't wait for an answer. "You boys come on in and wait in the parlor over there. I'll get the doctor." She went to the back of the house to find her husband sawing a long board in two. "Sam, there are two nice boys waiting to see you. One looks like he's hurt pretty bad."

"Okay, Martha. I'll be along in a minute." She returned to the boys with cookies and milk which even Claude devoured. She smiled when she saw how her baking was appreciated and went back to the kitchen for another batch.

Dr. Samuel Brown walked into the parlor. He was a short stout man in his late sixties. He was dressed in his overalls. The boys looked at each other wondering what kind of doctor they had found. "Well now, I'm Dr. Brown." The boys were well mannered and introduced themselves. The doctor addressed Claude. "What happened to you, young man?" Claude began to explain. Dr. Brown noticed the accent. "Where're you from, young man?"

"From France, sir. My Mother is an American," he hastened to mention.

"Ya don't say!" The boys thought he had a peculiar way of speaking.

"We are touring America on our bicycles." Just then Mrs. Brown, a little more round than her husband, walked in with more milk and cookies. "These boys are visit'n from France, Martha."

"France! My, my!" she said.

Implant

"Well, Claude," said the doctor as he was examining his arm, "I think you'll have to put the bikes away for a few weeks. The arm is broken. It'll mend fine but you have to give it four to six weeks. We'll need to get it x-rayed up at the hospital in Machias. Where're you stayin'?" The boys looked at each other. It was obvious that they had no place to stay and they were on a tight budget. Martha saw the picture immediately.

"Sam, they can stay with us in the guest room." She was excited. It was the most exciting thing in Milbridge in years. All the way from France!

"Sure, if they'd like. It ain't much but you're welcome."

The boys were happy to accept. Clean beds and showers... they hoped.

They stayed with the Browns for four weeks. After the first few days Dr. Brown had insisted that they telephone their parents. Sarah wanted Claude to come home immediately. Dr. Brown got on the phone, spoke with her and assured her that he would take good care of them. Reluctantly she agreed.

The Browns never had children of their own and they loved having the boys. Sam took them everywhere, even on his house calls. That was Claude's first introduction to medicine. He loved going with Dr. Brown. The boys were shown Acadia Park, Cadillac Mountain, Jasper Beach and Quaddy Head with its wonderful light house. They were like family to the Browns. The boys couldn't believe the couple's sincerity and soon there developed a close tie between them and the Browns. It would last for years after their return home.

The time in Milbridge passed quickly and Claude's cast came off in four weeks just as Dr. Brown said it would. The day arrived for them to leave. Martha cried as she prepared food for the boys to take on the road. The Browns made them promise to write. There were hugs, kisses and handshakes. And they were gone as though they had never been there. Claude was true to his word and corresponded with them over the next fifteen years. When Sam died in 1984 he wrote Martha a long letter of condolence and told her how Sam had influenced his seeking a career in medicine. He continued the correspondence with Martha until her death in 1986. He would never forget the kindness and love he was shown in America. He would never forget Sam and Martha Brown.

* * * * *

At about 5:00 AM the nurse heard unintelligible mumbling sounds from Marc's cubicle. As instructed, she immediately called Dr. Dumont. They leaned over him, trying to make it out. "No, please! Don't! Don't! Don't have it. Where? Ashley... Ashley... Help me, Ashley!" Dr. Marcus Hamilton was finally coming to. Dumont thought, "*Ashley*. Must be a woman. But of course." Marc became silent but continued to thrash about. They allowed him his restless sleep.

It was 6:30 AM. The 7:00 to 3:00 shift was coming on duty. While the head nurse was giving her report, they heard Marc calling for help and the noise of bed rails shaking. The head nurse and an attendant ran into the cubicle. They saw their patient trying to get out of bed. "Where am I? What's going on?"

"Dr. Hamilton, please lie down. You're at the Hospital St. Michel de Paris. You've been injured. This is the intensive care unit."

"What happened to me?"

"We were hoping you could tell us," said the nurse.

"How bad am I?"

"Doing much better now. You were in shock. You have some fractured ribs and a hemothorax. The neurologist found only a severe concussion, no actual brain damage. Several lacerations have been repaired. Your facial bone fractures will require attention." She had gone into much more detail about his condition than she would have with an ordinary patient but this was a doctor and would demand to know anyway. She felt this was the easiest way to quiet him. Habit, however, made her say, "But you're doing fine, just fine." He settled down, not reassured but merely confused. The nurse felt that he was stable, at least for the moment. She looked at the monitors. When satisfied, she left to finish her charting.

Marc remembered being injured and getting to a hospital. His pain was much less now. He realized that they must have given him something for it. He tried to think through the cobwebs and thick fog. If he could just concentrate. Think harder. Try harder. Then finally his efforts began to pay off. There were flashes, pictures, like a television screen being turned on and off, on and off. The hotel room. Working on his presentation. Room service. Oh God, room service! Only it wasn't room service! As he had opened the door they forced themselves in. Two men. Business suits. The larger of the two grabbed Marc's arms from behind, rendering him helpless. The other was asking questions while beating and pounding him in the face, chest, head, every square inch of his body, or at least it seemed so. They wanted something. What did they want? What? What...? A memo? The memo! Of course they wanted the memo. But he didn't have the memo. He really didn't have it and they wouldn't believe him! A huge weight fell on his head and then nothing. Now things were falling into place. The taxi. The hospital. The fear of death. Something was missing. Not the memo. He knew about that and why they had come. He had to meet someone. Meet Ashley. God, Ashley! He was supposed to meet Ashley! Again he tried to get over the side rails only to be restrained by an orderly. "Now just settle down, Doc. You're in no shape to get up."

"Ashley! I've got to get to Ashley! Please! Please!" he insisted. The orderly put in a call to Dr. Dumont.

"He's getting wild, Dr. Dumont. Can I give him a sedative?"

"No. He's had enough with a head injury. Try to keep him calm. I'm on the way." A few minutes later Dumont arrived to find that the orderly had placed Marc into restraints. He thanked the orderly and asked him to leave.

"Dr. Hamilton, I'm Dr. Claude Dumont. I took care of you last night." Marc's eyes were wide open as in a state of panic. Dumont realized that he was still disoriented.

"Nobody understands! I have to meet Ashley!"

"Who is Ashley?" he gently asked while releasing the restraints.

"Ashley."

"What is her last name?"

"Barton! Ashley Barton."

"Where can I find Ashley Barton?"

"At La Coupole... No, no... Hotel Splendid. Please call her. I've got to see her!"

Dumont phoned the Hotel Splendid and asked the desk clerk to connect him with Ashley Barton's room. He was told that the room was registered in the name of Dr. Marcus Hamilton. He knew this because all foreign passports had to be turned in to the authorities. The clerk rang the room. A sleepy voice answered, "Marc?"

"No, Madam. I am Dr. Claude Dumont. Dr. Hamilton has been injured and is at the Hospital St. Michel de Paris. He is in the intensive care unit. His condition is much improved and he is asking for you."

She was suddenly wide awake. "I'm leaving now." As she hung up the phone she thought, "He's alive! Thank God! He's got to be okay." She put on her shoes, grabbed her coat, ran down the stairs and into the street. It took a few minutes to find a taxi.

It seemed to be the longest wait she had ever known. "Hospital St. Michel de Paris, please. Hurry!" Her heart was pounding as the taxi drew up to the entrance of the hospital. She asked the first person she saw in a white uniform for directions to the intensive care unit.

She entered a large waiting room. All the chairs were taken. Several people were asleep on the floor and she took care to avoid stepping on them. She saw a priest. He sat near a group of people who were hugging each other closely. A young woman sat alone. Her dark hair was in complete disarray and her red eyes stared at nothing. Her face was frozen, motionless, without expression. It made Ashley think of how she must look and then immediately she felt guilt among these unfortunate people engulfed in their private pathos. She dismissed the thought and had only Marc's face in her mind as she approached the reception desk. "May I see Dr. Marcus Hamilton?" she asked of the elderly woman.

With a gentle smile and soft voice, the woman asked, "Are you Ashley Barton, madam?"

"Yes, I am."

"Dr. Dumont is expecting you. Please come with me." Ashley followed her out of the waiting area and a short distance down the hall to a door marked Private. "I shall let Dr. Dumont know that you have arrived."

"How is Dr. Hamilton?"

"Madam, I am only the receptionist. I am sure Dr. Dumont will explain everything to you. I hope your friend will be well soon." She opened the door for Ashley and gestured for her to take a chair. With a smile and a slight nod she turned and left Ashley alone in the small room. There were only the desk, two chairs and a lamp. There was no window. It was an unfriendly and ominous room. Ashley wondered how many people had been told tragic truths in this room. How many peoples' lives had been changed in this room? She wondered if she would be among them.

After a few minutes he entered. "Mdsl. Barton?" Ashley began to rise from her chair.

"Yes. Dr. Dumont?"

"Yes. Don't get up." He placed the other chair closer to her and said, "I'm pleased to meet you."

"How is Dr. Hamilton?" with urgency in her voice.

"I am happy to be able to tell you that his condition is now stable." She breathed a sigh of relief and at the same time observed the young face behind creases and lines that were premature and carved from fatigue. Behind the lines was concealed a handsome face. The dark brown eyes were dull from sleeplessness and yet they were reassuring. "Dr. Hamilton has been severely beaten. He arrived here in a state of shock from massive blood loss. I repaired several lacerations. He will need the attention of a plastic surgeon for his facial bone fractures. Except for a concussion and temporary recent memory loss, the neurologist has assured me that there is no brain damage. This is surprising in view of the severity of the attack." As he spoke he absorbed everything about her. She was stunning! He tried not to show his interest and hoped he had been successful in concealing it.

"Dr. Dumont, I am deeply grateful for all your efforts but may I see him now?" she asked impatiently, trying not to be rude. All she wanted was to see Marc... now!

"Of course you may in a moment. The situation is awkward and I need your advice."

"My advice?"

"I'm sorry. You don't understand. According to French law this incident must be reported to the police. It is obvious that this is no ordinary mugging or theft. I have called you here to clarify, for me, if you can, the circumstances that resulted in this incident. I do not wish to cause you or Dr. Hamilton any problems. If this were some simple crime, then perhaps calling the authorities would be to your advantage. I can delay for a while but eventually..."

"Then you haven't called the authorities yet?"

"Not yet."

"Dr. Dumont, I can only tell you this. Marcus Hamilton is one of the most honorable and ethical men you will ever know. He has become involved in a medical situation of global dimensions. Calling in the police and making this public now will place him and me in serious danger. Dr. Hamilton and I have come into possession of certain information that could be harmful to... certain individuals. They would kill to destroy that information. There is no question that they would kill us for merely having knowledge of those facts. If the data we have ever became public, it would have repercussions involving millions of women worldwide. I'm sorry I must be so vague, but I implore you to believe me. I can't expect you to jeopardize your position, but if you can give us just enough time for Marc to be well enough to leave, I promise that you will not become involved and you'll not hear from us again." He saw her eyes well up with tears. He believed her. He knew he would never make the call.

"Come. Let us see Dr. Hamilton," he said.

CHAPTER 8

In the late 1950s during his residency in plastic surgery at University hospital in Houston, Dr. Allen Greenberg had become fascinated with the concept of a breast prosthesis for augmentation mammaplasties. In most training programs the emphasis was on reconstructive surgery and the heads of these programs were looked upon as the leaders. These academicians who taught in their isolated ivory towers took every opportunity to condemn those who were performing cosmetic procedures. They took the position that any procedure outside of reconstructive was frivolous and demeaning to plastic surgery. Greenberg had applied for research grants to develop a breast prosthesis that was effective and safe. Not only were his applications turned down, but he nearly lost his residency.

After his last application was rejected, he requested a meeting with his chief, Dr. Jason Inglewood. He wanted his research project and somehow he would get it. He had no idea of what he was going to say to Inglewood as he knocked on the door.

"Come in, Greenberg. I think I know why you're here." Jason Inglewood was a large man. His size alone was impressive and intimidating, and he knew it. He used his frame and deep penetrating voice to maximum advantage. He could terrify his residents or bend the will of the plastic surgery organizations. It was not by mere chance that he was president of The National Plastic Surgery Society. As a speaker he was eloquent. He had the rare gift of being able to call forth the precise word or phrase, not only to express himself but at the same time to create a desired emotional response from his audience. He was impressive. So was Allen Greenberg but in a much more subtle manner. Greenberg could read people, understand their actions, anticipate their moves, zero in on their weaknesses and flatter their egos. He was a master manipulator. Although he didn't abuse this skill, he was not ashamed to use it when he found it necessary and this was one of those times.

"Dr. Inglewood, if you have a moment, I was hoping we could discuss Mr. Alfred Grimes."

"Grimes?"

"The 58-year-old man with the squamous cell carcinoma of the nose. I was wondering what your plan might be."

"What would you suggest?" asked Inglewood.

"Well, my thought was to remove the tumor tomorrow and to consider reconstruction as a second stage procedure a few weeks later." Greenberg knew that his chief nearly always preferred a one-stage operation with immediate reconstruction whenever there was a favorable chance for cure and this was such a case.

"Why the hell would you do a two-stage when you know you can cure him and do a forehead flap reconstruction in one stage?" Inglewood was irritated with his resident.

"Of course, sir, a forehead flap! I don't know what I was thinking! Perfect for a one-stage! I should have realized after all you've taught me. I just hope that one day I'll be able to see the best option as clearly as you do, sir."

"Well it takes time and experience," said Inglewood more calmly and now the wise teacher. "You have to see the entire picture. It's judgment, Greenberg, judgment!"

"But it's more than that, Dr. Inglewood. It's something special. I hope I'll have half that talent someday."

"You will, Greenberg. Work at it. It takes time," now with a fatherly smile.

The hook was in and only needed to be set. "I hope you're right, sir. I guess I'm just discouraged about my breast prosthesis project. Dr. Inglewood, I've been working with silicone gel for months in the lab. Every test shows that the gel is inert... nonreactive with animal tissues. The purified gel could be contained in a preformed silicone envelope and used as a safe prosthesis for reconstucting or augmenting the human breast. Chief, it's revolutionary! I know it will work! As you've tried to teach me, I can see the whole picture. I know my judgment is right but..." he said with a disappointed shrug and head turned away.

"You really think you can do it?"

"If I just have the chance!" Inglewood was pulling on his bushy eyebrow. For a moment neither one spoke.

"The research foundation turned you down again. They think it's frivolous and a waste of time and money."

"But, sir, isn't the quality of life important too? You've always taught me that. A breast prosthesis that is compatible with human tissues would change the lives of millions of women. Nothing would make me more proud than to call it the Inglewood Implant." Oh, God, did he overdo it?

Inglewood studied his resident and smiled, "You know I can't go over the research foundation's decision but if you could get funding from the private sector, you would have my permission on a six-month trial basis."

"Do you mean that, sir? Do you mean that? I've been talking with Alcott Laboratories and they're very interested in giving me a private grant. They just want to be sure that the department here will approve. Dr. Inglewood, this is going to be big! I know it!"

"Six months and no promises until I review your progress."

"Thank you, sir. Thank you."

"Just don't make a fool of me, Greenberg."

"You won't regret this, chief."

As Allen Greenberg, elated, left the office, his chief kept saying over and over to himself, "The Inglewood Implant, the Inglewood Implant."

* * * * *

In 1985 Marc Hamilton was finishing his last year of plastic surgery residency. He was scrubbing on a case with his chief, Dr. Allen Greenberg. They had a good relationship and Greenberg was pleased that his resident had taken such a deep interest in continuing research on the silicone gel breast prosthesis, the Inglewood Implant. As they were scrubbing, Marc said, "Congratulations, chief. I hear that the nominating committee was unanimous."

"Thanks, Hamilton. It will be a tough year as president of The National Society, but if I can get a few of my ideas through, it will be worth it."

"I'm sure you will, Chief."

"What are your plans for July?" asked Greenberg.

"Private practice. I can hardly wait."

"You know you should be teaching."

"I'm flattered, sir, but I need to work with people. It's definitely private practice for me."

"Well, if you ever change your mind..."

"Thanks, Chief. That means a lot to me."

"I want you to get your boards right away," said Greenberg. I want you to get your membership in The National Society while I'm president. I have a job for you."

"Sir?"

"I want you to be a one man committee, liaison between the breast prosthesis manufacturers and the plastic surgery organizations. With the FDA raising it's ugly head we need the communication and contact."

"That would be an honor. But I'm not sure. What's involved? I hope I'll be up to the job."

"You will be. I'm not worried about that. Not one bit."

Marc had never thought of himself as a politician and was uncertain about his effectiveness as one. At the same time it was flattering that his chief had so much confidence in him. He knew that he couldn't disappoint Allen Greenberg. They got the signal from the o.r. nurse. The patient was anesthetized and prepped. Marc followed his chief into the operating room.

July came quickly. Marc had been making plans to open a private office in the fashionable Galleria area. He had thought about this carefully. Nearly all the plastic surgeons were in the medical center but the city was growing rapidly and a large affluent community was developing around the Galleria. Although he realized that he would be dependent on trauma and reconstructive procedures for some time, his heart was set on the aesthetics of plastic surgery and this was where it was going to happen. He found an appealing small medical building a few blocks from the shopping center and inquired about the leasing arrangements and about the other tenants. There were several names he didn't know, but Thomas Jackson was a well known dermatologist and Ben Crosby, obstetrics and gynecology, had a fine citywide reputation. That would be all he needed for a start. He made appointments to see both potential referral sources.

Crosby welcomed Marc and was delighted to have a plastic surgeon in the building. Crosby was a young man who had been in practice about seven years. He had moved from the medical center two years ago when he realized the potential in the suburban areas. People simply didn't want the inconvenience of driving the congested freeways to the medical center. He had made the right decision. His practice was booming.

"Marc, this is great! Do you have any idea how many of my patients are requesting breast implants? Your research with Greenberg is common knowledge. I can't think of anyone in whom I'd have more confidence for breast augmentation," he said enthusiastically.

"Ben, I really appreciate that and you know I'll need all the help I can get."

"Trust me. You've got it!"

The visit with Tom Jackson was equally rewarding. Jackson needed a plastic surgeon he felt could accommodate his busy practice. Marc was promised all the lesions that required excision and reconstruction.

Armed with these assurances Marc committed to a five year lease in the building. He selected a ground floor space, about two thousand square feet. Now came the expense of finishing it out. For the first time he found it necessary to dip into the trust fund his parents had left him. He hired a decorator and an architect, explained his needs to them and proceeded to develop a functional and aesthetically pleasing office. In less than ninety days it was complete. The first morning he approached the door to his office he stood for a long moment admiring the sign on it:

Don Klein

Marcus Hamilton, M.D.
Plastic and Reconstructive Surgery

He thought about the long hours of study and work that had allowed him to arrive at this beginning. He wished that Marla had been here to share this with him, but he didn't dwell on that for long.

Marc had hired Mrs. Anne Warner, a nurse with adequate secretarial skills, to be his assistant. She had come from a general surgeon's office, was familiar with surgical terminology and had considerable knowledge about medical office management. She was brunette, thirty-four years old, presented herself well, had a pleasing voice and, most important, was outstanding on the phone. If the patient was seriously considering surgery, she could usually make the appointment. Marc announced the commencement of his practice by putting an ad in the Houston Daily Journal. He made a point of specifying, *specializing in cosmetic surgery of the breast*. The ad seemed to pay off.

"Good morning, Dr. Hamilton," said Anne Warner as Marc walked in.

"How's it going, Anne?"

"Lots of inquiries about all sorts of things. Most calls are about breast augmentation and I always mention your special expertise in that area. Made two augmentation appointments for next Thursday," she said proudly. Marc was delighted.

"Not bad for openers." It was really beginning, and he could hardly contain his excitement.

"Oh! You're to return Dr. Allen Greenberg's call. He'll be out of surgery after one o'clock," said Anne. He was sure his chief was calling to wish him well in this new phase of his career. At one o'clock he returned the call and was put through to his former teacher.

"Marc?"

"Yes, sir. How are you, chief?"

"I've seen better days. Have you heard about that sonofabitch Messerman?"

"Who?"

"Wade Messerman! The head of the FDA!"

"Oh, sure. What about him?"

"He's making noises about breast implants again."

"What's he saying?"

"The bastard is grandstanding. He's trying to use the *prior to 1976* ruling to reclassify silicone gel implants from class I to class III."

"Can he do that?"

"I hope not. It would be a disaster. Can you imagine what would happen if the two million women in the world with breast implants got even the suggestion that their implants aren't safe?"

"My God! Why is he doing this?"

"Politics, my boy. Politics!"

"What does he hope to gain?" asked Marc naively.

"Well let me ask you this. Do you think an aggressive bastard like Wade Messerman, M.D., PhD and lawyer would settle for a minor niche as head of the FDA? Shit no! He's aiming a lot higher! The sonofabitch is trying to get the attention of Congress and the White House. What better way to get the public stirred up? He wants a cabinet position, maybe surgeon general, and a groundswell of grass roots support wouldn't hurt."

"But there's nothing wrong with the implant."

"Christ, how can my best resident be so politically stupid? The truth doesn't matter! Only what you can get them to believe counts. Who's going to doubt the head of the FDA? Marc, I need you now! You know Chuck Walker at Alcott, right?"

"Right. I worked closely with him on developing the new generation of the Inglewood."

"Well, I spoke with him today and they are as concerned as we are. They want to talk with us through the National Society and develop a closer working relationship and possible future strategy. Sooner or later we're going to have to deal with Messerman, and a united front between the manufacturers and organized plastic surgery could be our best weapon. This is where I need you for liaison."

"But I'm not even an active member of the Society yet."

"You leave that to me. There's no one who knows the nuts and bolts of this shit more than you and I, and as president I have to be impartial. That leaves you. Walker is expecting you at the plant in Seattle on Saturday. Okay?"

How could he refuse. Besides, it was important. "Sure, I'll make my reservations!"

"No need. We've done that for you already. By the way, congratulations. I really mean that." Marc knew that the sentiment was genuine. He made plans for the trip to Seattle and told Mrs. Warner that he'd be back on Monday morning.

Chapter 9

When he exited the terminal building in Seattle, Marc saw Chuck Walker signaling for his attention. Marc had always been treated royally by the executive staff of Alcott Laboratories so he was not surprised to see Walker himself, the Vice Executive Director, and the familiar limousine. "Marc, good of you to come on such short notice, especially when you just opened your practice. Congratulations from all of us."

"Nice to see you, Chuck. What's going on?"

"Let's get in and we can talk on the way." Chuck Walker was forty-six years old and young for his position. He was medium height and physically fit. He worked out daily. It was like a religion with him. The face, which was too round, gave him a heavier appearance than he deserved. He had light brown hair and his thick brows that met in the midline created a menacing look. Alcott had recruited Walker from the FDA five years previously when J.T. Roswell, the CEO of Alcott, had met him at an early encounter with the agency. Roswell had been impressed with the subtle manner in which Walker had diffused the first sticky issue. Walker's knowledge and connections would be invaluable and his managerial skills were apparent. Roswell made him a handsome offer and Walker accepted. The transition from government to the private sector was easy for him. He was organized, knew his responsibilities to the Lab and set his priorities and long term agenda. He liked his work, and Alcott was pleased with their acquisition.

"There's a board meeting at two o'clock and J.T. wants you there. We can get a quick lunch at the Club first. The FDA is getting to be a real problem, Marc."

"Chuck, Greenberg gave me the basics but I'm no politician."

"Well, sonny, you're gonna learn fast and we're gonna teach you. We need a plan and mutual cooperation between all the manufacturers and organized plastic surgery."

"Can the FDA really attack the implant?" asked Marc.

"You bet your ass they can. Our job is to stop them."

"But can we? How?"

"That's what we'll discuss at the board meeting. Here we are. Let's get some lunch."

The board room at Alcott Laboratories was impressive. It was on the tenth floor and the row of windows on the south side of the room overlooked the lush green park below. All the walls were richly paneled in solid walnut that had been milled in squares with a four pointed star geometric pattern. On the south wall hung photographic color portraits of the members of the board of directors. In the center of the room was a long table also of solid walnut with twenty very comfortable leather-upholstered chairs around it. At the head of the table sat Jonathon Tyler Roswell who preferred to be called "J.T." by his board members. He had been CEO for twenty-one years and no one had ever challenged his position nor his authority. He was about sixty years old, tall and trim. He had thick white hair and small piercing blue eyes. He wore a medium solid blue double breasted suit and conservative tie. His bearing and stature were absolutely patrician. Behind him and to his right sat his private secretary, Virginia Moore, an attractive middle aged woman who sat, stone faced, attentively taking notes on a legal pad.

In the late 1950s Alcott Laboratories was a small pharmaceutical company manufacturing only a few minor products and was in financial trouble with enormous debts. The company had been poorly managed by the sole owner, Andrew Alcott, whose goal was to become a prominent figure in the pharmaceutical industry. He had no concept of fiscal responsibility and no managerial skills. Andrew Alcott had a pharmaceutical degree, an inheritance and a dream. The company was going down the tubes. He had always ignored the advice of his financial advisors to diversify and run a tighter ship. However, with financial disaster imminent, he finally listened and hired a young aggressive executive from International Energy Corporation, a growing oil refining company. His track record was amazing. He had singlehandedly reorganized the oil company, set goals for growth and put them into the international limelight.

That young executive was Jonathon Tyler Roswell. The board of directors of Alcott offered him an enormous salary, which they could not afford, and made him CEO. To save face they "promoted" Andrew Alcott to President, an office with a title and no official responsibility. J.T. was an organizer. He developed more products, got Alcott out of debt and with his marketing skills and international contacts he had the company in black ink within four years. Roswell had singlehandedly transformed Alcott Laboratories into a major player in the international industry. He was always aggressively seeking new opportunities, and when he heard of Dr. Allen Greenberg's research with the silicone breast prosthesis, Roswell contacted him and arranged for funding his project. J.T. had the foresight to see the worldwide attraction to the product and made it his personal goal to acquire all rights to manufacturing silicone gel. He had his battles with the FTC and FDA but finally prevailed. Alcott Laboratories by 1962 was the only producer of silicone gel, had the lion's share of the international breast prosthesis market and had established laboratories in every major nation outside of the Communist Bloc. This success story had earned him worldwide recognition and his picture on the cover of *The Executive*.

Chuck Walker and Marc entered the board room. The meeting had obviously been in session for some time. Nearly all the chairs were filled and volumes of papers lay in organized stacks about the table. Mrs. Moore was passing out folders to the board members as all heads turned toward the new arrivals. Of course they were expecting Marc. J.T. had made that announcement to them at the very opening of the meeting. Marc, during his residency had been working closely with Greenberg in developing a second generation of the Inglewood Implant, which resulted in an improved textured surface gel prosthesis. Greenberg had sent Marc as his emissary on several previous occasions to apprise the Board of his progress. They knew Marc, and the young surgeon was well liked by all of them.

J.T. stopped in mid-sentence, "Chuck, Marc, come on in and please join us. The rest of these reports can wait. Marc, on behalf of all of us at Alcott, congratulations on the commencement of your practice. No one knows better than we how well you have earned this milestone. Best of luck." This was followed by a sincere round of applause from the board. Each member stood and shook hands with Marc, while offering a few private congratulatory words. Marc was surprised by this almost overly enthusiastic display and was somewhat embarrassed but enjoyed it thoroughly.

Several men moved their places to allow Chuck and Marc to be seated beside each other at the table. Roswell began, "Marc, I'm sure that Chuck has given you the basics on your way here today. We are facing a crisis regarding the manner in which the FDA wants to perceive the *safety and efficacy* of silicone gel. If Messerman were to be successful in his condemnation of the product, it would open a can of worms that might lead to the withdrawal of the gel breast prosthesis from the market. That would spell economic disaster to the manufacturers and plastic surgeons and would cause the loss of one of the great advances of plastic surgery in our time.

Such a frivolous and unconscionable act on the part of the FDA would surely result in terrifying over two million women who have mammary implants when there is absolutely no scientific data to support the implied danger. Perhaps worst of all would be the deluge of class action lawsuits that would certainly follow. What a bonanza for the trial lawyers! We can't allow that to happen! The board has proposed a joint effort between all manufacturers and organized plastic surgery. As manufacturers we have the facilities to give the FDA the scientific laboratory data they want, and your organization can provide the necessary clinical data from an immense patient pool. A perfect marriage. Of course this has been discussed with Dr. Greenberg and he is presenting this to his board of directors as we speak." He glanced at his watch and continued, "It is our understanding that you will chair this new liaison committee and naturally, we couldn't be more pleased with Dr. Greenberg's choice. I'm sure you have some questions, so shoot."

"Mr. Roswell, I'm not clear on exactly what my responsibilities will be," said Marc.

"You will meet with this board once each month and we will present to you our scientific findings. The testing protocol has been brilliantly established by Warren Burns, chief of research. I'm sure you know Warren." Burns stood and extended his hand to Marc.

"It will be a pleasure working with you, Dr. Hamilton."

"Thank you," said Marc as they shook hands.

Roswell continued, "Your job, Marc, will be to present our findings to your board and to assist your society in supporting clinical studies and data throughout the country and abroad. Finally we will combine our respective findings and present them to the FDA with the hope that this will satisfy them."

"Excuse me, sir, but this plan will take years."

"Exactly! We'll kiss Messerman's ass and keep the implants on the market for as long as possible."

"Then you seem fairly certain that eventually the gel implants will be withdrawn," said Marc.

"We're buying time, Marc. Maybe we can get Messerman out before he causes any real damage."

"It seems such a waste when we have over twenty years of experience showing no serious risks with gel. Why not just go public with our current data?"

"Do you have any idea what sort of panic that would create? Even the suggestion that silicone might be related to a disease process would be chaotic. That's Messerman's ace in the hole. He knows we can't risk going public with the truth. But we must try to keep him from implying publicly that there may be a health risk. He has nothing to lose and a lot of recognition to gain. I'm afraid all we can do is stall. The bastard is determined."

"Isn't there some way to discredit him?" asked Marc.

"That's the whole point of our combined effort. This will make it as difficult as possible for him. Marc, it's our only chance and we've got to take it."

Implant

After the meeting the limousine took Marc to his posh hotel. He was exhausted after the trip and the meeting. As he lay in bed his mind began to wander and just before sleep engulfed him, there was an uneasy feeling. Was it the possible loss of the silicone implant? No, something else. Something intangible. Something frightening. Then the thought slipped away allowing sleep to obliterate all conscious concerns.

Chapter 10

Marc was at his desk reading his mail when Mrs. Warner's voice on the intercom interrupted him. "Dr. Hamilton, your last patient is here for her consultation. May I bring in her chart?"

"Yes, please."

Marc scanned the information sheet. The patient was female, twenty-eight years old, divorced and was seeking consultation for augmentation mammaplasty. "Mrs. Warner, would you please show Mrs. Barton in."

A moment later, "Dr. Hamilton, this is Mrs. Ashley Barton." Mrs. Warren exited closing the door behind her and returned to her office.

She stood there for a moment as tall and slender as a lily. Her shoulder length blond hair fell softly framing a face with lovely contours and delicate features. He rose to greet her and tried to be casual. "A pleasure to meet you, Mrs. Barton. I think you'll find that chair comfortable," he said as he offered her the light blue easy chair. He absorbed every graceful movement. She sat somewhat forward with her legs crossed. She was spectacular! Her makeup was subtle and just enough to accentuate her sparkling green eyes. He said, "I hope you haven't had to wait too long." The light rose colored lipstick suited her fair complexion while defining a generous mouth.

"Not at all, Doctor. Your office is beautifully done."

"Thank you but it's my decorator who gets the credit. I simply told her that I wanted a subtle and unobtrusive look, something definitely non-medicinal and an atmosphere which would allow a patient to feel comfortable and relaxed."

"I'd say you've achieved exactly that, Doctor."

"I understand that you would like to consult with me about breast augmentation." He had already noted her full cut olive silk blouse and made a concerted effort not to gaze at it while maintaining eye contact. Marc hoped that he hadn't brought up the subject of her visit too soon. He was nervous and was desperately trying to show a cool, professional demeanor.

"Yes, I've always felt that my breasts were, proportionately, much too small. Truthfully it has been a great source of embarrassment for me. A 34A just doesn't cut it. I hope you can give me some information about silicone implants and your evaluation of my problem." She said all this easily. He knew that many women had great difficulty with discussing their breasts, and for them a breast examination was a traumatic experience.

"Of course I'll be doing exactly that." He proceeded to obtain a medical history, which proved to be essentially negative. He pushed the intercom button and said, "Mrs. Warner, would you please drape Mrs. Barton for a breast exam in room four." Mrs. Warner showed Ashley into an examination room, helped her undress and get into a garment. As Marc entered he felt more composed. Ashley's smile and relaxed attitude helped.

After the examination he asked her to get dressed and return to the consultation room but not before smilingly saying, "There is hope for you... definitely!"

She laughed and said, "Oh, thank God!" They both laughed. He spent the next thirty minutes explaining the procedure and the possible risks involved. He suggested that an increase in breast size was indicated to achieve better proportions. The discussion turned to the silicone implant itself, including a history of the prosthesis, its known safety record as well as the FDA's current rumblings. He knew the words were coming out of his mouth. He heard them but they seemed to be distant.

His words were covering his conscious thought, "This is the most spectacular creature I've ever seen!" Her eyes never left his. Her lips were slightly parted. Was she really listening? "Yes, I think we're on the same wavelength with a C cup," he heard himself say. Was he reading something in her face that wasn't there or was she really on the same wavelength? He must be mistaken. She was a beautiful patient and that was it!

"Now, if you would like Mrs. Warner to schedule your surgery..."

"Yes, please. The sooner the better." He walked her to the door and let her go with an overly formal nod and smile. He actually let her go! He had always thought of himself as sophisticated and yet this woman, this patient, was making him feel an awkwardness he had never known. It was a tug-of-war between professionalism and the true man within. Professionalism won this round. He could have kicked himself. He was sure he saw something in her face. He was certain.

After she left, he asked Mrs. Warner, "Did Mrs. Barton schedule surgery?"

"Yes, Doctor. Two weeks from today."

"May I see her chart again?"

"Of course, Doctor." He noticed her quizzical expression.

"I simply want her phone number. There is something I forgot to discuss."

"Of course, Doctor," this time with a knowing smile and a slight elevation of an eyebrow.

"If you "of course, Doctor" me once more, you're fired!"

"Yes, Sir." They both smiled.

That evening Marc went home to his small but comfortable apartment not more than ten minutes from his office. He went through his usual rituals of washing up and changing into more casual clothes but he couldn't take his mind away from thoughts of her... the sparkling eyes, the sensuous mouth, the classic silhouette. He took a scrap of paper out of his wallet and reached for the phone. "Mrs. Barton"?

"Yes."

"This is Doctor-ah- Marc-"

"I know and I'd be happy to have dinner with you tonight."

He knew it! He had seen it! Oh, God, they were on the same wavelength! "Can I pick you up at eight?"

"Fine."

"Armando's okay?"

"Perfect."

"See you then." He wanted to jump in the air and click his heels.

Armando's was the *in* place in Houston. Besides his having outstanding cuisine, Armando was the perfect host. Though he had never met Marc before, when he heard "Dr. Hamilton" at the reservation desk and noticed the beautiful woman beside him, he quickly accessed the situation.

"This way, please, Doctor Hamilton. So nice to have you with us this evening." Armando's was the place where prominent, or aspiring to become prominent, Houstonians went to be seen. There was a definite pecking system completely and meticulously controlled by Armando. The more prominent and socially elite were automatically seated nearest to the entrance to be able to be seen and recognized. However there were exceptions and this was one of them. The couple was ceremoniously led to a discrete table for two in a quiet corner. "Thank you, Armando," said Marc, as though he knew him well. He was playing the game. At last they were seated and alone. The conversation in the car had been superficial and somewhat stilted but now that they were seated both seemed to relax a bit.

"Would you care for a drink?"

"Please... Martini, dry, cold, up and olive." Marc had the same. The waiter took their order.

"I'm glad you called," said Ashley. "I hoped you would."

"You knew I would, didn't you?"

"Yes," she said candidly. "I guess I didn't hide my thoughts very well."

"Apparently I didn't either." The drinks arrived. They clicked glasses. Nothing needed to be said. They were sipping while searching each others eyes. Finally Marc broke the silence, "You do have the advantage. You know who I am and something about me."

"Oh, quite the contrary, Doctor. I believe this afternoon you got to know me intimately," she teased.

"Please, no games," he said seriously. "I want to know all about you."

"All about me... Okay! I was born in California but grew up everywhere. I was an army brat. Never made the effort to form lasting relationships because we never knew when another transfer order would come through. Oh, don't misunderstand. I wasn't shy and never lacked for dates but I couldn't see the value of making a serious commitment. This all changed when I went to college, UCLA. I made a lot of close friendships there. Kind of making up for lost time. That was were I met Bob Barton, Robert

Barton, Jr. He was handsome, suave and at the head of his class in the school of engineering. I was a sophomore undergrad. We met by chance in the campus coffee shop. We hit it off and I fell for him completely. We were married shortly after his graduation. I left school to become a housewife.

Somehow everything went wrong for Bob. Every promising job offer turned to dust. It was a bitter time. He was so talented but lacked sound business sense as well as the ability to understand people or to gain their confidence. I did what I could to be supportive. I suggested business courses but he wouldn't hear of it. Maybe this was the male ego thing. I got a job with an advertising company. My background was in communications. Without a degree I could get only an entry level position. It was enough to pay for groceries and mounting household bills. Bob began to drink and things went from bad to worse." The tears began to well up. "When he was loaded he became abusive and when he was hung over he was apologetic. I felt that I was on a merry-go-round and had to get off. How do you help someone who doesn't want help? It finally ended in a divorce about two years ago. I won't go into the gory details. It was messy. I went back to school and got my degree in communications. Now I'm back in advertising with a solid job and career goals I hope to achieve. And that's the short version of the life story of Ashley Barton."

"Pretty tough. I think you deserve better," he said.

"Your turn!"

"Okay... Let's see... Doctor's son, born in Ohio, graduated Harvard. By pure chance I found my niche in plastic surgery. I did my training here in Houston and recently started my practice and here I am."

"That's it? I'm not letting you off so easily. I didn't ask for a CV. What about *you*? Any women in your life? I assume you're single."

"You're tough! Yes, there was a woman. Marla. She was a nurse at the hospital where I trained. She was beautiful, smart and fun to be with. We fell for each other hard. Finally toward the end of the general surgery residency we were married. I thought we were happy. I couldn't see beyond my own happiness to notice her loneliness. Residents don't have much time. I figured that was understood, her being a nurse and all. I couldn't see her needs and couldn't understand that she didn't want to share such a time consuming career with me. My acceptance of the plastic surgery residency was the last straw for Marla. She loved me. I know that. But she had supportive needs and I simply wasn't there to fulfill them. One day she left. No warning. No letter. I found out the story from our best friend, Dave. Apparently she had confided in him and just couldn't face me. I didn't think I'd survive but I guess adversity has a way of building strength... or is it caution? God, I'm sounding paranoid."

"No, your not. I understand. I went through the same thing. For a long time I didn't want to meet another man. So I guess you're divorced."

"Well, not exactly."

"Not exactly! What's that supposed to mean?"

"Neither of us ever filed for divorce. Don't ask me why. I don't really know. Maybe some burning embers. I found out that she left Houston. I haven't seen or heard from her since. That was a few years ago. I've dated but nothing serious. I try not to think about it. It's painful."

"Trust me," she said. "You have unfinished business. It will hang over your head and be painful until you deal with it head on. There must be a closure. I'm talking too much. It's really none of my business."

"You made it your business by asking," he said gently.

"I guess I did."

"I'm glad you did. I've never been able to discuss this with anyone before. Somehow it's easy with you."

Dinner was served but neither of them ate. They picked at their food during the conversation. They were too engrossed to think about eating. They had coffee. The check arrived. Ashley glanced at her watch. It was half past eleven. "I didn't realize it was so late. I'm a working girl, you know."

"I enjoyed this. I hope we can do it again. Home?"

"Please." The room was nearly empty now. On the way home the conversation turned to the forthcoming surgery. "How soon will I be able to return to work, Marc?"

"We're operating on a Thursday so with a little caution you should be able to return to reasonable activity the following Monday. I hope to see you before that."

"I'd love to," she said. "How about dinner at my place the Saturday evening before? I'm not a bad cook."

"Great."

They arrived at her apartment and he took her to the entrance. "May I come in for a few minutes?"

"It's really rather late and I have an early meeting." Marc wondered if he had struck out. His face must have shown the disappointment.

"Marc, I really want to but in view of the surgery I think I would feel better, more comfortable, with keeping it cool. I don't want to mix my emotions. I think that could spoil things and that's the last thing I want to do." He bent toward her without another word. She met his lips eagerly, hungrily. Her mouth opened slightly and their tongues explored. He felt her warmth and eagerness. She was aware of his erection in their tight embrace. It was more than just a good night kiss. It was an assurance that more would come but with caution. They'd both been burned and both still felt a certain remnant of that pain. At least they had that in common. Although it was difficult, he respected her wishes and admitted to himself his own insecurity. He didn't want to complicate this relationship. Her responses were real and she showed her genuine feelings toward him. He gently let her go.

"I'll call you tomorrow," he said.

"I'll be home after seven." With that she smiled and disappeared through the entrance.

Marc couldn't sleep. Thoughts of Ashley spun in his brain like a windmill. Was it real? He thought it was the real thing with Marla. Could he trust his feelings? "Well, buddy, you'll never know until you try," came from somewhere inside and he knew it was truth.

They spoke daily, laughing, teasing and learning to know one another. The Saturday night dinner was a success from every standpoint. There were long lingering kisses. Marc thought about touching her breasts and then canceled that. That was forbidden territory for now. She was emotionally too focused on her breasts and his amorous explorations could spoil everything. Ashley was right. He would keep it cool for now. The day for surgery arrived. She accepted his offer to pick her up that morning to take her to the outpatient surgery ward. The operation was uneventful. He was satisfied with the aesthetics. It was a strange feeling for Marc. Although he had performed this operation many times before, this time was different. He had been creating only for the patient before. Now he was also creating for himself. He was glad they had kept the flame low. More could have interfered with his judgment. He knew she would be pleased with the result. Soon when her self confidence level rose, she would be ready for him and he would wait patiently until that moment.

She spent the night in the hospital. In the morning Marc took her home. Since he had canceled his schedule, he was able to stay with Ashley to help through the first uncomfortable days. He needed to do this and she was grateful for his tender care. "Gentle Marc," she said lovingly to him. He gave her a soft kiss.

As promised, she was able to return to work on the Monday following surgery. Marc returned to his increasingly busy practice. They spoke on the phone daily and during the next four weeks they often dined together. When she was up to it, they took short walks. Ashley was delighted with her result. A strong feeling of self confidence quickly replaced the former insecurities that so many have who seek this surgery. By the fifth postoperative week she was blossoming. Marc saw this and took pleasure in knowing that she was pleased. One evening after dinner and a walk together she asked, "How about a night cap? I have a surprise for you." Marc wondered if this was show time at last.

Once in the apartment after offering Marc a brandy she excused herself. He nervously waited. After a few minutes she entered the living room where Marc was sipping his drink. She wore a dark blue lace negligee. Her soft hair fell gently on her shoulders. Her eyes were flashing. Her head tilted to one side as she approached him as if to ask, "Well, what do you think?" He answered by slowly walking toward her. He drank in every feature, every contour as though she were a delicate art object which might break if roughly handled.

Again their lips met, eager and hungry lips which slowly parted for tongue to seek tongue. This time deeper thrusts while they tightly embraced. Suddenly Marc backed off. She said, "It's all right. They don't hurt any more." She always seemed to be able to read his mind. They kissed again and embraced as his hands ever so gently touched her nipples beneath the lace. They were hard. He bent down to kiss one and she drew his head closer to her breast. She sighed as her head extended backward. Her finger touched his zipper and she slowly drew it downward. Finally her hand cupped his erection. They swayed to and fro deliriously for a long time. Then she took his hand and led him to the bedroom. As he removed his shirt she let her garment fall to the floor. She stood there for a long moment allowing him to see her nakedness. She then walked toward Marc and slowly undressed him. He felt a hungry aching deep within.

Then they were in bed. They gently explored one another. He loved to touch and follow every curve of her body. She felt alive only where his hands touched her. As he approached her thighs he felt the luxuriant growth of her hair and he thrilled as she sighed deeply while he ran his fingers through it. His hands explored further and at last he felt the familiar soft, warm contours and inviting wetness. As he touched her there she gasped from pure pleasure. Slowly he entered while being careful to keep his weight from her breasts. As he penetrated deeply he was overcome with emotion and said in a throaty voice, "Ashley, I love you." She responded with an ecstatic moan, "Me too, Marc, me too." Their bodies moved in perfect harmony, both seeking the same thing. He sensed that she was ready. At that moment she said, "Now!" His thrusts became faster and deeper, faster and deeper until the inevitable crescendo consumed them. They didn't move for a very long time and they fell asleep in each other's arms.

It was Sunday morning and Ashley awoke first. She put up the coffee. The aroma of the fresh brew awakened Marc. He stayed there reflecting on the delicious evening. She came into the bedroom with fresh cups of coffee and with a broad smile. "Good morning," she said.

"Good morning. I love you."

"Oh God, I love you too!"

They sipped the coffee while their eyes maintained searching contact. They both knew it was real! Without another word they put down their cups, embraced and devoured one another again.

Later that morning they showered together. Marc was drying Ashley's back with a towel when he said, "I have to go to Seattle next Thursday. Can you come with me?" She turned toward him.

"I'd love to. I'll make arrangements to get covered at work, but what's in Seattle?"

"Alcott Laboratories," said Marc.

"Am I supposed to know what that is?" She was puzzled.

As Marc finished patting her dry, he said, "Honey, do you remember my mentioning the FDA when we first met in the office?"

"Not really. I guess I was concentrating more on you rather than on what you said." She gave him a hasty peck on the lips and then wrapped a towel about her. "So tell me. What did I miss?"

He continued. "Alcott Laboratories is the primary manufacturer of silicone gel. Although there are other companies making breast implants, the gel comes from Alcott. They're big, very big."

"And you buy the implants from Alcott," she said.

"Yes, but there's more to it. My chief, the man who was head of the department of plastic surgery during my residency training, was Dr. Allen Greenberg. He invented the silicone breast prosthesis and knows more about it than any man alive. During my training, I worked closely with him and was involved in several research projects. There has been continuous research on the implant and the gel itself for about thirty years. As I told you during your initial consultation, we have found the silicone implant and gel to be safe, effective and inert when in contact with human tissues. The clinical studies of plastic surgeons throughout the world have proved this to be the fact and furthermore these studies coincide with the laboratory findings of Alcott."

"Now I remember," she said. "I felt more comfortable after you explained the safety factor to me. But I still don't understand why you have to go to Seattle?"

"Well, I'm not finished." He tried not to show his irritability over her impatience. Nevertheless she got the message.

"Sorry."

"That's okay... Anyway, the FDA was given authority by Congress to investigate the safety and effectiveness of implantable devices that came on the market prior to 1976, when FDA requirements for use were less stringent. So with this new power they've decided to reopen the silicone issue."

"But why? You just said that studies for the past thirty years show how safe they are." Ashley looked down at her breasts. "And I'd say they're definitely effective!"

He laughed. "Its not quite that simple. Politics seems to be playing a major role. Alcott and other manufacturers, even Allen Greenberg, are pretty pissed off about that. The FDA doesn't want to look at the scientific data. Messerman, Commissioner of the FDA is pushing this forward for his personal purposes. He wants recognition and power. Nothing would please him more than to tell the world that silicone breast implants are unsafe and must be removed from use."

Ashley protectively folded her arms across her chest. "Oh no! They can't have mine!" When she saw that Marc was serious, her expression changed. "So how are you involved more than other plastic surgeons?"

"Allen Greenberg is now the president of the National Plastic Surgery Society, the NPSS. He feels that we must have a joint effort between organized plastic surgery and the manufacturers to try to change the attitude of the FDA. Allen appointed me to serve as a one-man liaison committee. My function is to carry the laboratory findings of Alcott, who represents the other manufacturers as well, to the NPSS. Then the NPSS coordinates Alcott's findings with current clinical studies from plastic surgeons around the world. Finally I take those results back to Alcott for evaluation and coordination with their own lab data. And that means a meeting about once a month in Seattle where I can parley with the lab director and the executives to keep things perking."

"Marc, that sounds like a very big job. Do you think its possible to change the course the FDA is taking?"

"I don't know, Honey. But I'd like you to come with me Thursday. See what you think. You're in the business of creating public opinion. I'd respect your view. I don't know whether or not all this can make a difference, Ashley. If Messerman is determined, this effort may be in vain. I just don't know."

CHAPTER 11

During the first week in October, 1989, the FDA was holding hearings regarding the *safety and efficacy* of the silicone gel mammary implant. If fact finding were the genuine purpose for the hearings and if science had prevailed, the information gathered by the years of research from the tedious labors of the national plastic surgery societies in the United States and elsewhere, as well as from the laboratories of the manufacturers of the implant would have been admitted and heard.

Every plastic surgical society, every plastic surgeon and every manufacturer were barred from admission to the hearings. Commissioner Wade Messerman had meticulously orchestrated the event. He had pathologists who reported on the tissue changes surrounding the implant. Of course it was common knowledge that a layer of scar tissue developed around every implant and that occasionally it could cause hardness. That was a procedural risk that every patient who had the surgery understood and was willing to accept. He had immunologists on the government payroll who stated that any free silicone *might* cause an autoimmune response, which *might* trigger various collagen diseases such as rheumatoid arthritis or lupus. He had other government experts, some of whom had never even seen a gel implant or the operation performed, who claimed that any free silicone *might* result in a woman having a deformed fetus and even *suggested* a link to breast cancer.

The key words were *might* and *suggested.* These innuendoes were published and circulated among those in government who could influence health legislation and to the manufacturers of the implant. After thirty years of experience with the device, logic would dictate that all this was false. Where were all these diseased patients? Were they all hiding in the dark cellars of plastic surgeons? But it wasn't logic that prevailed. It was unscientific, unadulterated terror that ruled. Messerman had a stacked deck and he won the first round. The silicone gel mammary implant, after a thirty-year safety record was reclassified to a III status, meaning that more research, government research, would be needed to prove that these horrors did not exist. Class III status dictated greater FDA control over these devices and possible withdrawal from use.

* * * * *

It was late afternoon. The last rays of the sun filtered through the tenth-floor windows and cast long ominous shadows on the walnut paneling of the board room at Alcott Laboratories. The room, usually seen in bright sunlight as a friendly place, assumed a completely different character. Four men sat at the far end of the long table in a kind of huddle with their backs turned away from the empty chairs. They remained there for a long time, even as twilight fell. Perhaps they felt more secure in the approaching darkness. The near silence was broken only by the low murmur of whispers that accentuated the dark mood. Jonathon Tyler Roswell sat at the head of the table. On his right sat Chuck Walker. On the left, bending toward his boss was the manager of the research laboratories, Warren Burns. Beside Burns sat a man who seemed out of place. He had the attentive yet empty gaze of someone wanting to understand but not completely comprehending. He was in his mid forties, large with gross facial features. His clothes merely fit and lacked the fine fabric and tailoring that the others wore. He sat uncomfortably in his chair. While trying to look interested and involved, he twirled a pencil this way and that between his thick fingers. J.T. was speaking. "Well, I guess it's happening. Class III means more work for you, Burns. How do you plan to approach it?"

"Sir, I thought I'd start with some animal studies to show the integrity of the implant covering. Maybe later I could go on to study tissue specimens from areas injected with free silicone."

"Okay, but remember, I don't want any surprises. We had enough of that a few years back, if you catch my drift."

"No, Sir... I mean yes, Sir. No surprises. I'll keep you informed all the way."

Chuck Walker added, "Warren, we have to comply with the FDA's request for more research, kind of busy work. It's already been researched to death and any unusual findings can only hurt us. This is just part of Messerman's show before he lets the news media and lawyers have at it. We don't have to make it easier for him. We just have to comply."

"Yes, Sir. I understand."

"Burns," said Roswell in even a lower whisper, "are you sure there is nothing in the files or in the computers from the unfortunate 1976 episode?"

Implant

"When I first took over the lab from Matt Wertheim in January of 1976, I made certain that everything was clean. I'm sure."

Roswell continued as he turned toward the large man, "Conners, give me an update of your situation."

"Well, Sir, we're ready for anything. This plant is secure. I have several agents around Seattle at strategic areas working for TV stations and newspapers. Same in other cities where the gel is manufactured. Same in Area X. If anything gets out of control I'll know it!"

"Area X?"

"Yes, Sir," in a whisper, "Europe. I have eight men in London, six in Paris, nine in Amsterdam..."

"Okay. I got the picture. I assume they know what to look for."

"Yep! Besides the usual security breaks and leaks they are to report any activity by Wertheim. Right now he's working for a biochemical company, Gibson Global Industries, in Atlanta. He makes frequent trips abroad to their subsidiary plants. No unusual moves. He has no idea he's being watched. We even know when he takes a piss. Anything unusual, I'll let you know that minute."

"God damn that Wertheim! I haven't slept well since I fired him. I want to know the second he has any contact with the FDA. The sonofabitch knows too much... knows it all. Even if he would have spilled his guts before, he was no real threat. We could always discredit him. Now with Messerman looking into our labs, I'm getting worried. He could say something out of spite or just because of his damn principles. He could destroy us."

"Boss, you just say the word..." said Conners as he punched his right fist into the palm of his left hand.

"Are you nuts? That would lead a trail straight here. No! Hopefully we'll never need to deal with that... On the other hand if we have no choice... Just keep me informed!"

"Absolutely! By the way what about Hamilton?"

"What about Hamilton?"

"Can you trust him?"

"Christ, this all happened way before Hamilton! He doesn't know anything. You spooks are all alike! Conners, are you paranoid?"

"No, Sir. Just trying to do my job."

"Chuck, you're closer to Hamilton than any of us. Do you have any reason to believe he knows anything?" asked Roswell.

"No. I'm sure he would have discussed it with me. No. Hamilton is clean. He'll be here Thursday for his monthly visit."

"Well, that settles that," said Roswell as he stood up from the table signaling the end of the meeting.

Chapter 12

Ashley and Marc spent every free moment together. They went to the symphony, theater, movies and long quiet dinners followed by spending the night at one or the other's apartment. Sometimes if Marc finished surgery early enough they even managed to have lunch together. Marc's practice was growing faster than he could have hoped. He was rapidly gaining the reputation of being an excellent and caring surgeon. He had joined several hospital staffs and became active on various committees. This was the best way to become known by the other doctors in the community who might become referral sources. He was well liked. Marc always accommodated his referring doctors in the emergency room or the operating room at any hour of the day or night. They knew they could rely on him and when asked by a patient for a referral for an elective cosmetic procedure, Marc's name was usually at the top of the list. Of course the best were the patient referrals, pleased former patients who recommended him to friends and family members. That was the foundation of a cosmetic practice.

Ashley's career was skyrocketing. With Marc's encouragement she left her position at Multimedia Advertising and went into private consulting work. She was considered a genius in public relations and marketing and was in constant demand by the most prestigious firms to handle their advertising and marketing programs. Her greatest asset was her ability to understand people and their specific needs. She based her recommendations on these. She laid out the best plan for the budget she was given. If she encountered resistance, she never pushed but gave alternative approaches. Without effort she exuded confidence, and this was absorbed by her clients.

Although very much in love, neither Marc nor Ashley had actually made a firm commitment to their relationship. The painful experiences of past marriages loomed over them. Sex was easy. They indulged themselves freely and gave of themselves wholly. It was the emotional investment they both feared. They understood this and made their compromises. They finally agreed to pool their resources to make a down payment on too large a house for too much money in the very affluent Memorial area. About a year after they had met they set up housekeeping and found that the arrangement and necessary adjustments came more easily than either had expected. Gradually they began to trust their feelings and the old wounds began to heal. The emotional barriers were falling away like a wall around an ancient city ruin.

Ashley occasionally accompanied Marc on his monthly excursions to Seattle. She was charming, and the executives at Alcott liked her and treated her with appropriate respect. She was always invited to dinner, but at those times business was not discussed. Despite this exclusion Ashley felt comfortable with the executives at Alcott and liked hearing how they praised Marc's work. For the first time she really understood the full importance of what he was doing. She encouraged Marc to continue with his liaison efforts in the hope of altering the course of the FDA.

They had been living together for over three years and during this time Marla's name was hardly mentioned. Ashley rarely brought up the subject but Marc could see that if their relationship was to continue, and he desperately wanted that, he had to close the door on that episode of his life. But he didn't even know where to find Marla. Then the obvious came to him. Dave Stein had probably stayed in touch with her.

* * * * *

After residency Dave had joined a well respected group of general surgeons. He was considered the expert in the surgical treatment of breast cancer, not only by his peers, but by the public as well. Dave and Marc often worked together on breast reconstruction cases. They enjoyed one another and had remained best friends. Occasionally they met for lunch or went for an early morning jog together. Dave was still single. He had never been able to get Sharon completely out of his system. Although he dated often enough, he compared every date with Sharon, and every date came up short.

Marc and Ashley were away on one of their Seattle trips and Dave found himself alone for the week end. He could have called a number of people for dinner or a movie but decided not to bother. It had been a tough week. His new BMW had been creamed by a pickup truck and he was having a difficult time getting the other driver's insurance company to settle with him. He was still sore from the muscle spasms in his neck caused by the sharp jolt of the collision, but luckily there were no serious injuries to either party. He simply didn't feel much like company. It was Saturday night, about seven o'clock. A spring shower had started just as he pulled up with his rented car into the parking area of Grover's Restaurant. It was his favorite place for a hamburger and a beer. He managed to find a parking space near the covered entrance. Grover's was always packed and the foyer was thick with people waiting for tables. They took no reservations. Dave squeezed his way toward the young girl making table assignments at a podium. "How long?" he asked.

"About forty-five minutes, sir.

"Okay." He hated to wait but he had no place to go anyhow. "It's just for one... S-T-E-I-N. Nonsmoking area, please." He turned and began to weave his way through the crowd to find some breathing space near the bar. He was almost there when they collided. Her drink spilled across the front of his shirt. "Oh, God! I'm so sorry! Are you okay? Here, let me get that off." She withdrew a handkerchief from her purse and began to dab at him. He let her dab. Her touch was sensuous. "You're soaked and its all my fault."

"Nonsense! It's just as much my fault for not looking," said Dave.

"Lange party, Lange. Your table is ready," came over the speaker.

"That's me!" she said. "Are you with someone? I mean, if you're alone, I'd be happy to share my table with you... I mean, I don't want to..."

"I am alone and I'd like that very much," he said.

"It's the least that I can do." She smiled at him. He couldn't take his eyes from her. She was beautiful. She was mid thirties, about five foot seven, long silky dark brown hair, eyes the color of ripe olives. Her mouth was outlined in crimson. Her makeup was certainly not subtle but definitely complimentary. He followed her to the table while watching every movement, every contour... and she knew it. They were seated in a booth across from one another.

"I'm Dave Stein, the victim," he said with a broad smile.

"And I'm Victoria Lange, the perpetrator." They laughed. He liked the way she immediately picked up on his humor.

"How did I get so lucky to find the most beautiful woman in the house?"

"Oh, sir, you make me blush," but she didn't. "Actually I hate dining alone."

"Ah, now I see! You go around spilling drinks on innocent single guys in restaurants just so you can have a dinner partner."

"Innocent? Any guy who would say he was innocent has to be lying. I think you're lying, Dave."

"Damn! Caught again!" said Dave with a telling grin.

"So what do you do, Dave?"

"What would you like me to do, ma'am? I'm very accommodating."

She was laughing. "No. You know what I mean. What do you do for a living?"

"I'm a surgeon. And you?"

"I eat surgeons for lunch! I'm an attorney. I handle mostly personal injury cases. Does that end our short but violent meeting?" She was smiling but nevertheless she was half serious.

"Of course not. I never met a lady lawyer before and I'm too curious to end this torrid affair." The waiter came and they ordered. "Have you 'eaten' any surgeons lately?"

"Chewed him up and spat him out!"

"Ugh! I guess I had better be careful around you," he said with mock concern.

"I give you fair warning, Doctor. I have a very nasty bite."

Their dinner arrived.

They had ordered hamburgers and after the first mouthful Dave said, "This is the world's best burger!"

"You see, we can agree on something," said Vicky.

"Yes. Do you think we could build a relationship based on that?" They were still fencing.

"That depends on what you mean by a relationship."

"I know we're not cousins, so it can't be that. Let me think... You're not my patient and I'm not you're client so it can't be those. So by the process of elimination I believe I have solved the problem."

"Yes...?"

"How about social... boy-girl type stuff?"

Vicky was silent for a long moment. Then with a serious expression and a midline furrow between her brows she said, "Dave, you seem to be a nice guy. Let's just leave it as it is. I just got out of a bad situation two weeks ago. That's why I was alone this evening. I am sorry about spilling on you. I thank you for sharing this evening with me, but that's all. I'm not ready for anything more just now."

"I understand. How about possibility number two... an attorney client relationship? Strictly business."

"Strictly business?"

"Strictly business and no strings!"

"Do you really have a problem... or is this just...?"

"Vicky, I really have a problem and I need a lawyer."

"If you're being sued for malpractice, I can't defend you. I only represent plaintiffs."

"No. It's nothing like that." He proceeded to give her the details of his recent car accident.

"You are serious! Can you come to my office tomorrow evening? You'll need to sign some papers so I can get things rolling. This should be a piece of cake."

"Sure. Can we make it late? I'll need to finish my hospital rounds."

"I work late too. How about eight o'clock?"

"How about dinner?"

"There you go again! I can't trust you!" she scolded.

He threw his hands up defensively. "Okay. Okay. I'll be good."

"Promise?"

"Promise."

The waiter brought the check. Vicky insisted on paying it. He saw that this was important to her, so he didn't even reach for his wallet. "What a beautiful woman. What a fascinating and bright woman. This is just the beginning, Vicky," he thought. They left the restaurant together. It was raining heavily and Vicky had parked her car a good distance away. "My car is right here. Let me drive you to yours. No point in getting soaked."

"I'd appreciate that." She got in and he started the engine but didn't back out just yet.

"Thanks for dinner and the company," he said. It was all he could do to keep from stroking her hair. He restrained himself from any advances. He knew that when the time came for it, Vicky would take the lead. He wasn't sure about how he would accept her obvious need to be aggressive. It might be very interesting. He'd deal with it then. He drove to her car.

"No. Don't get out. Why should you get wet too?" she said.

"Okay." It made sense.

"Thanks, Dave."

"For the ride?"

"No. For not pushing me. Thanks for understanding."

"For understanding that you want to be in control?" Maybe he had been too blunt. She didn't speak. She only stared at him. She was amazed. They had been together for a mere hour and he read her as clearly as an open book. Vicky was impressed.

This might be very interesting, she thought. She smiled. She wasn't offended.

"See you tomorrow," Vicky said as she stepped out of the car

She worked on the case for about six weeks. She was wonderful and no match for the rather complacent insurance company lawyers. Vicky had won a generous settlement for Dave. He was so impressed with her professional ability that he had bragged about her to Marc and Ashley. They met more often than necessary, but it was business only until the evening that she handed him the check from the insurance company. "Vicky, let's celebrate. Dinner? Please don't say no." He had kept his word and she couldn't say no. She didn't want to say no. They went to the Black Rose, an intimate little bistro near her office. They ordered cocktails, toasted one another and sipped in silence. After a few minutes, "Councilor, tell me who you are? Who is Victoria Lange?" She sipped her drink and silently searched his eyes. Maybe she could trust those eyes. She wanted to trust him. But could she? She had never been able to trust any man completely. Should she chance it?

Vicky put down her drink and began. "I was born in Ridgetown, West Virginia. My daddy was a miner. God! How I loved him when I was little. Momma raised six of us and she was an old woman by the time she was forty-five. I was fifteen when he left, and I was glad he did."

"But you just said you loved him." Dave could see that she was fighting back tears. Now he was sorry he had asked but it was too late.

She looked away and fell silent again. Then after another sip, "He'd start drinking on Friday night after he got his pay check. Sometimes Momma would send me to Charlie's Bar to try to get him to come home before he drank away the grocery money. We were dirt poor then. He would always leave with me when I came for him but I dreaded his coming home. As soon as he walked into the house he'd start in on Momma. He beat her mercilessly and she always took it. I hated her for being so weak. Then, one night he came to my room..." She choked up and couldn't continue.

"Oh, God, Vicky. Stop! You don't have to go on. I'm so sorry I..."

She looked straight at him again. "No. I want to tell you. I've never told another soul. I have to tell you. I need to." She continued. "We never really knew for certain but we heard that he had a girl friend. Momma got a job as a maid cleaning house. All the kids had to leave school and get jobs to support the family. I made up my mind when I was fifteen years old that I would never end up like Momma. I was mature for my age. They believed me when I told them I was eighteen so I could get work at the shirt factory.

Mable Slaughter was the only person who was ever kind to me in that dirty old town. She was a school teacher and she tutored me in the evening after work. She helped me get a full scholarship to the University of West Virginia. I worked my way through law school and got my degree. I sent out forty or fifty applications for jobs with law firms, any law firms. It's tough, especially for a woman. Finally I was accepted by Lovelace, Randall and Bates here in Houston. I stayed with them for two years. I dealt mostly with battered women and abused kids. Then I went out on my own. My practice is growing as I'm getting more involved with personal injury cases. Dave, I've made it out of the gutter and I'm going to stay out at any cost... AT ANY COST. I'll never be weak like my Momma. Never!" Her eyes were flashing.

At first Dave was sympathetic, and then he saw how she was consumed with anger and hostility. It frightened him and he wanted to back off. She was a goddamn weightlifter with balls of steel! And she was beautiful and smart as a whip. She had proven that to him when she stood toe to toe with the insurance company. How could such a spectacular facade conceal the venom behind it? It was this mystery that beckoned and intrigued him. He had to know more. He had to know all of it.

Vicky was glad that she had told Dave. She had never been able to be that open with anyone before. Still she had the need to be cautious with him. She would never let her emotions get in the way of her aspirations. She would never depend on any man. She would never be weak.

They started meeting regularly on the weekends. It was dinner, a movie or just talking. Dave knew that he had to take it very slowly. He had mentioned Vicky to Ashley and Marc many times and they were eager to meet the woman who had bewitched their best friend. Finally the schedules meshed and they went to dinner together. It was Dave's suggestion that they meet at the Top Hat. Ashley and Marc had arrived first and ordered drinks. It was only a moment later that Dave arrived with Vicky on his arm. Marc got up from the table to shake hands with Dave but his eyes were on Vicky. It was very clear to Ashley that he liked what he saw. "I'm so pleased to meet you. This is Ashley," he said. The women smiled at each other. Marc sat down and Vicky positioned herself between the two men. "We just ordered cocktails. Let me call the waiter back," said Marc.

After the drinks were ordered Ashley leaned forward toward Vicky and said, "What have you done to poor Dave? He hasn't been able to speak of anything but you for weeks."

"Well, I hope it's not all bad," said Vicky.

"No, quite the contrary. He told us about how great you were with the insurance company in getting the claim settled out of court."

"Dave tends to exaggerate when it comes to me. It was actually an easy case to win."

"I'm sure you're being modest," said Ashley.

"I'm never modest about anything," said Vicky with a sober expression and a firm, almost angry tone.

"I only meant..." said Ashley almost apologetic as Dave interrupted,

"You have to understand Vicky. She's candid to a fault." Marc sensed the tension in the air and changed the subject.

"Dave, you've been keeping Vicky all to yourself. I always knew you were selfish." Marc turned to Vicky and said, "Dave said that your practice is largely personal injury."

"Yes. I enjoy it. It's a challenge." Ashley was gazing into her drink and seemed lost in thought. She barely said another word for the rest of the evening. They ordered and chatted over their dinner. Most of the conversation was monopolized by Dave and Marc.

After coffee was served Ashley excused herself to go to the ladies' room and gave Vicky a questioning glance. Then Vicky responded with, "I'll join you." They left the men at the table.

Ashley was looking into the mirror of the ladies' lounge as she carefully applied her lipstick. She saw Vicky's image behind her and turned around to face her. It was Vicky who spoke first. "Ashley, I'm sorry. There was no need for me to be rude. I guess I feel a little nervous about meeting Dave's closest friends for the first time. Please forgive me."

"I understand. There's no problem. I'm happy for Dave and you," she said with noticeable coolness in her voice. Ashley returned to her lipstick. She wasn't sure about Vicky. Perhaps she was reading more into it than was there. The poor girl probably felt like she was under a microscope. Who wouldn't be nervous under such circumstances. She had to give her a chance. Vicky was still standing behind Ashley and was assessing the last comment. It was an awkward moment for both. Ashley turned around again and extended her hand. "I want to be friends, Vicky. I trust Dave's judgment."

"I want that too. Thanks... You're lucky you have Marc. He seems to be a fine person. I understand there is a stumbling block in the way of your marital plans... There I go again... I'm getting too personal.

"That's okay," said Ashley. "It's certainly no secret that Marc is still married. I hope to get that resolved soon."

"I'm sure you will. I'm glad we talked. I may need some advice about Dave. Will you have lunch with me if I call you?"

"Of course I will. I'd love to. I think it will be easier without the men." They exchanged knowing smiles. "Shall we join them?"

When they arrived at the table they found Marc and Dave laughing and holding their sides. It was apparent that a new joke had been told and that the women had not been missed. Although this first evening together had been awkward, the two couples went out occasionally. The women began to trust each other more and made the effort to be friendly, but in reality it was mostly for the benefit of the men.

* * * * *

Even when Marc was alone with Dave, the subject of Marla never came up. Marc never asked and Dave was too tactful. Finally, one August morning after jogging they collapsed onto a park bench. It was eight o'clock and already getting hot and muggy as only Houston can be in summer. They were thoroughly spent and dripping with sweat. Between rapid and labored breaths Marc puffed out, "Dave... huhahu... you ever... huhahu... hear from Marla... huha?"

"Yah... Phone... once in a while.

"How is she?"

"She's fine. She lives in San Antonio. She's been working in CCU at St. Vincent's Hospital there. Last I heard she was still single and still looking for the perfect guy. A couple serious affairs but they all end the same way. Zero. Sweet kid. Always asks about you, which is more than I can say about..."

"Okay, okay! I deserve that. I know."

"Shithead, you could have at least asked about her before! She was... is your wife!"

"I'm asking now." Marc realized how selfish he had been, playing the martyr all these years. After all, it was she who had walked out. No warning! No discussion! He knew there was her side of the story as Dave had tried to tell him so long ago. He hadn't wanted to hear it. Only now when he needed her did he even inquire. He should have realized that Marla was Dave's friend too. He hung his head in shame while waiting for Dave's next lashing. There was silence between them. Marc knew that Dave was really angry.

"C'mon! I was hurt and tried to erase it." His ego wouldn't even crack.

"You want sympathy from me?"

"Please, Dave. Don't! I know I've acted like a schmuck." The first admission of any guilt. Dave stared at him for a long moment and decided that was enough. He let his anger subside.

"You want her phone number?"

"Please," he said still not looking up. He couldn't bear to look into his friend's angry eyes.

"Call me at home tonight. I'll give you her number."

Marc nodded, "Thanks... Friends?"

"Friends." They shook hands, got up and went in opposite directions.

Marc called back over his shoulder, "I'll call around seven. Okay"?

"Fine."

It was nearly seven o'clock when Marc arrived home. Ashley had been working longer hours than usual for the past several weeks. She had worked hard to get the Texas-American Oil Company account. Now she had to work even harder to keep it. She had to come up with never ending new marketing strategies, which meant long evening meetings with her client. Marc was relieved to have arrived home first. He wanted to talk with Marla alone. Although there were no secrets between them, he would have felt awkward and embarrassed with Ashley present. He called Dave as arranged and got Marla's phone number.

What do you say to your wife after not having had contact for over four years? What would she say? Would she be angry? Hell, he was the one who had been hurt! No warning, no explanation, nothing! But she must have been in pain too. He cooled down. Dave had gotten through his thick head. She was his wife and he hadn't even made the effort to find out how she was doing or if she needed anything, and he knew Marla would never ask him for help. He only knew the reason for the split through Dave. He had always thought of himself as a caring person. He was realizing how selfish and cruel he could be. Somehow it was in him. He was capable of being a real sonofabitch. Suddenly he thought of Richard Welch. Was Welch too good a teacher? No, he wasn't like that, but Marla deserved better. What an example to show Ashley!

His hand was unsteady as he dialed the number. "Hello?" He remembered her voice.

"Marla, this is Marc." There was a shocked silence.

"Marc, you've caught me off guard. I wasn't... ah... well, how are you?"

"I'm fine. And you?"

"Fine, fine."

"I got your number from Dave. I hope you don't mind." He was testing the waters.

"How is Dave? I haven't heard from him in a long time."

"Oh, Dave is fine. We often operate together and, you know, we jog and sometimes have lunch together."

"Yes, he's told me. It's great that the two of you have kept up your friendship for so many years. I understand that your practice is doing very well. I'm glad but I wouldn't have expected otherwise."

"You obviously know more about me than I do about you."

"Well, I've inquired." Marc wondered if that was a dig. That wasn't the Marla he remembered, but in nearly five years one could change.

He said, "I've behaved rather badly on that score."

"I didn't mean it that way, Marc." He relaxed a bit.

"Tell me about yourself. I know you're still in nursing."

"Yes, I'm in the coronary care unit at St. Vincent's here in San Antonio. I've been here since I left... ah... about four years."

"That's a long time to be in a CCU."

"Yes, I'm about burned out. I guess it's time for a change."

"You're making some plans?"

"Plans? Well, I'm not really sure what but I've had my fill of CCU. I guess you know what I mean." Marc realized that this conversation was going nowhere. It was his call. The ball was in his court.

"Marla, would you mind if we met and talked?"

"No, I'd like to see you. I'm off on the week ends."

"I could drive down Saturday, if that's convenient."

"Sure. What time?"

"I could be there around noon."

"Good. Do you know the Alamo-Grande Hotel on the River Walk? The mezzanine lobby?"

"Yes. That's fine. Till noon then, on Saturday."

"Till noon on Saturday. Bye."

The conversation was so superficial that he felt more as though he were making a blind date than talking to his wife. But, he realized, what could he expect? He heard the door open and Ashley had arrived. "Marc," she called.

"I'm in the study." She found him in a pensive mood as she planted a kiss with hardly any response.

"Something wrong, Honey?"

"No, something right for a change. I called Marla. I'm going to San Antonio to meet her on Saturday." Just like that, cool and resolved. She tried to conceal her surprise at his sudden decision. She knew the meeting was inevitable and had been hoping for this moment. What she didn't expect was the anxiety she felt. Although she had more than hinted at his facing Marla and ending it, she knew better than to push Marc. She understood his pain, frustration and anger. It was delicate and she didn't want to lose him. She hoped that he would someday be strong enough to do it. It had to be his decision. He had to love her enough to go through the pain of a closure to that episode in his life. She had been patient. God, how patient! Often she was inwardly furious with him. She had chewed it up and swallowed it. At the same time she was possessed by her love for him. This was the moment she had been waiting for... and now this anxiety. She couldn't understand it at first.

"Oh, good. You know you need to do that," she said convincingly.

"Yes, I need to."

Even as sure as Ashley was about him, this was foreign territory and, logically, anything could happen... a reunion... burning embers becoming a flame. It was a risk that had to be taken if they were ever to move forward and she wanted that desperately. He read her face and said, "I need to see her for us." She sat in his lap with her head on his shoulder and they held on to each other for a very long time.

* * * * *

On Saturday morning he headed west on Interstate 10. The road was familiar. During the tough years of residency training, after Marla had left, he, Dave and one or two of the guys would drive to San Antonio and just let loose. They would cruise the River Walk and find some willing girls who were looking for the same thing. Sometimes they would get bombed out on Margaritas and sometimes they would score. There were plenty of hotels along the river. He had tried to get Marla out of his system. He had tried to keep his sanity. He hadn't thought about those days for a long time. Now his mind was flooded with thoughts, some simple and some complex, some questions for which he had answers and some for which he had none.

He thought that life had been extraordinarily kind to him, except for his marriage. He still couldn't completely understand what had destroyed it. He remembered their love for one another and there was no bullshit about that. But now he had Ashley and wasn't going to let her go. My God, she must love him to have hung around this long. He was sure about her, and his love for her was boundless. But hadn't it been as real with Marla? He thought so and the thought made him uncomfortable. Perhaps he didn't remember exactly. After all it had been such a long time ago.

The more he dwelled on it the more uncertain he became. Could he still have something for Marla or she for him? No! The bitch left him without a sign or warning! Now anger was taking over. How was it possible that he couldn't have seen her instability? How could he have been so naive? And yet, he admitted to himself, he was frightened to see her again. The more he thought, the more muddled it all became. Would she agree to a divorce? Did he want the divorce? It certainly took him long enough to get this far. Would she suggest a parting fuck? Oh, shit! He turned it off in favor of the anger. That was the fuel for the courage to meet this encounter. And then he heard himself say, "I want Ashley! Oh, God! I want Ashley."

    He arrived in San Antonio at 11:30 AM and made his way to the downtown area. Parking lots were already full. On Saturdays the Alamo and River Walk were popular attractions. After circling for about ten minutes he finally found a space in a fairly remote lot. He crossed the wide avenue and headed toward the River Walk. Marc knew the area well enough and followed the sounds of music. He looked nervously at his watch. Ten more minutes. The signs directed him to the stone steps that led down to the river. The crowd was thick. There was no way around or through the throng so he paced himself to their rhythm and moved along in the direction of the Alamo-Grande Hotel. The sounds of jazz flowed and mingled with Mariachi melodies from restaurants and cafes to set the happy mood reflected in the faces surrounding him.

    His eye caught the Giant Iguana. That was where he and his buddies had spent many afternoons girl watching and downing the enormous Margaritas while watching the passing parade. He remembered how they had been caught up in the revelry and had eagerly joined the Mexican dancers who had coaxed them on. Although he had been trying to forget his troubles then, there were some carefree moments and treasured memories. He let those thoughts dissolve. This was now and he was not a participant. He had a specific destination with a specific goal and an uncertain result. He pushed on and with each step the nervousness of meeting with Marla became more intense. He entered the hotel from the river entrance and walked past the trendy shops. He took the escalator to the piñata-decorated and fiesta-colored lobby and then rode the elevator to the mezzanine level. He stepped out and looked about for an instant only. There she was, not twenty feet away sitting in a comfortable chair facing the elevators.

Even though he expected to find her here he was taken off guard by seeing her the instant the doors opened. He must have looked foolish, he thought, and with that he immediately regained his composure. She stood up and waited for him to cross the distance and as he approached she smiled. He noticed that she was dressed for the occasion in a floral patterned cotton short sleeved dress. He saw the familiar flashing dark eyes and curly, shining, brown hair. Her lipstick was too red and the long gold-plated earrings seemed garish to him. In that instant he couldn't help comparing her to Ashley. Marla was still as beautiful as he remembered, but there was nothing subtle in her appearance or demeanor.

As he walked uncertainly toward her she noticed his tan Palm Beach suit and pastel tie. The face was the same, perhaps a few lines around the eyes. The untamable lock of hair falling carelessly upon his forehead was still there. He had remained slim and he walked with the manly grace she so often recalled.

"Hello, Marc. You look wonderful."

"Hi. You too. It's been a long time." He allowed a wary smile.

"Yes, it has." There was a momentary awkward silence. Marla spoke first. "I've kept in touch with Dave. He's told me all about you, your work and success." He wondered if she had said this to emphasize the fact that he had never inquired about her until now. Was this going to be a power game?

"I guess I've been pretty lucky," he said.

"Come on, Marc! You always made your own luck. Please sit down," she said gesturing toward the chair beside her. This all seemed unreal to Marc, too staged, or was it just his uncertainty in this uncharted territory.

"You mentioned that you were getting burned out in the CCU. What are your plans?"

"I haven't made any definite plans. Maybe I'll travel a little before I take on something new." Now a longer silence.

"How about a drink?" Marc asked. She declined more firmly than necessary.

"Thanks but I'd rather not."

"Oh, sure. Okay," he said awkwardly.

She waited for a long moment and then began, "Marc, remember, you called me. Shall we talk about it?" She was going straight for the heart. The smile was gone. She intended to make him uncomfortable. He was now certain of that and she was succeeding. She had all the chips and this was going to be her game.

"Marla, I was floundering for months, shocked and hurt when you left. Oh, sure, Dave explained. I didn't even suspect there was a problem."

"Of course you didn't. You were too busy to know I was alive," she said with bitterness.

"Now that's not fair! You knew what to expect of a resident."

"You're right. I did know, and I placed you and your work first and my needs and happiness were neatly tucked away in some dark corner."

"But I thought we were happy."

"You thought you were happy," her voice now became a pitch higher. "It was a one-way street. I loved you and catered to your needs until finally I couldn't deal with it any longer. I really didn't want to hurt you or your career. So I simply left."

"But without a word! Not even a hint," he continued to press his point.

"Would it have made any difference?"

"I don't know. You didn't give me a chance to figure it out."

"Marc, it only would have created more problems and frustrations, and making you change your career would have caused guilt for me, resentment for you... and I couldn't see it end like that. But surely you didn't come to talk about our past. I hear you have a lovely companion."

"I guess you mean Ashley. Yes, she is wonderful. We are very much in love. Is there someone special in your life?"

"Do you really care?"

"Marla! I know I should have..."

"No! I'm sorry," she avoided his eyes. "I didn't mean for this to be an angry encounter. No, no one special. I suppose your relationship is serious, though. Do you want to marry her?"

"Yes, but..."

"I would never stand in your way, Marc. A divorce as soon as possible is fine with me. Why didn't you ask for a divorce earlier?"

"Marla, this isn't easy. I guess I was playing the martyr and my almighty pride wouldn't let me contact you. Then I met Ashley and it got serious, but I wanted to be sure and Ashley needed to be certain about me as well as herself. We both had a past and we had to work through it. Now we know. We couldn't be more positive. But you've been in contact with Dave all along. Surely you knew my circumstances. Why did you wait until now?"

"I was trying to hold on to a dream and no one had come along to fill the void. I couldn't face you after leaving the way I did, even though it was the right thing to do... for me. I wanted you to contact me. When you didn't call, the guilt turned into anger and then, finally, acceptance."

"You're being very reasonable about this."

"Why not? We were in love once. It was a mistake. We can correct it, so let's do it." She was being so logical he could scarcely believe it.

"Well, I have a lawyer. I'll have him contact you."

"No problem. I don't want anything."

"But I think you deserve something," he said.

"How do we put in monetary terms what we had? It was good, Marc, but it's been over for a long time. I just want a clean break."

"Can we be friends?"

"After all this time, friends?" She couldn't help one more thrust. "I think not."

"Will you be okay?"

"I've been fine. I'll be fine."

"Then I guess there's nothing more to say," he said with a shrug showing his acceptance of her rejection of any friendly relationship.

"No, I suppose not."

Friends. How childish and unrealistic! It was a clumsy attempt at an apology and of ridding himself of the guilt he bore. He realized, though he got what he had come for, she had won the game hands down. As she got up from her chair, Marc stood up and took a step toward her still expecting some sort of signal, a hug, a parting kiss. She extended her hand and he took it, even now disappointed at her coolness and then realizing how absurd it was to expect more than her generosity.

"Goodbye, Marla."

"Bye, Marc. I wish you the best." He turned and walked toward the elevators. She looked away seeming to study the arrangement of paper flowers in the vase behind her.

Implant

The elevator doors parted and he entered and turned. The doors closed as a punctuation to the end of a chapter in his life. He couldn't see the tears in Marla's eyes or know her thoughts at that moment. For Marla the words of an old song echoed in her mind... *It's so easy to remember, but so hard to forget."*

CHAPTER 13

Marc left Ashley sitting at the breakfast table still sipping her coffee. It was 6:00 AM and he had surgery at 7:30. The night before, when he arrived home from San Antonio, they had been up late discussing his encounter with Marla. They would soon be free not only of Marla but also of the pain of the past. On Sunday they talked for hours planning and dreaming of their future together. Their love making was more intense than ever, a joyous celebration of freedom and commitment. Marc had mentioned the international plastic surgery meeting in Paris in October and Ashley was excited about going with him. She smiled to herself as she thought about seeing him in action when he would moderate the panel on breast augmentation. The trip to France was to be a honeymoon. They were going to be married as soon as the divorce was final, although the honeymoon would probably come first.

Her reverie was broken by the ring of the telephone. "Hello?"

"May I speak with Dr. Hamilton?" asked a male voice.

"I'm sorry. He's left for the day but if you're a patient he can be reached at..."

"No, no. I need to talk with him personally."

"May I have your name and number? I'll have him phone you."

"No, no," said the nervous voice. "He can't call me!"

"Well, you can try the office later." Ashley tried once more, "Who shall I say is calling?"

Click. He hung up. How bizarre, she thought but then dismissed it as probably another phone solicitation for purchasing insurance or for a joint venture in a diamond mine in Sierra Leone.

At about one o'clock, following a lengthy surgery, Marc arrived at his office.

"Dr. Hamilton," said Mrs. Warner while following him into his consultation room. "You have several calls to return but the strangest thing! I had three calls from a very nervous gentleman who insisted on speaking with you personally."

"What's his name?"

"Well that's it! He wouldn't leave his name or number. He said he'd call back. I was surprised when he wanted to know when you were planning your next trip to Seattle."

"Oh? What did you say?"

"Well, of course I didn't give him any information and told him he might reach you here in the office at about five o'clock."

"Hmm! I guess he'll call back if he wants me." It was 4:45 when Marc had finished with his last patient. He was on the phone with Dave relating to him the meeting with Marla when Mrs. Warner came in and signaled him urgently. "Dave, I'll have to call you back. See ya! Jog Saturday? Fine."

"It's that man again, Dr. Hamilton and he's very persistent. Shall I tell him you're with a patient?"

"No. I'll take it."

"Line two," she said.

He picked up the phone, "This is Dr. Hamilton."

"Dr. Hamilton, it is of the utmost importance that I speak with you."

"Who is this?"

"Please not on the phone! I'm calling from Atlanta. When will you be in Seattle next?" Although his trips to Seattle were no secret he had not made a particular point of discussing them outside of plastic surgery circles. He was taken aback by the question.

"Seattle? Well, I'm not sure... Who is this? What do you want?" he asked with noticeable irritation.

"Believe me, Dr. Hamilton, this is urgent. I must meet with you in Seattle."

"Well, I don't think I can do that."

"Never mind. I'll find you!" There was a hang up click and he was gone.

Marc thought about the peculiar phone call all the way driving home. Ashley had a Martini waiting for him. She greeted him with an embrace and a soft, lingering kiss. "Dinner will be ready in about half an hour. Good day?"

"Not bad. Ashley, have you spoken with anyone about our next trip to Seattle?"

"Maybe casually to a secretary at the office. Why?" He mentioned the unusual phone call. "Well, I wonder... Did he sound nervous?"

"Yes. Very! How did you know?"

"I'm not sure, but just moments after you left this morning a man called asking for you. He sounded nervous and wouldn't leave his name. I thought he might be some sort of salesman or promoter as usual but now that you mention it, it must have been the same person. What did he want?"

"He wouldn't say and was very secretive. He said he'd find me in Seattle."

"Strange," she said.

"Very! Well, maybe we won the lottery or a free trip to Waxahachie." They laughed, had dinner and forgot about it.

* * * * *

Ashley arranged for a long weekend off and was able to accompany Marc to Seattle on his last trip before the Paris meeting. He wanted to get the latest test results on silicone and make his monthly report to Greenberg.

They were met, as usual, by the limo at the airport and taken straightaway to Alcott, except for dropping Ashley with the bags at the hotel. Marc and Burns had a brief meeting where Burns gave him the latest data on the subcutaneous injection of silicone in rabbits. The results were completely negative, as expected. There were no unusual reactions. Burns took Marc to the lab to show him the silicone injected animals as well as the control group. This was routine and completely necessary for Marc's report to the Society. Burns was cordial as he always was and invited Marc and Ashley to dinner. This time Marc tactfully declined and indicated that he and Ashley had planned on dinner alone as they had some important things to discuss. Burns gave him an understanding wink and,

"Sure. We'll catch up next time. Let me call the limo for you."

At about four o'clock Marc arrived at the hotel. Ashley had made reservations for them at the Seven Seas for eight o'clock. A few minutes before eight they went down to the lobby to get a taxi. Just before they stepped outside to get the attention of the doorman they noticed a man staring at them from a wingback chair near the entrance. He was slight in build, about late sixties with thin silver hair. Dark rimmed bifocals partially concealed watery light brown eyes. His cheeks were sunken and his lips were pursed. There was something desperate about him as he nervously clutched a black attaché case. Suddenly he uncoiled himself from the chair and darted at the couple. Marc took a step backward but the man was still in his face and said in a whisper, "Dr. Hamilton?"

"Yes," said Marc totally taken off guard while drawing further back as a reflex.

"May I speak with you privately for a moment?"

"We're just going out..."

"Dr. Hamilton, please excuse this intrusion. There is a very urgent matter I must discuss with you."

"Who are you?" asked Marc.

"My name is Matthew Wertheim, former head of the research labs at Alcott. We must talk!"

"Did you call me in Houston about two weeks ago?"

"Yes. I'm sorry to alarm you and Mrs. Hamilton but we must talk... alone... not here."

"We're just going to dinner," said Marc in an effort to avoid the man whom he suspected of having a few loose screws. He had certainly never heard of him at Alcott.

"Now, Dr. Hamilton! Now!" The man's eyes widened with the command and Marc had to take notice of his desperate persistence while Ashley, terrified, began to clutch Marc's arm. The man again leaned toward Marc and whispered, "Meet me at Barney's Deli. It's just two blocks away. I'll go first. You follow five minutes later. Dr. Hamilton, you may think I'm nuts but if you will please give me a few minutes I can explain." His tone now changed from commanding to pleading. He looked at Ashley and added, "Come alone."

"Mrs. Hamilton comes with me, or forget it!"

Ashley tugged at Marc's coat sleeve and said in a low voice with utter disbelief, "Marc, surely you're not going!"

"We'll meet you at the deli in five minutes," said Marc. "And this better be good!"

"I'd rather not have Mrs. Hamilton present," said Werthiem.

"Then buzz off," said Marc taking a step toward the door.

"Okay! Okay, if you insist. Please, please be there." With that Wertheim hastily turned and walked rapidly through the door. In an instant he was gone as though he had never been there. Ashley gazed after him wondering if this was real. Had this actually happened?

"Marc, are you crazy? You're going to meet this nut?"

"Maybe he is nuts. Let's see what this is all about. The deli must be a public place. I really don't see any danger, but you should stay here."

"Not on you're life! Oh, God! What am I saying? I'm going with you. Just one promise?"

"What?"

"If he's a kook we leave and call the police. I don't like how he was waiting for us and seemed to know you."

"Okay. I promise." He raised his right hand taking an oath. "Whatever it is, he's desperate to talk with me." He glanced at his watch and they waited the five minutes. Ashley had given up. She knew that when he was like this, it was impossible to dissuade him. They asked the doorman for directions to the deli. Just as Wertheim had said, it was two blocks away. They found it easily. As they entered they noticed that the place was packed with well dressed people. This allayed some anxiety. They were surrounded in the entryway by the chattering crowd waiting for tables. While the delicious aromas of corned beef, chicken soup, pickles, salami and sharp cheeses enveloped them, they scanned the room. A waving newspaper caught their attention. It was Wertheim, who had managed to hold a booth at the back of the bustling and almost chaotic restaurant. They walked toward him. Wertheim courteously stood up and urged them to get into the booth. His eyes were darting everywhere.

"Thank you for trusting me. I am fully aware of how this must appear. I assure you I'm not mad. If after ten minutes of your time and my explanation you are not convinced of my honorable intent you are free to leave and I'll never contact you again."

"Okay," said Marc. "You've got ten minutes." A waiter came to get their orders. They had coffee all around.

Wertheim began. "I went to work for Alcott Laboratories shortly after J.T. Roswell became CEO. In fact he recruited me to head the continuing research on silicone gel and the silicone mammary implant. I had an open budget. Any equipment I asked for I got, no matter what the cost. I had a wonderful salary. It was the dream of every research scientist to have such a position. In return I worked hard providing them with all the scientific data I discovered. All my exhaustive tests in the lab over many years indicated that the gel and implant were safe for use in humans. I even went beyond the studies required by the FDA guidelines to prove "safety and efficacy." My data was used in marketing strategies as in the sale of the gel to other implant manufacturers. It was the primary information disseminated to the plastic surgeons, such as yourself, in the form of *Dear Doctor* letters from Alcott to you. On this purely scientific basis we informed you of the inert qualities of the gel and implant and the probable survival of the implant for a lifetime. Of course there were logical exceptions, namely the occasional severe trauma of a steering wheel injury or as you know, a penetrating breast or chest wound. This was the information that the sales representatives had, and which you conveyed in good faith to your patients."

"Yes." Marc acknowledged all this and realized the man seemed to know what he was talking about. "Please go on."

"Bottom line, a safe implant, nonreactive in human tissues with no relationship to breast cancer or any other disease process. To be sure, surgical complications, such as thick scar tissue formation remained as known and usually accepted risks. I was working on solving that very problem when one day the unexpected occurred. Fifty white rats were chosen for an experiment. Specific quantities of silicone gel were injected into each animal subcutaneously in order to study the rate of fibroblast proliferation." Ashley looked at Marc for an explanation.

"He means how fast scar tissue will grow around the injected silicone."

"Precisely," said Wertheim. Ashley nodded that she understood. She was now thoroughly engrossed in Wertheim's words. After all he was talking about her body!

By this time Marc was listening intently and realized Wertheim was relating genuine scientific data. Wertheim continued, "Then the most unfortunate error in my entire career occurred. My lab assistant had accidentally selected the Alpha 1060-Delta III strain of rats. These animals are so inbred that many recessive characteristics show up in far greater proportion than in the normal rat population. Among these are the frequent development of carcinoma and autoimmune disease. I must emphasize that this is the only strain of lab rats so sensitive, and naturally this bears no relationship to any other mammal. In the course of the study, sadly, I could not find any clues to the problem of scar tissue formation but did find that a statistically significant number of injected animals eventually developed carcinoma and/or autoimmune disease... not at all unusual for that strain of lab animals. As a dedicated scientist I had to report all my findings, favorable or not, for that is the scientific method. My formal report went through the usual channels to the executives at Alcott. Needless to say they are businessmen and not scientists. Two days after I presented the findings I received an internal memo from the board of directors signed by Roswell himself. I was ordered to destroy the rats as well as all the data to be sure that this "sensitive and improbable information" not be disseminated to other implant manufacturers and especially not to the doctors."

Marc interrupted, "I have difficulty accepting that. I've been intimately involved in their research and never had any hint of holding back or altering data. I've had only complete cooperation."

"Dr. Hamilton, I have the proof, the very same memo, here in this attaché case."

"What did you do?" asked Marc.

"Of course I went to J.T. himself to verify this strange request, especially since the results were so predictable. He said that if the slightest hint of any potential problem, real or not, scientific or not, ever got to the news media it could create mass panic..." Ashley was nodding affirmatively. "...and bring a rapid demise to augmentation mammaplasty and of course, economic disaster to Alcott. He said he'd worked too long to let a lab test with questionable results destroy the industry."

Ashley interrupted, "If the test results were as questionable as even you admit, why not go along with their wishes?"

"Because, Mrs. Hamilton, as I said a moment ago I am a scientist, and the scientific method demands that all results be reported, even undesirable ones. Otherwise it is not science. Otherwise where should we draw the line between what should be reported and what should not? Science is a demanding and unrelenting taskmaster. Who knows the future? Someday another scientist, in another place, in another time may need this data to prove or disprove an hypothesis. I explained my position to Roswell and was fired on the spot. If I published the data they could easily discredit me and my findings and take away my pension, which he threatened to do.

It came down to caving in to them and leaving with a letter of recommendation, a huge bonus, hush money if you wish, and keeping my pension and all retirement benefits. If I acquiesced I could obtain a good position elsewhere. If I didn't, I would have left with my work discredited anyway by their next head of the lab but maintain my honor and dignity as a scientist. Unfortunately honor and dignity won't feed a family of five. In any event I would have to break all ties with Alcott. It was blackmail. I'm sad to say that I gave in. Fortunately I found a fine position with Gibson Global Industries in Atlanta where I work today. But before I left I was able, secretly, to make a personal file of my work and all the unfortunate occurrences surrounding it." He tapped the top of the attaché case.

"If all of what you say is true," said Marc, "that may be what Messerman needs to clinch the FDA's case against the silicone implant. The nature of the study won't mean a thing to the politicians and the public who really don't understand the scientific process. Just the hint of the possible occurrence of breast carcinoma or autoimmune disease will be all he needs to create the groundswell and grass roots support he's been hungry for. Perhaps destroying this unimportant data would be the best road to take."

Matthew Wertheim's eyes flashed with rage as he pounded the attaché case with his fist. Through clenched teeth he said, "Have I been wasting my time? Have you heard anything of what I said? For God's sake, Hamilton, you're a scientist! Suppose there is the one in a million chance or the one in ten million where there is only the faintest hint of the possibility of a problem. How can you ignore that? Use it to disprove the significance, if you will. How would you feel if the study had the slightest merit and even the far-fetched possibility of a linkage to any disease process, perhaps only in the rare super sensitive human? The test was done! I believe the results to be of little merit if any, but it must not be destroyed! Alcott realizes the significance. I've had my phones tapped. I'm followed everywhere. This is not paranoia. They suspect that I have not destroyed the data. I've carried this burden for thirteen years. I'm a wreck. I can't sleep. I can't live with this any longer!

I've been aware of your involvement with Dr. Greenberg and the National Plastic Surgery Society. In view of the FDA's interest and the fact that I will be retiring next year, I feel that you would be in a better position to make the decision about releasing the data. Incidentally I have no more affection for that fake scientist and opportunist, Messerman, than you do. Everything is clearly documented, including Alcott's desire to cover it up. I've watched your career and know you are an honorable man. I won't bear this burden any more! I've already dishonored myself by not coming forward. They might believe you. It will be hell when it hits the fan. You're the only one I know who can make the decision. Please, don't think too badly of me." With that he gently placed the attaché case on the table, stood up and left. Marc and Ashley couldn't believe this was happening. In desperation Marc called after him, "No! You can't! I can't! Wait!" It was in vain. Wertheim was gone.

They sat staring at one another in disbelief. Was this a dream, a nightmare? When the initial shock began to wear off, Marc said, "Ashley, what the hell do I do with this?"

"God damn it, Marc!" She was furious. "I tried to stop you from meeting with him but you wouldn't listen! Now look at the mess you're in!"

"Oh, come on, Ashley! Don't tell me you would have ignored the guy!"

"You're God damned right that I would have ignored the sneaky little shit!"

"But this stuff may be genuine. It might be important."

"Jesus, Marc! Does it have to be your responsibility because he said so?"

"But we haven't even looked at it yet and you're having a fit about it!"

"Right! That's exactly what I'm trying to tell you. You haven't seen it but you've bought it. It's all yours now! And you're asking me what to do with it? You really want me to tell you what to do with it?" She was hot! It was their first big fight. He knew she was right. He had stuck his head in the noose and there was no one to blame but himself. He tried to calm her down.

"Well, I guess I wasn't too smart." Ashley's eyes were still sparking with anger. "And I guess it's too late for regrets," he said sheepishly. There was a long moment of silence. Ashley spoke first.

"There's no point in sitting here and brooding about it, I suppose." She gave in a little. After all he was apologetic. "Let's go back to the hotel," she said resignedly. They left and walked to the hotel without speaking. Both were immersed in thought.

Neither one wanted to continue the wrangling but each was too stubborn to break the cold silence.

In the heat of their argument at the deli they hadn't noticed the burly man who had been watching the entire scene from a table in the far corner.

CHAPTER 14

PASSAIC, NEW JERSEY, 1955

"Wade, supper will be ready in ten minutes. Better wash up." The elderly woman called from the kitchen of the simple frame house to the boy sitting idly on the back porch steps. He was only a few feet from the screen door of the kitchen and yet he could have been miles away. Indeed he wasn't really there at all. It was 5:30 on a hot late summer afternoon. The sun was low and shone directly on the boy's face. It reflected in the hundreds of beads of perspiration on his forehead and nose and in his thick wire-rimmed spectacles. His rust colored hair was wild and dull even in the bright sunlight. While there was nothing unusual about a twelve year old boy wearing jeans, a tee shirt and sneakers, there was something definitely different about his appearance. His clothes were clean, not a speck of dirt. There was no ball, no bat and no other kids around. His face was an expressionless mask. He sat staring into space and was lost somewhere in time.

"Dr. Messerman, may I pass you your scalpel?" asked the spectacularly gorgeous blond nurse.

"Yes, but be quick about it! This patient is very sick," he answered. The operating room was all white and while all the nurses and doctors surrounding him wore white scrubs, he was the only one wearing brilliant green.

"Oh, Dr. Messerman, you're the only one who can save him," said the beautiful nurse.

"Yes. It's my new operation and only I can save him," he said. Suddenly his green scrubs turned into a long black robe. He sat on the bench with a gavel in his hand. "You are in contempt of court," he said to the lawyer standing before him. He banged down the gavel and said, "Bailiff, lock up Larry Block and the fine is one million dollars! If he can't pay it, stick a garden hose up his ass and turn the cold water on!"

"No, Judge Messerman! Please have mercy. The quality of mercy is not strained. It droppeth like bird turd. Oh, please, Your Honor! What will my mom say? I promise never to make fun of you again or to trip you in the aisle in school or to steal your lunch and I promise never to call you a dork."

"It's too late, you dumb shithead. I have sentenced you..."

"Wade! That boy is at it again! Wade, you know your grandfather doesn't like to be kept waiting. Supper's getting cold. Wade!"

"Uh... what? Uh... Okay, Grandma. I'm coming."

Victor Messerman was in the South Pacific in 1942 when his son was born. He and Rose Grose were married just a few months before he was drafted in World War II. He never saw his son. He was killed somewhere in the Philippines. Rose and the baby moved in with her parents. It seemed the logical thing to do under the circumstances. After an appropriate period of grieving, she began to entertain thoughts of marrying again. Wasn't she still young and attractive? She should marry again...

as soon as it was decent. After all the baby needed a father. There was just one problem. During the war there were very few available men at home. They were either too young or too old or too sick.

Dates were rare. At last a friend of the family introduced Rose to a forty-eight year old German-Jewish refugee. He was desperate to marry an American woman as a way to obtain United States citizenship and Rose was desperate for some kind of future and security. Sam Goldberg had a small grocery store. It was a perfect match! Besides she'd be able to get food without rationing stamps. That was no small matter. But desperate as he was to marry, he had one major condition. No kid! *Oy vey!* She was genuinely torn. Despite this obstacle her parents encouraged Rose to marry him. They would take wonderful care of the baby. After all the Bronx wasn't so far away. She could see the baby any time, and it was certain that as they grew more fond of each other Sam would want Rose to be happy and would relent.

They married in 1944 and things seemed to be going fairly well. Rose was working in the store but managed to see the baby at least once a week. The love affair was not exactly blooming. It was more a partnership than a marriage. The storm came a few months before V-J Day. Sam got a letter from his best friend, Jake, in Charlotte, North Carolina. Jake was in the construction business and business was booming. He needed help, a reliable person. Sam was the man he wanted. He offered a good salary, and after a year Sam would get a significant piece of the action. Rose thought about it. She wouldn't have to work anymore... and what a future and security! It was too good to pass up. Rose's parents encouraged the move to Charlotte and assured her that they and the baby would visit often. Rose, the thoughtful mother that she was, knew it was for the best and off they went leaving

Wade with the adoring grandparents, Sadie Grose, age 61, and Morris Grose, age 64.

* * * * *

"So Sadie, how is the baby?" asked one of the mahjong players.

"To tell the truth, not because he's my grandchild, he's the most beautiful baby. And smart... you wouldn't believe! He and Morris are having an afternoon together and that's heaven on toast to my Morris."

"That's wonderful, fantastic!" said the friend. "But I don't know how you do it. A two year old! It's a *mitzvah*! Sadie, you're an angel from heaven."

"What do you talk, Molly. He's such a good baby. You wouldn't believe!"

"So when is Rose coming to visit?"

"Soon, very soon. They are so busy! The business can't do without them."

"Fantastic!" said Ida as she glanced at Molly for a fraction of a second. "Is Rose working in the business too?"

"Not actually *working* in the business but she's helping Sam get established. My Rose is now a regular southern bell and, you know, she's always been such a *macher*. She's in everything, the temple sisterhood, Haddassah, Red Cross volunteer and now the country club with the golf. She's so busy! I don't know how she can come even twice a year. I'm sure when things get settled she'll come every chance. Molly, please excuse me. I need to powder my nose."

"Go. You know the way." As she left the room, all eyes followed her.

"Girls, I don't care what you say, a mother's place is with her child. That Rose was always no good. Selfish... I can't tell you. Leaving the baby with her parents... a crime! Not that Sadie and Morris aren't wonderful but they're not getting any younger... and raising a two year old!"

Sadie was sitting on the toilet sobbing silently. It took a few minutes for her to regain her composure. Her anger helped. "Those bitches!" she thought as she powdered her nose.

Back at the table... "Now, I heard that Morris almost is having a nervous..."

"Shush! Here she comes... So Molly, for the cookies you use real butter?"

* * * *

When Sadie arrived home the baby was screaming and Morris had the radio blasting. "Morris! Morris! The baby!"

"I can't shut him up. I've tried everything, diaper, bottle, toys. Sadie, I can't stand it. I love him, God bless him! I just can't stand him. The screaming! It never stops."

"What do you know!" she said as she picked up the child who stopped crying instantly. "See," she said.

"Yeah. Now put him down and see."

The household was chaotic. As Wade grew up, he ran the household with rings through the noses of his grandparents. Whatever Wade wanted he got. "Nothing is too good for this angel," was Sadie's motto. He had tantrums until age six. He almost destroyed the house by the time he was ten. Morris and Sadie always gave in. It was all that their energy would allow. Wade had no friends. He was never included in games. But what he lacked in interpersonal relationships was compensated, to some degree, by his brightness. He soon learned that the only source of recognition for him was to excel in his studies. Books were his only friends. They were his refuge. He would show up his classmates by always knowing the answers, and they hated him for that. He was the butt of jokes and a wonderful target for schoolyard fights. Wade had no idea of how to defend himself and would usually run home crying. His insecurities grew, and the more they grew, the more he withdrew into books and daydreaming. "Some day I'll get even. I'll show them all, especially that Larry Block of shit," he would often think.

At least Sam Goldberg was generous with the financial help he gave the grandparents. He had even set up a trust fund for the kid's education. Wade had everything, even medical school. Rose didn't attend his graduation, but she bragged on and on as though she had everything to do with this achievement. She bought him a new Thunderbird as a present and when she came to Wade for a thank you kiss, all she got from him was a curt, "Thanks," and his withdrawal. He hated her but he was determined to take anything and everything he could get, including four more years of education in law school at NYU.

By the time he finished law school Morris had died and Sadie was in a nursing home. He never visited her. Wade applied for a position with a law firm in Washington, DC, and was accepted for a very junior level opening. He had applied, in the first place, because he would be involved primarily with medical malpractice cases. It was payback time. For the first time in his life he felt accepted. The senior members of the firm praised his work. He screwed every doctor and almost always won the case for the plaintiff no matter how frivolous the suit. He would never settle a case out of court. That often made the seniors in the firm nervous. To Wade Messerman a settlement was the equivalent of losing the case. He was an absolute shit with everyone in the office, secretaries and colleagues alike. But he used his medical knowledge skillfully and was brilliant in the courtroom. He was soon recognized as one of the most competent attorneys in medical malpractice.

Implant

Wade was making big bucks for the firm as well as for himself. He was a rising star and he had plans, big plans. Through his legal contacts, he had met Philip Purcell, the current head of the FDA. Purcell admired the gutsy lawyer-doctor's track record and told him there would be a place for him with the FDA any time he wanted it. That was the beginning, a position with much less to offer monetarily but with the potential for power, big-time power. He gave the firm a month's notice and accepted Purcell's offer. The firm begged him to stay. They offered him a full partnership, benefits, perks, bonuses. The more they pleaded with him, the more delicious became his departure. They didn't understand that he had no appetite for money, only for power, an insatiable appetite for power. For now the FDA would do. It was a stepping stone, and Wade Messerman was going to be very sure footed.

Chapter 15

When they arrived at the hotel they went straight up to their room. The silent walk from the deli had allowed Ashley's anger over the situation to subside. Her anger with Marc was replaced by anxiety concerning the Wertheim incident. Marc placed the attaché case on the small round table and stared at it for a long moment. Ashley was noticeably irritated. "Marc, now that you've got it, for God's sake open it! It's not Pandora's Box!"

"You're right. Probably just a can of worms." The case had a combination lock but the latches sprang open when he slid the square levers outward. Inside was a manila folder, fairly thick, and on top of it lay what appeared to be a single blank sheet of white paper in a clear plastic covering. It all looked so harmless and yet Marc's hand trembled as he reached for the paper. Ashley was looking over his shoulder. He carefully removed the plastic covering and, as he suspected, the top sheet concealed another which was not blank. They read it together.

Implant

INTERNAL MEMO

To: Matthew Wertheim, Director   April 4, 1976
Research Laboratories
From: Board of D\irectors

    We have carefully reviewed the data submitted on April 1, 1976 regarding the rate of fibroblast proliferation in tissues directly injected with silicone of varying viscosity. As there was a serious error in the method of testing, that being the selection of inappropriate animals, the Board of Directors finds the results to be inaccurate and conclusions from those results to be tainted. By unanimous vote you are immediately directed to destroy the animals as well as all associated data in order to ensure that this study never be misunderstood or used to mislead purchasers or users of Alcott's silicone gel. This false information is not to be disseminated in any manner to other manufacturers, laboratories and specifically not to the plastic surgeons. This data has not been given to the sales staff. The matter is now considered closed. You are further instructed to continue your otherwise excellent work in the area of fibroblast proliferation. However, such serious errors in the future will not be tolerated by this Board.

                            J.T. Roswell, CEO

"Wow! That's some slap on the wrist of the director of a research lab! Normally such an error would simply be overlooked or seen for what it was, only a lab error. But *destroy the animals and don't tell the doctors...* That has a very bad odor," said Marc.

"Let's look at the folder," said Ashley impatiently. Marc slowly turned around and looked at her with a surprised expression. He saw that patience was not her long suit.

"Come on! Just open it!"

"Okay, Okay." He began thumbing through it and scanning the data. *Alpha-1060 Delta III... carcinoma... autoimmune responses... statistically significant...* These caught his eye. "Wertheim was telling the truth. The memo absolutely proves a cover up of this data."

"Marc, what are you going to do?" He sat down in a chair and read further. Finally he looked up at Ashley with a frown and then a shrug.

"Remember what Wertheim said? No data is completely worthless even if it seems erroneous." He held the papers out toward her. "This report is probably insignificant, but it had to be documented. Wertheim was right."

"What are you going to do?" she repeated.

"I don't know. Shit! I really don't know. This is thirteen years old and certainly by now, after about thirty years of research and clinical findings, if there existed any link to cancer or to autoimmune disease we would have seen it. But we haven't. Still, if the FDA got hold of a cover up... can you imagine how they would publicize it? And goodbye implants!"

Ashley was quiet for a moment. Then she said, "You can't release this to anyone, science or not. Two million women with breast implants will panic every time they sneeze or have a headache. I'm not kidding, Marc. I know how I feel, even though I may be better informed because of you. Still there is that tiny but persistent doubt."

"I understand, but surly you know..."

"Yes, yes I know. Intellectually I know! But a woman's breast can't be easily separated from her emotions."

"Are you telling me? Involved with emotions? I only deal with these women daily!" He was noticeably very irritated by her remarks. They fell silent. She realized that subconsciously he was trying to protect the implant and scientific integrity at the same time. It was a conflict without resolution.

"I'm sorry," she said, "Look who I'm telling about breast augmentation."

"No. You have a very valid point and we really agree about all of it. I'm just afraid if we don't release this now it may bite us in the ass later."

"And if you do, every plaintiff's attorney will be lining up to bring suits against the manufacturers and… oh, my God, against the plastic surgeons!" They suddenly realized that possible legal implication.

"I need some help with this… Greenberg! No! This is the end of his term as president of the National Plastic Surgery Society. I can't do that to him… What about Vicky?"

"What about Vicky?" she asked.

"She'll have the best perspective… a woman and a smart attorney and whatever we discuss will be privileged. Perfect. I'll call her as soon as we get home."

"Marc, are you sure?"

"Yes, I'm sure. What's the problem?" He was annoyed with her question.

"Well… I'm not certain that she's the best one to ask about this."

"Why not?"

"Oh, I don't know. It's just… I guess it's just me."

"Ashley, I know that you're not crazy about her. I know that you only tolerate Vicky because of Dave but…"

"You're right. Forget it. I'm being silly. You're absolutely right! Vicky will have the right perspective." Ashley was determined not to let her emotions become an obstruction to good judgment.

* * * * *

Victoria Lange had a small office near the medical complex in Houston. She preferred having a solo practice. It worked out for the best since most larger firms weren't involved in her other areas of interest, those being child abuse and battered women. The former issue was dirty business and the latter was boring and neither was very profitable. For Vicky these were crusades. Her personal injury practice was slowly growing. She learned a great deal about medicine by listening to Dave's and Marc's discussions. In addition she had contact with various doctors in the medical center and this further expanded her medical knowledge.

Marc had insisted on an appointment to see Vicky and this surprised her. Why was he being so formal? It must be something more than could be discussed over dinner or cocktails. He would be here in a few minutes. She checked the mirror, reapplied her lipstick and added a dab of perfume behind her ear lobes for good measure. A moment later her secretary announced him. She checked her watch. He was exactly on time. Marc was always so damn precise! She didn't know why that bothered her.

"Hi, Marc. This is a surprise." She leaned toward him for a peck on the cheek. She got one.

"Thanks for seeing me, Vicky. I need your professional opinion."

While she was going over the material Marc was closely observing her and he noticed the similarities between her and Ashley. Both were beautiful women, both were smart and both sexy as hell. He could easily understand Dave's attraction. As he saw it, a major difference between the women lay in the thinking process. Where Ashley expressed herself more on an emotional level Victoria was more analytical. She had become aware of being observed and liked it. She was fond of Marc and it didn't disturb her at all.

She looked up and removed her reading glasses. "Well, my friend, you're fucked if you do and you're fucked if you don't. Holding this back in the present climate with the FDA breathing down your neck could be construed as conspiracy in view of your close association with Alcott."

"But this was just thrown in my lap. I had nothing to do with it! What if that stuff, memo and all, just disappeared?"

"Marc, grow up. Too many people know about this," said Vicky.

"No. No one. No one knows except Wertheim, and he surely wouldn't say anything.

"Oh no? At least he was under duress to cap it. A court of law might take that into consideration. But who's forcing you to withhold what may be construed as essential information? And no one else knows? Be real, only the entire board of directors! If push comes to shove, they'll talk to save their asses. Believe me. This is my business. How do you know how many hidden copies of this memo are out there? Remember, thirteen years is a long time. Allegiances change. Someone may have a copy and want to use it against Alcott, or for the benefit of the FDA, or against the plastic surgeons... or against you. If this came out now, the first person approached would be Wertheim. He got the memo originally. Someday, in some deposition, when asked to produce the original memo you can bet he'd tell what he did with it to save himself. He's already shown you how weak he is. Talk about scientific integrity! What about plain ordinary morality? He didn't give a damn about involving you! He was bought and he'd sell you out in a New York minute. Face it. You are involved!"

Marc had never seen all those ramifications and possibilities. He never realized he was so naive but he knew Vicky was right. It was perfectly logical. "Vicky, what should I do?"

"Strictly from a legal standpoint, I'd have to advise you to take this directly to Wade Messerman and say, *Sir, this was just dumped in my lap. I don't think it's significant but I think the FDA should have it.* That would probably save you, ruin the industry and unnecessarily terrify millions of women and their families. Class action suits would grow like Johnson grass in a field."

"I can't..."

"I know. Of course you can't do that. Lord, what a mess!"

She didn't say anything for a long moment. Finally, "When do you go to Paris?"

"We leave October second. Why?"

"Leave this with me. I'll put it in the safe. Let's buy some time. Go to Paris. Y'all have a ball. Forget it for a while. Nothing's going to happen right now. It might never... but if Messerman is as aggressive as they say, that's doubtful. At least it will give us time to think. Meanwhile you'll have some peace of mind by having it out of your hands. As for me, it's privileged information between attorney and client."

As soon as Vicky took possession of the memo he felt much better. "Vicky, you're great!"

"Tell me that a year from now and I might believe you. Now go!"

"Thanks." He gave her another peck and returned to his office. The issues were far from resolved but he felt relieved of a huge burden, at least for the present.

After Marc left, Vicky stood in the doorway studying the memo once again. She looked up, smiled, put the papers in her safe and thought, "Don't worry, Marc. I'll take care of everything."

* * * * *

It was Monday and Ashley was still worrying about the memo and the toll it was taking on Marc. She had never seen him in such a state. He didn't eat. He couldn't sleep. He thought about nothing else. She prayed that his meeting today with Vicky would give them an answer to it all or at least some relief. The phone interrupted her thoughts.

"Hello."

"Hi, Ashley?"

"Yes. Who's this?"

"Chuck Walker. How are you guys doing? I missed seeing you the other day in Seattle. Even old Warren Burns was disappointed in not having dinner with you the other night. Why, one might think you were trying to avoid us," he said with a chuckle.

"Well, Marc and I..."

"Oh, not a problem," he explained. "You two wanted to be together and alone. Hell, I understand but I still missed you," he said in a friendly manner. "By the way, where did you go?"

"We, ahh... had reservations at the Seven Seas."

"Excellent choice. Is the big guy around?"

"Marc will be home at about six. You can reach him at the office. Is something wrong?" This was the first time anyone from Alcott had called at home.

"No. Not at all. Just need to talk with him. May I try again later this evening?"

"Sure. I'll tell Marc you called. Oh, and regards to..." He hung up before she could finish. She wondered what the call was about.

Ashley was relieved after Marc related the details of his consultation with Vicky. He explained how much he thought of her professionally. They had just finished dinner when the phone rang. It was Chuck. Ashley had mentioned his call to Marc when he had arrived home. He didn't seem to think anything of it so she let it go.

"Hi, Chuck. What's up?"

"How are you doin'?"

"Fine. What's..."

"Oh, well, I never had a chance to ask you about your panel and the presentation you planned for the Paris meeting," he said casually. "I was wondering what the specific subject was. I know you'll wow 'em no matter what. Just wondering..."

"The topic is postoperative complications in augmentation mammaplasty," he said. "I'm moderator so I'll be making comments about the panelists' presentations."

"You mean like scar tissue and post operative bleeding?"

"Exactly. Why?"

"Oh, you know. We always try to keep track of the accomplishments of our favorite plastic surgeon." Marc was experiencing that putrid odor again. "Well, you and Ashley have a wonderful time in Paris and we'll want to hear all about it when you get back."

"Sure thing. Thanks, Chuck. Nice of you to call. See ya."

The anxiety was back and stronger than ever. Walker knew something, Marc was certain. Why was he so curious about his presentation?

"Ashley, what did you say to Chuck?"

"Nothing. As a matter of fact he was in such a hurry I couldn't even send regards to Jean. He hung up in my mid sentence."

"I know he suspects something. It makes no sense for him to be concerned about what I say or discuss at the meeting... unless... he believes that I have the memo... Shit! That's it! He's afraid I'll blow the whole thing wide open at the Paris meeting."

"No!" she said silently, only mouthing and in disbelief. "But how would he know?"

"Alcott has an enormous security system in place. Maybe they saw us with Wertheim. Hell, I don't know! But Chuck knows something. I'm sure of it."

"I'm scared, Marc. I'm scared!" She began to cry. He held her close and kissed away her tears.

"It's going to be okay. We simply need to be careful for a few days and then we'll be a world away." He tried to reassure her. "Ah, Paris! It'll be great!" He was reassuring himself as well. Neither of them slept that night. Not a word was spoken. They didn't even think of making love.

* * * * *

The Carnival Cafe was noisy and the smoke hung like a blue veil above Earl Conners as he sat at the small table drinking his beer. He had been observing Chuck Walker in the phone booth for the past five minutes. Finally Chuck hung up the phone and joined Conners at the table. Chuck had a worried expression which was accentuated by the deep vertical frown furrow in the center of his forehead. He was engrossed in thought and Conners knew it was best not to interrupt him. After a few seconds of silence, "I spoke with both of them. You were right, Earl. Neither one said anything about Barney's Deli or meeting with Wertheim. Not a word about the attaché case."

"I told you! My man's been tailing Wertheim from the time he arrived in Seattle."

"Well, shit, Earl, we've never known for certain what Werthiem had in his possession and we still don't."

Conners was visibly upset with Walker's denial of the obvious. "Mr. Walker, be real! What would Wertheim pass on to Hamilton that could be of the slightest interest to him?

Wertheim must have had the original memo and he kept it for insurance in the event that Alcott might ever try to compromise him or his research again. He was no dummy but after thirteen years of seeing strange shadows every day of his life, no matter where he was, Atlanta, London, everywhere, he finally broke. He couldn't bring himself to destroy it so he took his chances and dumped the shit in Hamilton's lap. Hell, I don't blame the guy. We let him know he was being watched and he caved in under the pressure."

Chuck persisted, "I asked Marc about his presentation at the Paris meeting and he seemed pretty cool about it."

"Did you think he'd say, *Oh, by the way, I'm going to let the world know about the memo?*" asked Conners sarcastically.

"No. No, of course not but I know Hamilton. He doesn't want this to blow up in his face either. I think he'll keep it quiet." Now Conners was really annoyed with Walker's protective attitude toward Hamilton.

"Mr. Walker, security is my business. Please listen to me. We must assume the logical. Wertheim passed the memo and research data to Hamilton. If that ever comes out you know Wertheim will talk to save his ass. He's pure chicken shit! When he talks, the weasel will point his finger at Hamilton and Hamilton will have to make a decision—destroy everything or tell all." Connors waited a few moments to let it sink in, to let Chuck absorb it. Then, "What do you know of the FDA's schedule and plans?"

"Our inside sources," said Chuck, "indicate that Messerman knows nothing of the data or memo. If he did know surely he would have used it by now. It seems safe to assume that he will continue his plan to come down hard on the manufacturers, probably by the end of this year. Damn him! He wants to bury the silicone gel implant and could care less about the repercussions. All this is in the name of *safety and efficacy*! What shit!"

"Sir, if the FDA got hold of the data, especially the memo, it would be pretty incriminating, right?"

"Yes," said Chuck with a dejected look while staring into his mug of beer.

"Then you have to let me do my job. I understand your close relationship with Hamilton and I think he's an okay guy, but you know J.T.'s orders."

"Yeah. I do." He frowned again. "What about the girl?"

"I'm really sorry about her. She's real sweet but this is too important for emotions to get in the way of duty."

"God! Her too?"

"You saw the report. She was at the meeting in the deli. She knows it all."

"When and how?"

"Sorry, sir," said Conners. "Even J.T. won't know. It's best you not know, for your own protection. I'll make it as easy as I can on them. After all I'm not a barbarian. This is just routine business."

"You mean there have been others?" Conners silence said it all. "Earl, thanks for seeing me and giving me a chance to try."

"Sure, Mr. Walker, I'd do the same for a friend of mine." With that Walker got the check. They shook hands and left the cafe walking in opposite directions.

Chuck could only think, "Shit! Shit! Shit!" When he got to his car he kicked the front tire as hard as he could, got in, closed the door and then loudly, "God damned fucking shit!"

Chapter 16
October 3, 1989

Ashley and Marc arrived in Paris at nine o'clock in the morning. The nonstop flight from Houston was smooth. As they landed they were disappointed by the cloudy day and the threat of rain, but they were determined not to let it bother them. Neither one had slept and both were exhausted, but this was Paris.

They checked into the Hotel Splendid in the Rue St. Jacque and hastily unpacked. Then they took a taxi to the Place de la Concorde, marveled at the Obelisk of Luxor and at the beauty of the square itself and strolled along the Champs Elysees toward the Place de l'Etoile. As they walked arm in arm they talked excited happy talk, observed the latest fashions irresistibly displayed in the elegant shop windows, paid homage at the Tomb of the Unknown Soldier beneath the Arc de Triomphe and finally stopped at a little bistro near the George V Hotel. Over lunch they planned the rest of the day. Marc needed to make some final corrections on his presentation and said, "Ashley, no point in your sitting in the hotel with me. This is Paris. Go see the sights and I'll meet you for dinner. Make reservations somewhere for six o'clock and I'll be there at five for cocktails. Okay? Just say where."

"Great!" she said excitedly. "I'll spend the afternoon at the Louvre. I know of a wonderful restaurant in Montparnasse. It's supposed to be a popular meeting place for the artsy-fartsy crowd. La Coupole, okay?"

"Sure. Perfect."

Ashley dropped Marc at the hotel. They kissed on parting and Ashley called out to him through the taxi window, "Remember, La Coupole, Montparnasse, five sharp."

"Right," he acknowledged. She instructed the driver to go to the Louvre.

* * * * *

It was five o'clock in the afternoon on October 3rd in Atlanta. Matthew Wertheim had finished for the day at Gibson Gobal Industries and was thinking about his next business trip to Frankfurt as he walked along Peachtree Street toward the parking lot. The pedestrian traffic light had just turned green. He stepped off the curb and never saw the van turning the corner at high speed. He was thrown into the air about ten feet. His head crashed into the pavement. Blood trickled from his left ear and there was an expanding pool of blood exuding from somewhere beneath his head. His legs were contorted into a grotesque position that made him look like a limp marionette. Later, witnesses said it was a late model black paneled van that hit him. No one saw the license plates or the driver. It was over in merely a few seconds. The paramedics worked over him for only a short time. They indicated that any further efforts would be useless. Matthew Wertheim was dead.

* * * * *

Marc changed his clothes into something more comfortable before tackling his work. He was in the midst of writing appropriate questions to be asked of the various members of the augmentation mammaplasty panel when there was a knock at the door.

"Room service," called the voice.

"I didn't order anything. Must be a mistake," he called out.

"No mistake, sir. Compliments of the management." Marc unlocked the door and before he could comprehend what was happening two large men quickly forced their way into the room and locked the door behind them. The fat one with light hair spun Marc around and got a head lock on him. The taller man with thin hair landed a pounding blow into his solar plexus. The crushing pain made Marc's knees buckle and his world was turning dark. He could barely hear the deep voice say, "Doc, this can be easy or tough. Depends on you." Marc was completely immobilized. He was gasping for air and heard himself ask, "What... ahh... do you... ahh... want?"

"The data and the memo, Doc, now!"

"What?"

"Don't shit me, man!" said the fat one as he pounded into Marc's right ribs from behind. The pain was unbearable but he was starting to understand. "The memo, Doc. Just tell us where it is and we're out of here like crap through a goose. THE MEMO!"

In a coughing whisper, "I... don't... have... it." *Bam,* went a fist to the right side of his face. A crunching sound resonated.

"Have it your way!" said the deep voice as he smashed Marc's nose with full force. Blood tracked down his upper lip. He was still conscious.

"THE MEMO!" shouted the other.

"I... don't..." and three more ramming fists, two to his head and the third to his ribs again. Marc slumped into unconsciousness.

"Let him go. We'll find it," said the balding attacker. They emptied all the drawers and dumped the contents on the floor. Next was the closet. Nothing there. They scattered the papers on the desk and slashed open the pillows and mattress. In desperation they pulled the pictures from the walls and still nothing. The room now looked like a war zone.

"Nothing!" said the fat one.

"It's got to be here someplace," said the other. Marc was coming to. Again the fat man put a strangle hold on him. By this time Marc's face resembled something like a box of squashed strawberries. The thinner man shoved a thirty-eight into Marc's line of vision and said, "You want to buy it, big man, buy it right now?" Marc saw the gun but didn't have the strength to answer. This enraged the man. He took the butt of the thirty-eight and slammed it again and again into Marc's skull. Marc heard a distant cracking sound and passed out again. The last blow splattered blood on the wall behind him. They let him fall onto the carpeted floor a few feet from the door.

"Christ, don't kill him!" shouted the fat man. "We need him to find it."

"Maybe the girl has it."

"Right. If he had it, he would have talked. They always talk, Ed. Always."

Marc's head now lay in a pool of blood. He was motionless. Ed checked for a carotid artery pulse.

"He's still alive."

"We'd better split! We can finish this job later. We gotta find the girl. We can use him as bait." They stepped over Marc's body and made a hasty exit down the back stairs and disappeared in the Rue St. Jacque.

Chapter 17
October 4, 1989

Although the meeting officially began with a welcoming reception on the evening of October 3rd, the scientific program opened on the morning of the 4th. The auditorium was packed with well dressed men and women. An echoing cacophony resulted from the multilingual chatter in the audience mixed with the screeching feedback of microphones. At the left side of the podium was a floor to ceiling projection screen. About the walls of the huge room were the flags of the countries represented at the gathering. The annual meeting of the Aesthetic Society of France was about to begin. The officers of the Society stood at attention at the drum roll. The entire audience came to their feet and fell silent. From the back of the hall the brass band played the haunting Marseilles. Then followed welcoming speeches and the introductions of officers.

Finally the presidential address was being given. Dr. Allen Greenberg was listening attentively through earphones which gave him the instant translations from French into English when a young woman in an official blue blazer handed him a note:

> Dr. Greenberg,
>   Please meet me immediately in back of auditorium near exit. Urgent!
>   Dr. Jean-Paul Ducett

"What could Jean-Paul want so urgently?" thought Greenberg as he made his way to the rear exit. As he approached he saw the familiar face but without the usual generous smile. Ducett, who was short, stocky and balding was the program director for the meeting. He had an unmistakably professorial demeanor and was unmistakably very nervous. He motioned to Greenberg to step out into the foyer. Immediately Greenberg saw his agitation. They quickly shook hands. "Jean-Paul, you look terrible. What's wrong?"

"Mon ami, I need your help. The mammaplasty panel! Dr. Hamilton is not here. He is not registered at the desk. You must help me! Please, will you moderate the panel?"

"Jean-Paul, of course you know I will, but that's not like Hamilton. I haven't seen him either."

"Allen, you will do it? Thank you! I will make the announcement of the change." Ducett quickly returned and made his way toward the podium leaving Greenberg deeply concerned. He knew Marc was coming to the meeting. They had spoken about it only a few days ago in Houston. In fact they had made tentative arrangements to have dinner together one evening. He let the thought go for the moment to allow himself to shift gears. He hastily jotted down a few notes, thought about them and then scratched them out. This was his subject. Greenberg knew more about the implant and the surgical procedure than any one else and really didn't need notes. He returned and found his chair. He caught Jean-Paul's eye and nodded to him indicating that he was ready. Jean-Paul made the announcement.

The panel went well. There were so many questions from the audience that the session went twenty minutes over the allotted time. As soon as Greenberg finished thanking the participants he went to the nearest phone to call the Hotel Splendid. Marc had mentioned that he and Ashley would be staying there. The hotel operator acknowledged that Dr. Hamilton was indeed a guest, however there was no answer from his room. Greenberg was genuinely concerned. Where the hell was Marc! He returned to the scientific session but couldn't keep focused on the presentations. Now he was worried and began to imagine all sorts of terrible possibilities. It was completely out of character for Marcus Hamilton to slough off a responsibility. Besides Greenberg knew that he had been looking foreword to the panel for months.

The room was darkened for the slide presentation. A smaller screen at the far left of the podium was for messages. Suddenly the screen lit up and Greenberg saw his name.

Dr. Allen Greenberg: please call 07-32-7000

He immediately left the session and returned to the phone to make the call. He knew something was wrong. The operator said, "Hospital St. Michel de Paris." He had called hospitals countless times during his career but had never experienced the chill down his spine which he now felt. He identified himself and the operator acknowledged by saying, "Ah oui, Dr. Greenberg. Un moment, s'il vous plait."

He heard a click and then a female voice, "Hello?"

"This is Dr. Greenberg speaking."

"Dr. Greenberg... Allen, this is Ashley."

"Ashley! For God's sake, are you all right? Is Marc...?"

"Allen, Marc's been seriously injured. Please come. Room 702. Get a pass for a patient by the name of Louis Perras. We need you. I'll explain when you get here."

"I'm on my way—702, right?" He turned away from the phone and briefly noticed the heavy-set, light haired man sitting in a chair only a few feet from him. The man looked very busy with a newspaper. Allen was sure that same man had been sitting in the auditorium just across the aisle from him. He had noticed him because he seemed so out of place. It was his lack of interest in the program that had gotten Allen's attention. "Strange," he thought. "Must be security for the meeting." He had observed all this in an instant and it was as quickly forgotten. Marc needed him and that was all he could think about.

Allen found a cab and in a few minutes he was at the hospital. He got a pass from the lobby receptionist to visit Louis Perras. At the bank of elevators stood a hospital security guard. He motioned to Allen to show him the pass and then asked for identification. Allen was surprised at that but showed the guard his driver's license.

"Dr. Allen Greenberg?"

"Yes, I am." The guard looked at a sheet on the clipboard he held.

"Bon, Monsieur. Le ascenseur a la gauche, s'il vous plait."

Allen entered the elevator while wondering, "Louis Perras? Security check? What the hell is going on?" He took the elevator to the seventh floor, turned left and found room 702. The name on the door was *Louis Perras* as Ashley had said. Allen was totally confused. He was about to enter the room when he heard, "Allen! Thank God, you're here." It was Ashley walking rapidly toward him. "I just stepped out for a moment."

"But..."

"I know. The wrong name. Let's find a place to talk." She looked terrible. Greenberg had never seen Ashley in such a state before. Her hair was disheveled, no makeup, red swollen eyes.

"Are you okay? What the hell's going on? Where's Marc?" They stepped into an alcove just beside the door to Marc's room.

"Allen, it's a long story. I'll explain but, first, Marc's been badly beaten. He has serious facial bone fractures and other injuries. He needs you. He wants only you."

"Ashley, calm down." He saw that she was in such an agitated state that further questioning would get him nowhere.

"Just come see him, Allen, please," she implored. They walked into the room. Marc's face was so bruised and swollen that Greenberg almost didn't recognize him.

"Allen, Chief, thanks for coming," said Marc in a barely audible voice.

"What on earth...?" Ashley cut him off.

"I promise to explain but please come with me now. Dr. Dumont has his x-rays. He's waiting to show them to you."

"Chief," whispered Marc, "I don't want anyone else, just you for the surgery. Please, Chief, just you." Greenberg saw that he was speaking through severe pain.

"It'll be okay, Marc. You need to rest. I'll be back in a few minutes." He left the room with Ashley.

Ashley seemed to relax a little now that Greenberg had seen Marc. As they were hastily walking down the corridor she brought Greenberg up to date about Alcott, the memo, the beating and Marc's injuries. He listened but was obviously upset, bordering on angry. "Why the hell didn't you and Marc let me know all this. Maybe I could have helped."

"How, Allen? How? Besides you know Marc. He didn't want anything to spoil your year as president of the NPSS."

Allen was furious. His face was crimson. Through clenched teeth he said,

"Stupid kid! God, I thought my residents had some smarts! Spoil my year as president...! That's more important than his life? Shit! This didn't have to happen. I could have straightened it out with Alcott! They wouldn't have dared! Ashley, why didn't you call me?"

"What could we do? Going public wasn't a reasonable option. He couldn't destroy the data or the memo. So what could he do? What could you have done? Allen, this has been tearing him apart inside. You have no idea... and now..." she was choking back tears, "...Dumont says it's a miracle he survived."

They reached Dumont's office and knocked on the door. "Entrer, s'il vous plait. Oh, Mdsl. Barton and this must be Dr. Greenberg." The men shook hands. "Dr. Greenberg, please come with me. Mdsl. Barton, we will be back in a few minutes." Ashley got the message. This was going to be doctor talk and she didn't mind waiting. She knew that Allen wouldn't exclude her from knowing the facts. She trusted him completely.

The two doctors went into the x-ray viewing room and Dumont began, "He is finally stable. Last night he arrived in shock with a cerebral concussion, memory loss, a right hemothorax and multiple facial bone injuries. I have been able to tend to all but the face." Dumont put down the x-rays, turned toward Greenberg and said, "Mdsl. Barton has explained to me some of what this is about. I do not need to know any of the details. It is enough that I know that she and Dr. Hamilton are in great danger. He is admitted under the name *Louis Perras* and so far I have managed to keep the police out of this. Even the hospital administrator doesn't know anything. I have done what I can."

"Dr. Dumont, I understand the risks. You are doing far more than you should. At this point I can only assure you that they have done nothing wrong. I am very close to them and I know that they are honorable. The degree of danger to them is obvious. I learned of the situation only upon my arrival at the hospital. Our gratitude to you will never be forgotten." Dumont nodded indicating that he understood. He asked no questions.

"Please, Dr. Greenberg, here are the films. I hope they are what you need." Allen placed the facial bone series on the fluorescent viewing box and studied the films carefully.

"You see here, Dr. Dumont, the right cheek bone areas. There is no question that there are severely comminuted fractures of the zygomatic complex. I haven't had a chance to examine his vision, but I'm reasonably certain of a blowout fracture of the right orbit. It's amazing... the left maxillary sinus is normal as are the facial bones on that side. The nasal bones are displaced and will also require reduction." Allen was silent for a moment. Then, "Normally I would wait a few days for the facial swelling to subside but every moment he is here, he is in danger. What do you think of his condition and ability to withstand a general anesthetic?"

"Although he is stable, he has lost a great deal of blood. I must advise at least three units of blood prior to surgery. I am sure he will require transfusion during the procedure. The amount will depend on the blood loss at that time."

"I agree. Forgive me for asking but with respect to HIV, how well controlled is your blood bank?" asked Allen.

"There is always some risk but it is minimal. We screen our donors as carefully as possible."

"How quickly can he be transfused?"

"He is scheduled to receive two units today and one tomorrow," said Dumont.

"Good. Hopefully his edema will be down enough by then for surgery. You have been so kind. I am embarrassed to ask if somehow I might get temporary privileges here. Marc wants me to do the surgery but we will understand if..."

"I can arrange it," said Dumont. "He will be on the surgery schedule with my name as the surgeon. I shall tell administration that you are an expert in this procedure and that I am very fortunate to have such a distinguished plastic surgeon visiting and willing to assist me. Of course, I will be assisting you. We have had visiting surgeons before. It should not be a problem."

"Again, I am eternally grateful. I can borrow all the special instruments I will need from Dr. Jean-Paul Ducett. He owes me a favor anyway. Shall we plan for the day after tomorrow?"

"Fine," said Dumont.

"I'll explain all to Ms. Barton and Dr. Hamilton," said Allen.

Ashley had been sitting alone in the small room. She had become restless while waiting for Allen and Dumont. It had been over half an hour and she decided to return to Marc's room. She knew Allen would realize where she had gone.

* * * * *

Just a few minutes after Greenberg had arrived at the Hospital St. Michel de Paris, a large fat man entered the lobby. He had been watching Greenberg all morning at the plastic surgery meeting and knew the doctor would lead him to Hamilton and hopefully to the girl. He had followed Greenberg's taxi to the hospital and all the while kept repeating to himself, "702, 702." That was the only part of Greenberg's telephone conversation that he had overheard. He guessed it was a room number. As he walked in he saw Greenberg at the reception desk. He stood at a distance and concealed himself behind a marble pillar. Here he could watch and not be observed. He saw Greenberg get the pass and show it to the security guard. Shit! The guard was checking

IMPLANT

IDs against a list! What should he do? He knew it was room 702 but how the hell was he going to get there? God damn! The guard was walking toward him. "Keep cool," he thought to himself.

"Monsieur, que voulez-vous?" asked the guard.

"Oh, sorry! I don't speak French. I believe I'm in the wrong hospital."

"What hospital are you looking for?" asked the guard in fairly good English. The fat man fumbled in his pockets.

"I wrote it down... and... how stupid of me... I must have lost the note. I'll have to check with my sister. Thank you anyway." The fat man turned and slowly walked out the exit door. He saw the guard take a few steps toward him. He held his breath as he felt an adrenaline rush. He checked for his gun in the holster under his suit coat and hoped he wouldn't have to use it here in plain view. The guard stopped and stood in the doorway watching his departure.

"God! That was close!" he thought. He couldn't hang around the hospital now. The guard was waiting and watching to see him leave the area. The fat man walked to the street and found a waiting taxi. He got in and asked the driver, "Can you suggest a restaurant nearby?" The driver didn't speak English and merely looked at him curiously.

"R-E-S-T-A-U-R-A-N-T," spelled the gunman.

"Ahh... Oui, Monsieur." The ride took less than ten minutes. He paid the driver and he found himself at the entrance of a small cafe. The cab sped off. After a few minutes the man walked to the corner and easily found another taxi.

"The Hospital St. Michel de Paris. Emergency entrance, please." The taxi pulled up into the emergency driveway. The driver was paid and left. The fat man walked through the glass doors into the emergency ward. It was chaotic. Doctors, nurses and gurneys all seeming to be going in every direction. Patients and their families sat in chairs, leaned against the walls and some paced about aimlessly. He melted into the confusion and casually headed toward the elevators. No guard! He pushed the button for the seventh floor and remembered 702.

He found the room and ignored the name on the door. He silently slipped inside and was sure he hadn't been noticed. Marc had been given a sedative and was asleep. The fat man pulled the telephone wires from the wall with a single hard jerk and then disconnected the intercom and call button. Marc began to stir. He felt himself being shaken awake. Then he saw the fat face that he would never forget! Panic shot through him like a thunderbolt. He tried to scream but no sound came from his open mouth. He could only stare wide eyed. The fat man saw that they had done too good a job on him and further efforts at interrogating Marc would be useless. He would wait for the girl. He wasn't sure that Marc could see the gun or comprehend the situation but he shoved the thirty-eight toward Marc's face anyway. Then the gunman positioned himself flat against the wall behind the door so as to be concealed when the door opened.

The lobby security guard was suspicious of the fat man from the start. When questioned he seemed cool but the guard had seen this facade many times before. He knew phony answers when he heard them. He had been keeping a lookout for the fat gentleman and the longer he waited, the more concerned he became. He was simply too cool. He thought he'd better play it safe and alerted the security team on his radio. He described the man and the incident and told them he was heading for the seventh floor.

Ashley walked down the corridor passed the bank of elevators to Marc's room. As she entered she immediately saw that something was wrong. Marc was lying in the bed and he was absolutely motionless. He looked rigid with his eyes and mouth wide open in a silent frozen scream. In that instant she thought he had had some sort of relapse. Ashley started toward him when from behind the door came the huge hands of the fat man seeking and finding her throat. She was terrified. She tried to call out but couldn't. She tried to squirm loose but he was too strong. The silence was broken by the fat man's raspy voice. "Now, little lady, I'll loosen my grip if you promise not to make a sound." He removed his right hand from her throat to reach for his gun. His huge left hand alone held her immobilized. "If you scream or try to make a run for it, see this thirty- eight? Your boyfriend gets it right between the eyes. Do we understand each other?" Ashley was too terrified to respond. Then louder, "Do... we... understand... each other?" Finally she nodded affirmatively. Marc was still motionless and silent. The fat man slowly released his left-handed grip on Ashley's throat only to put the gun to her head. His back was to the door. "Now we're going to slowly walk out of the room, go down the stairs and out into the parking lot. You won't get hurt if you do as you're told but remember, I'll have this gun on you all the while. Trust me. I'm not squeamish about using it." Marc still hadn't made a sound.

Ashley called out to him, "My God, Marc! Marc!" It was in vain. He couldn't hear. He couldn't see. His brain was on overload.

"Shut up or you get it here and now." Ashley's mouth was so dry from fear that she could hardly speak.

"What do you want?"

"We'll discuss that somewhere else where it's nice and private. Turn around slowly," he commanded and moved the thirty-eight to the center of her spine. "Okay, let's start walking..." He still had his back to the door when it suddenly flew open. The security guard with gun in hand instantly assessed the situation. He spotted the fat man's thirty-eight. In the same moment the guard saw that he had a shot clear of Ashley. He pumped twice, sending two bullets into the back of the would-be assassin's head. The fat man never had a chance to turn around. He fell to the floor. Ashley was covered with his blood. She began to scream uncontrollably. Just then Greenberg walked into the scene. He was speechless and horrified when he saw Ashley. She ran to him. "Allen! Allen! They tried to kill me, Allen! Oh, my God!" He put his arms about her protectively. Finally he found his voice.

"Good Lord, what is this?" he asked turning to the security guard.

"It's just lucky that I noticed this ape in the lobby a few minutes ago. Dr. Dumont had told us to keep a special watch on this room. Lucky for you, ma'am." Ashley was sobbing in Allen's arms.

A nurse burst into the room in response to the shots. When she saw the blood and the body on the floor she threw her arms upward and screamed, "Mon Dieu! Mon Dieu!"

A crowd had gathered at the doorway. The security guard barked at them,

"Allez-vous-en!" Just then Ashley's legs were going limp. Allen yelled at the nurse,

"Don't just stand there! Help me get her on the sofa." The nurse came to her senses at the command and helped carry her.

"Marc! Marc!" Ashley called with her last remnant of strength. There was no response. Marc was as still as a pillar frozen in time and space.

CHAPTER 18

Earl Conners lived in a two-bedroom apartment on the eleventh floor of one of the most prestigious highrises in Seattle. From the window of the master bedroom on a clear day he could see Puget Sound. He earned a good enough salary from Alcott to enable him to lease the apartment and to have it tastefully furnished by an interior decorator. It seemed completely out of character for this homely, obese and clumsy man who had only a tenth grade education. He lived alone and preferred it that way. He had been divorced twice and had lived with women for brief periods. Now, most of his sexual encounters were one-night stands.

He enjoyed showing off to his guests and especially loved to see their shocked reaction when he showed them about and discussed the paintings, prints of various French impressionists, throughout the apartment. He had memorized, from an encyclopedia, details of the artists and their work. The ladies whom he entertained were always impressed. His guided tours had a definite sequence. They began with the benign Mattise still life in the living room, then continued to the Degas ballerina in the dining room. The tour finally progressed to the master bedroom with the Renoir nude bathers and usually ended successfully in the sack.

Conners was alone and deeply asleep when the phone rang. He awakened with a start. He glanced at the clock. Three AM. He fumbled for the phone, not yet fully awake, and said in a hoarse voice, "Yeah?"

"Earl, you awake? This is Ed."

"Yeah?"

"Bad news, Earl. Barnes is dead."

"Yeah?" he said while rubbing his eyes. "What happened?" His voice was casual and matter of fact.

"Did you hear me, Earl? I said Barnes is dead!"

"I heard you. I heard you! Now are you gonna tell me about it or is this twenty questions?"

"He was at the hospital in Hamilton's room trying to get the girl when a guard, an ordinary hospital guard, walked in right in the middle of it all. Poor sonofabitch bought it with two slugs in the head. He never even saw it coming."

"A hospital guard! Shit! Did he have time to do the girl?"

"Hell, no! He didn't want to do her there. He was gonna squeeze it out of her and do her after, somewhere else, like we planned. Poor bastard!"

"And Hamilton?"

"He's so out of it, he ain't worth a turd."

"What about the cops?" asked Conners.

"She's too freaked out to talk with them. They're gonna try to get a statement from her later today. I don't know, Earl. Maybe we played this wrong. She's so scared she might spill the whole thing."

"That's why she won't talk. She's too scared. Now she knows we can get to them... anywhere."

"But, Earl..."

"Shut the fuck up! Let me get some sleep! Call me later. Find out what she says."

"Okay, Earl. Okay. Call you later." Conners slammed the phone down, turned over and went back to sleep.

* * * * *

Dr. Dumont had given Marc another sedative, which allowed him to fall into a fretful sleep again. It was his hope that when Marc awoke his mind would be clear of the last traumatic moments that he had expressed as an hysterical paralysis. Marc's mind had simply shut down protecting him from a psychological overload.

Allen Greenberg had remained in Marc's hospital room with Ashley. She had calmed down and was beginning to think more clearly again. Dumont had no choice. He couldn't stop hospital security from calling the police, but at least he had been successful in delaying their contact with Ashley until she was able to cope with them. It was now late afternoon and the police were returning at five o'clock for a statement from Ashley. "Allen," she said, "What can I tell them?"

"How about the truth, Ashley."

"You know that if I tell them the truth, it will be headline news in every major newspaper and on television. All we've tried to prevent will be lost. Messerman wins big time and the implants will be gone. Millions of women will be in a state of panic. I can't do that."

"That might save your asses. Alcott is seriously playing for keeps."

"I know," she said. "But there must be another way. When are you operating on Marc?"

"If he's well enough, the plan is for tomorrow, or the day after."

"Does he have to remain in the hospital for recovery? Can he be moved? Allen, I'm terrified of staying here! They know where we are!" He saw that she was getting upset again.

"Ashley, calm down. Everything will be okay. Once the surgery is finished, he'll need only dressing changes and general support. No, he doesn't have to remain in the hospital. I can show you what to do... Ashley, what do you have in mind?"

"Suppose I make up some story, say, just enough to satisfy the police for a few days. After all, we haven't committed any crime. We're the victims! Suppose we disappear, simply vanish?"

"For God's sake, that would make them suspect something foul! How can you just disappear? Where would you go? How would you travel with Marc still recovering? Alcott would be breathing down your neck.

"I don't know! I don't know! Marc would know what to do. He's got to come out of it! He'd know. The only thing I'm sure of is that Marc didn't want this mess to be made public. We spoke of that often enough."

"That was before either of you were attacked. Don't you think he'd change his mind now?"

"No, now more than ever, no."

"It's simply not worth all the risks, Ashley. I won't take the responsibility..."

"No one is asking you to take responsibility for anything. I don't mean to sound rude but it's not for you to decide, Allen... They'll be here in a few minutes. Excuse me while I freshen up." He knew he couldn't fight with her once she had made a positive decision. He knew he would support them and help in any way he could.

Ashley was in the bathroom putting on her makeup. Marc was still fast asleep. There was a soft tapping at the door. Allen cautiously opened it a crack. It was the hospital security guard. "Sir, the police are here for Ms. Barton's statement. They're waiting in the lounge at the end of the corridor." Hospital security now kept constant vigil at the door.

"Yes, please tell them that she'll be there in a moment." Ashley asked Allen to go with her. As they entered the lounge they were greeted by a tall, slender man in his fifties with thinning gray hair and a salt and pepper mustache. At his heels was a shorter, heavier man, perhaps forty-five, with a round red face and very serious expression. The taller man smiled at Ashley and smoothly made the introductions.

"Ahh, Ms. Barton! It is a pleasure to meet you. I am Inspector Raymond Moreau of the Paris police, homicide division, and this is Assistant-Inspector Victor Leoncour. I'm sure this has been a terrible experience for you. Such an unfortunate way to be introduced to Paris. How is Dr. Hamilton?"

Allen responded, "He's been badly injured and is sedated just now. I shall be taking care of his facial bone injuries. He should have a full recovery."

"I'm pleased to know that," said Moreau. "You are apparently friends attending the same plastic surgeons' meeting?"

"Yes, that's right."

"And what do you know of this unfortunate incident?" Moreau asked of Allen.

Before Allen had a chance to respond Ashley interjected, "Dr. Greenberg came by only this morning when he heard of Dr. Hamilton's injuries. I think I can give you any information you wish."

"Thank you, Ms. Barton. That would be very helpful. Shall we all sit down?" Moreau turned toward his associate. "Leoncour, please find another chair somewhere."

"Yes, sir." In a moment he returned with a chair. He sat down, flipped open a notebook and began taking notes.

"Please, Ms. Barton, continue."

"Last night Marc, Dr. Hamilton, was late meeting me for dinner. I waited for some time, about two hours, I think. Finally I called the hotel. There was no answer. I was very worried since Marc is never late... So I took a taxi to the Hotel Splendid."

"Where were you waiting for Dr. Hamilton?"

"At La Coupole in Montparnasse."

"A fine choice. I suppose there was a crowd... but someone would remember seeing you there?"

"Well, I didn't speak with anyone but after sitting at the bar for two hours, I'm sure at least the bartender would remember me."

"Yes, of course. Please continue."

"I arrived at the hotel and found that the room had been torn apart and Marc was gone. I was frightened. I didn't know what to think."

"I'm sure you must have been terrified. We have seen the room and the blood. Why did you not call the authorities? Surely the blood..."

"I fainted and the next thing I knew was that Dr. Dumont was on the telephone telling me about Marc. My only thought was to get to him."

"Hmm... of course, and yet, all the blood...?"

"When I came to I could only think of getting to Marc. I was grateful that he was alive."

"Yes. Well, that explains it. You are very close with Dr. Hamilton?"

"Yes. We are going to be married soon."

"Have you any idea what might have been the cause of such a vicious attack?"

"Obviously robbery. There was about five thousand dollars in cash. It's gone now."

"Ms. Barton, have you not heard of travelers' checks? Carrying such large sums in cash can be very dangerous."

"I see that now, Inspector."

"How would anyone know that Dr. Hamilton would be carrying so much cash?"

"I have no idea. They must have seen him enter the hotel... and... picked him at random."

"Indeed... *at random*," said the inspector while pulling on his mustache. "Now, what happened here, to you, at the hospital?"

"I walked into the room and that horrible man began to strangle me." She raised her hand to her bruised throat. She had been telling partial truths. She couldn't tell if Moreau was buying it all or not. Allen kept out of it and continued gazing at the floor.

"And why would that man attack you?" Ashley had no good answer so she feigned anger.

"How should I know! He could have killed me if not for that security guard."

"It must be a memory you want to forget! But why you, Ms. Barton? Why you?" Moreau was smooth as silk and as persistent as an itch.

"I think he was trying to rape me!" she blurted out.

"Disgusting fellow, Ms. Barton. I'm so sorry... But why you?" Ashley was beginning to lose control and tears of frustration filled her eyes.

"I don't know why me," she said angrily. "I was in the wrong place at the wrong time! Just chance, I guess. Random."

"Oh, I see," said Moreau with more than a hint of skepticism in his voice. "So we have two random occurrences, only hours apart, involving two visitors engaged to be married to each other... allegedly a robbery where five thousand dollars is stolen from the gentleman and shortly after, at another location, his fiancee barely escapes being raped... a *random* choice for the would-be rapist who ends up dead in the hospital room of the original victim! I'll have to run those probabilities on our computer but offhand I'd say..." Ashley was now openly sobbing. Moreau softened a bit. "Perhaps tomorrow after some rest things will be more clear. I wish you a good evening and I hope Dr. Hamilton continues to improve." In the next moment they were gone.

Ashley turned to Allen, "Do you think they believed me?"

"Ashley, you're a terrible liar."

On their way out of the hospital, Leoncour turned to Moreau and said, "She's lying or at least holding back."

"Sometimes you amaze me, Leoncour. You are so astute!" Leoncour fell silent after this rebuff from his superior. "But why is the victim holding back? What has she to hide? We'll try again when she is more calm and hope for better results. As far as we know they have done no wrong and until we learn otherwise there is little we can do." Moreau began to pull at his mustache again.

* * * * *

Marc slept straight through until morning. Allen Greenberg remained with Ashley all night in Marc's room. They felt safe enough with the hospital security guards just on the other side of the door. Ashley slept on the sofa while Allen pulled two chairs together to make a very uncomfortable bed. Although she had urged him to leave and get some sleep at his hotel, Allen refused to leave her after such a traumatic ordeal. Besides he knew he would have to return early anyway to evaluate Marc's condition for surgery.

They were awakened by Marc's calling, "Ashley?" They went to his bedside.

"I'm here, Marc. How are you feeling?"

"Like I was hit by a truck!"

"That's about how you look too," said Allen. He was relieved at seeing Marc so alert.

"I think something happened... I'm not clear... I remember both of you leaving. Then... there's something missing. I can't fill in the blanks."

"You simply had a sedative and slept through," said Allen. There was no point in going over the whole thing with him now. He would probably remember it soon enough. There was plenty of time for that. "Well," he continued. "Your edema is down a little. How do you feel about some repair work later today?"

"Will you do it, Allen?" asked Marc.

"If you still want me to." Marc didn't answer. He only smiled. Allen wished there would have been less swelling. Under normal circumstances he would have waited with surgery for a few more days but he felt it too risky for Marc and Ashley to remain in the hospital a moment longer than necessary. The close call from last evening made him certain of that. "Let me track down Dumont and see when the surgery schedule will be open." He turned to walk out and called back over his shoulder, "I'll let you know as soon as we can make arrangements. By the way, nothing by mouth, not even water."

Allen had Dumont paged. Dumont was finishing his rounds and agreed to meet Allen in the cafeteria in about twenty minutes. Allen had found a table and was already sipping his coffee when Dumont arrived. "Claude, he seems alert and stronger this morning."

"Yes. I believe the transfusions have helped."

"I wish there would be less edema, although it has decreased a little," said Allen.

"You are anxious to operate?"

"Only because I think it's too dangerous for them here. I don't think they'll stop trying to get them."

"You are probably right. I know that the schedule in surgery is full all day. We could operate him as an emergency case after hours, perhaps at about seven o'clock this evening."

"That would be perfect. It will give him all day to get stronger and give me a chance to borrow Ducett's instruments."

"Good. Then I shall arrange it with surgery and anesthesia."

"Claude, one more thing. Do you think we can move him elsewhere without anyone knowing? And please, no name on the door."

"Yes. I have a thought," said Dumont. "Let me have him moved to a holding area in surgery. Only authorized personnel are permitted as it is a sterile floor. Anyone out of place there would be immediately noticed. What do you think?"

"Excellent! We'll keep an IV open and keep him n.p.o. I'll tell them the news. Thank you, Claude."

Allen returned to Marc's room and explained the plan to them. Ashley's first thought was to remain with Marc until the last possible moment. "Okay," said Allen. "We'll have you change into hospital clothes and you can stay with Marc... on one condition."

"And what condition?" asked Ashley.

"That I stay with Marc now and you get something to eat."

Ashley smiled, pretending to surrender. "Okay. You win." Actually she was starved now that she thought about it. She couldn't remember when she had eaten last.

"A fine thing!" said Marc. "Talking about food while all I get is an IV!" He hadn't lost his sense of humor. Ashley bent down and kissed him and then headed for the cafeteria. While she was away Allen found a scrub suit, cap, mask and shoe covers for her. She returned just in time to see two orderlies come to move the bed to the surgery floor. They waited until she changed her clothes and then she accompanied them. As they were leaving Allen said, "See you later. I have to find Ducett." He felt that Marc and Ashley would be safe for the moment.

* * * * *

When Earl Conners awoke, it was seven AM. He went through his morning rituals while planning what to say to his boss. It was too early to make an appointment to see J.T. but he went ahead to Alcott Laboratories anyway. By the time he had finished breakfast in the cafeteria it was nearly nine o'clock and he was fairly certain that Roswell would be in his office. The secretary asked him to wait for a moment and then motioned for him to enter the office. J.T. was already busy looking over his schedule for the day when Conners walked in.

"Have a seat, Earl. What brings you here so early this morning?"

"It's not good news, Boss. Barnes was killed trying to get the girl at the hospital. A security guard got him."

"What did you say? A fucking security guard? You sonofabitch, I thought you only worked with professionals! How the hell did that happen?" Roswell was fuming.

"Boss, I'm sorry. It just couldn't be helped. For some reason the security guard decided to check Hamilton's room and Barnes was there at that exact moment. The guard nailed Barnes just as he was going to walk out with the girl. He must have seen the thirty-eight and didn't think twice about firing. And that's it."

"And that's it!" mocked Roswell. "And that's it!" Conners was bracing himself for more chewing out. "So now we have cops involved!" continued Roswell.

"I'm afraid so, sir." But Barnes had no ID on him. I never let my men carry any ID when on a job."

"So dummy, you don't think that Hamilton or the girl will put two and two together and run to the cops for protection?"

"Sir, with all due respect, I don't think they want to blow this wide open. Besides, the girl's too scared to talk. She knows we can get to them... *anywhere*."

"And the doc?"

"He's in no shape for conversation. He'll be history before that."

"You'd better pray you're right, Conners. If any of this gets traced back here, I'm taking you down with me. Now get out of my sight!"

"Boss, I promise you, we'll get 'em." Conners sheepishly made his exit with Roswell's eyes burning holes through his back.

* * * * *

It was eight o'clock in the evening and the surgery was in progress. All was going well. Dumont was assisting Greenberg as he had promised. "What a mess," said Greenberg. "We have to reconstruct the orbital floor too. They really did a number on him. Christ, it's just not worth it. They should have spilled it. This probably wouldn't have happened." By Dumont's silence Allen realized that he didn't understand. As only could happen in a close relationship, such as surgery, a bond had developed between the two surgeons. Greenberg realized that Dumont had stuck his neck pretty far out for them and had never even asked for a reason. He felt that Dumont deserved some explanation and was sure Marc would have trusted him as well.

Allen waited to explain. He was afraid to go into details with the nurses present. He didn't know whom to trust and he was taking no chances. They had finished the suturing. The dressing was next. It had been a grueling four hours in surgery. Dumont and Greenberg left Marc in the hands of the anesthetist and then proceeded to the locker room where they removed their surgical masks and caps. As they were dressing Greenberg began to unravel the story to Dumont whose eyes were wide in disbelief.

"Mon Dieu! If this is true, they are still in grave danger."

"I'm afraid so," said Allen.

"I have a thought," said Dumont. "Obviously it is too dangerous for them to remain at this hospital. While Dr. Hamilton is in recovery I will check on him. You go with Ms. Barton back to their hotel and get their passports from the desk clerk. Since they are not suspected of any crime, the police would have had no reason to keep the passports. Besides they were probably returned to the hotel before all this occurred."

"Good thinking, Claude."

"Wait. I am not finished."

"Sorry."

"My brother has a small cottage in a wooded area only a few kilometers north of Paris. It is quite secluded and my brother never uses it. They will be safe there for several days while Dr. Hamilton recovers. As soon as he awakens from the anesthetic, I'll take him to the cottage in my car. You can meet us there. I'll give you directions. Bon?"

"Bon," said Allen. "But what about the police?"

"We will say that they decided to leave the hospital. They did not ask for permission and simply slipped out. To make it look good, I'll telephone them later in the morning to show my good intentions. After all, there is no crime though I'm sure they would like to talk with them further. If the police don't find them in a few days, there will be little incentive to execute a serious search for crazy Americans. When all is quiet, they can go anywhere with their passports. What do you think?"

"It's good, Claude! It just might work. Let's check him in recovery. I'll let Ashley know all is well and we'll go ahead and get the passports. I just pray that they are at the hotel and not in the hands of the police."

Allen found Ashley where he had left her in the holding area. "It's all over and he's going to be fine." She threw her arms around his neck and began to cry silently. "Hey, no time for this. We've got to get busy now. Here's what we're going to do."

Chapter 19

Marc had been resting quietly in the recovery room for over an hour. Dumont was keeping him mildly sedated, just enough to take the edge off of his postoperative pain. He couldn't give him too much medication since he had to get him out of the hospital and to the cottage in a few hours. Finally Ashley was convinced that he was doing well and she agreed to go to the hotel with Allen for the passports.

It was about one o'clock in the morning when Ashley and Allen made their way through the basement to the service entrance as Dumont had advised. They were still very conscious of the danger of being seen and were relieved that they were unnoticed as they passed the central supply room and the laundry. The hospital never slept but at this hour there were fewer personnel milling about and it seemed to be on automatic pilot. They made their exit through the service entrance and found themselves on a side street. There wasn't a taxi in sight so they began walking toward the emergency entrance. Since they knew that the emergency room was probably being watched, they avoided the sliding glass doorway. They felt like thieves lurking in the shadows but the best chance for finding a taxi at this hour would be here. They turned up their collars for a measure of protection from the cold, damp wind while taking their chances waiting for a taxi to discharge some poor soul in need of emergency care.

About fifteen minutes passed. They were nearly frozen when at last a taxi pulled up to the emergency entrance. They watched a woman helping a man who was clutching his coat in the area of his chest. He seemed out of breath and they walked very slowly. The taxi driver helped them get a wheel chair, turned back to his vehicle and opened the door. He was about to get in when he took a step back in surprise as two figures suddenly emerged from the darkness and walked rapidly toward him. He felt vulnerable and quickly jumped into his cab. Driving a taxi at night was dangerous business. The two figures were furiously waving for him to wait. When he saw that it was a man and a woman, he decided that they were probably just ordinary fares and meant him no harm. He waited and the breathless couple got in and thanked him for waiting. "Hotel Splendid, Rue St. Jacque, please... ahh... s'il vous plait," said Ashley.

"Ashley, what the hell are we doing? This is nuts, lurking in the shadows, hoping not to be seen or worse yet, hoping not to be killed! Is it worth it?"

"I don't know, Allen. We're in this mess and there must be a way out. What else can we do? I don't think even going to the police and trying to explain would be of much help. What would memos and breast implants mean to them? They'd most likely see it as some foolish American issue. How could they protect us or even make the effort. It's not their problem."

"Ashley, I can't believe that they would turn their backs on us."

"What if they did believe us? How do we deal with the publicity? Don't you think Alcott will keep trying more than ever to get the memo and destroy it before anyone can prove their involvement in a conspiracy? Allen, Alcott is absolutely convinced that Marc or I have the memo. Since they tried with Marc, nearly killing him and without succeeding, it seems they are pretty sure that I have it. Why else would they try to kidnap me?"

"I guess you're right. What a nightmare!"

They pulled up in front of the hotel, paid the driver and walked in. The clerk was asleep behind the desk. Allen loudly cleared his throat and was successful in waking him. The clerk was embarrassed at being caught napping and quickly came to his feet and to attention. "Good morning. May I help you?"

"Yes, please," Ashley responded. "May we have our passports? We want to check out of room 424." The night clerk seldom saw any of the hotel guests. Without another thought he assumed that Allen was Dr. Hamilton. He turned to the letter boxes and withdrew the two passports and a white envelope. He handed the passports to Allen along with the envelope.

"An overseas telephone message for you, Dr. Hamilton. The passports were returned late yesterday. Is there a problem that you are checking out so soon? I see you were booked for a week."

"Not at all. We've simply decided to tour the chateau country along the Loire and thought we would get an early start."

As he was getting the bill prepared. the clerk said, "Very wise, sir. You will miss the morning traffic." Allen tore the envelope open:

To: Dr. Marcus Hamilton
From: Ms. Victoria Lange

Marc: Matthew Wertheim killed yesterday while crossing street in Atlanta. Have serious concerns. Please call. Be careful.

                                                            Vicky

Ashley had been holding her breath until the passports were in Allen's hands and then breathed a sigh of relief. "Thank God!" she said to herself. Allen showed her the note.

"Oh, no!" she whispered. "That was no accident! My God!"

"Is this note referring to Matthew Wertheim, the research scientist?"

"Yes, I'm afraid it is."

"Good Lord! I was very close with him in the early days of silicone implant research. I can't believe it! Hit by a car!"

"Allen, it was no accident!" He looked at Ashley and shook his head. He didn't want to believe it, but in view of the past events he couldn't ignore the possibility. Ashley and Marc had to find safety and for now, Claude's solution seemed the best course.

"Is there a car rental agency open at this hour?" Allen asked of the desk clerk.

"Sir, the only one I know is in the Place de la Opera. It is just next to the Hotel La Grand." They left the Splendid to search for a taxi. They didn't see the hotel clerk make a phone call.

The cab dropped them near the side entrance of the La Grand just a few feet from the car rental agency. There was not a soul in sight. They had taken only a few steps toward the rental office when they stopped in their tracks startled by the flicker of a cigarette lighter in the alley directly in front of them. It made the man's face glow for a moment. He obviously wanted to be seen. "Good evening, Ms. Barton," came out of the darkness. The sound of her name overwhelmed Ashley with terror. She tried to scream but couldn't. "You will both come with me, please. There is a gentleman with a very persuasive gun behind you. I would rather he didn't have to use it."

Ashley grasped Allen's coat sleeve. "Okay," said Allen. "Just take it easy. We'll do as you say. What do you want?"

Implant

"Just to talk with Ms. Barton. That's all. There's a car parked around the corner of the hotel a few yards behind you. Please turn around slowly." They did as instructed. "That gentleman is George. He'll lead the way to the car and we can have a little chat there... very privately. By the way, now I have a little persuader at your backs. Let's move very carefully and very slowly, please." Ashley was now walking on the inside, between Allen and the hotel wall. They marched as though they were in a funeral procession. Her panic was giving way to an acceptance of her fate.

She began to think, "I'm probably going to die anyway. Why not try?" They were approaching the side entrance to the Hotel La Grand. Suddenly Ashley let her ankle turn and at the same moment loudly called out, "Oh! My ankle!" She grabbed Allen's arm, pretending to prevent a fall. The two men were taken completely off guard by the shout. Ashley took advantage of the moment and gave Allen's arm a firm jerk toward her. They tumbled and literally fell in through the entrance onto the floor of the hotel salon.

There were a few late-nighters chatting or having a drink at the bar. Allen wasn't quite sure of what had happened when he heard an angry voice from outside, "Fuck it! God damn, sonofabitch!" The salon became silent and all eyes were on the two sudden intruders sprawled on the floor. For a moment it seemed like a slap-stick comedy from an old silent film. Allen helped Ashley up. They brushed the dust from their clothes as they made their way toward the safety of the bar. The silence and the stares seemed to require some sort of explanation. Ashley said simply, "Sorry. I twisted my ankle and tripped." That seemed to satisfy the onlookers, who resumed their socializing and seemed to forget about them completely. Allen led Ashley to a small cocktail table. Neither one spoke for a few minutes while trying to collect themselves. A waiter came over to take their orders. Allen looked at Ashley and waited for her request. She said, "A double gin Martini, up, and forget the olive."

Allen said, "The same, please." He looked at Ashley for a long moment. "You're some lady!"

"Oh, what the hell! What could we lose?"

"I don't know. Maybe our lives?" he said.

"Allen, shut up. Besides you look like shit!"

"Typical woman! We nearly get shot to death and all you can say is that I look like shit!" They began to laugh. Allen noticed that Ashley's laugh was turning into sobs. She began to tremble and was trying to choke down her tears, a reaction to the past few unbelievable minutes. He came over to her and reassuringly put his arm around her shoulders. "Ashley, we're safe now. Thanks to you, we're safe." The tears now flowed freely. He held on to her allowing it all to come out. At last the drinks came. They clicked gasses. "L' chaim," said Allen.

It was four o'clock in the morning. The bar had closed and the few stragglers finally gave up and went to bed. Ashley and Allen moved into another salon. They looked around carefully but saw no one suspicious. As they sat down on a sofa Allen began, "We're not safe here for much longer. Obviously they know where we are. Also I think we'd best forget the car rental agency."

"Do you think they're still waiting for us out there?"

"I doubt it but I'm not going to take the chance."

"We've got to get transportation to the cottage somehow," said Ashley. "Do you think we could arrange for a car through the hotel?"

"I don't know. We're not guests here but usually money talks." They went into the main lobby. The concierge was not at his desk. It was much too early. They had to leave the hotel soon. Allen went to the front desk and approached the clerk. "Good morning."

"Bon jour, Monsieur. May I help?"

Implant

"Yes, please. I need a rental car immediately."

"Sir, if you will just step around the corner..."

"I know. There is an agency there but my wife is ill and she won't let me leave her here alone. Can you arrange for them to bring the car here?"

"That is impossible, sir!" Allen pushed a $100 bill, palm down on it, toward the clerk. The clerk glanced at the note and smiled broadly. "I will arrange it. The Hotel La Grand always does its best." Allen felt like throwing up. Ashley saw his expression and almost laughed out loud.

Within ten minutes a young man walked up to the desk. The clerk said something to him and nodded toward Ashley and Allen who were still sitting on the sofa. He approached them. "Good morning, sir and madam. I understand that you wish to rent a car."

"Yes," said Allen

"Well, this is most irregular. We must go to the agency office."

Allen thought, "Then why are you here?" Then it came to him with no surprise. He withdrew his wallet and offered the young man $20.

"Sir, I don't know that this can be arranged. It is very difficult." Allen took back the $20. It was apparent that the desk clerk had clued in the agent.

As he was replacing the $20 bill Ashley whispered to him, "Cheapskate." He gave the agent a $100 bill. The fellow accepted it without a flinch and reached into his coat pocket for the rental papers. Allen signed the forms and placed the charges on a credit card.

The young man said, "Thank you. Here are the keys. It is a white Citroen parked at the front entrance."

"Thank you," said Allen. "Can you direct me to the highway out of the city toward Argenteuil?"

* * * * *

Dr. Claude Dumont had been driving for about an hour. It was still dark when he passed through Mantes on the road heading northwest toward Rouen. His passenger was sleeping comfortably in the front seat beside him. He had given Marc fifteen milligrams of morphine by injection as soon as they got into the car. It would keep him asleep until they reached the cottage. Claude had driven about ninety kilometers when he slowed up as he approached an obscure unmarked road lined with tall trees which were now nearly bare. He had been following the valley of the Seine and now turned westward away from the river. He followed the road for about twenty minutes to a flashing yellow light and turned left again onto a dirt road. Within a few minutes the terrain changed to thickly wooded rolling hills. He made a sharp right, went about 100 meters and stopped. They had arrived.

Claude got out of the car and went around to the passenger side. He shook Marc gently to awaken him and carefully helped him out of the car. Marc was able to walk but with rubbery legs. At least his mind was clearing a little. They walked through a grove of trees with Claude's arm supporting him. "Just a few more meters, mon ami." There were three steps up to the door. The cottage was simple, wood frame with roughly hewn shingles and a window on either side of the solid front door. Though his mind was hazy, it reminded Marc of a hunting lodge. The sky to the east was showing the first signs of dawn. Claude had to let Marc lean against the door so he could get to his keys. He fumbled in his pocket for a moment, withdrew a key ring and turned toward the dim morning light to find the cottage key. They entered the dark room. Claude helped Marc to a chair beside the fireplace. Next to the chair was a table with a kerosene lamp. Claude found matches beside the lamp and lit it. The light cast long surrealistic shadows on the walls.

Implant

They were in a parlor very simply furnished. The floor was wood planks with a rug in front of the fieldstone hearth, which was the focal point of the room. Above the hearth, on the stone wall, hung a shotgun secured by brackets on both ends. Opposite Marc was another fireside chair. An old, worn sofa and a long library table completed the furnishings. The walls had dark paneling upon which hung a few nondescript pictures. There was a small kitchen to the left, and to the right was a bedroom.

Claude's first thought was to get Marc comfortable in bed. After Marc was settled, Claude went into the kitchen and brewed a pot of strong coffee. He filled two mugs and handed one to Marc who took a few sips. Next he went out back. Beside the outhouse was a woodshed. He carried in several logs and built a fire. In a few minutes at least the chill was out of the room. Claude found two more blankets and covered Marc with them. He hoped the heat from the hearth would reach Marc soon.

"Mon ami, it is getting light and I must return to Paris. I have to call the police to let them know I just discovered that you and Mdsl. Barton have left the hospital without permission. And of course I have no idea of where you might be. Before I leave I will give you another injection of morphine. When you awaken, if all went well, you should find Mdsl. Barton and Allen here. I will return this evening with provisions, and we shall celebrate with a party. Bon?" He gave Marc a reassuring smile.

"Bon," whispered Marc. "Claude, how can I ever repay you?"

"Repay? No. This is what friends do. It is only natural." He reached for the hypodermic. "And now a stick… and now you must rest." Within five minutes Marc was asleep. Claude stood in the doorway of the bedroom and watched his regular deep breathing. He was confident that his patient and friend was doing well. As he stood there he said softly, "Mon ami, I hope this works out for you. You have courage, my friend. But I think also you are a little stupid... I wonder what I would do."

As he walked to his car he noticed the light of early dawn. The sky was orange and clear with the promise of a beautiful fall day. Thank God, the cold rain and wind were gone for now. Dr. Claude Dumont hoped that this day would be better than the last. "How could it be worse?" he thought.

Chapter 20

Ashley had excused herself and made her way to the ladies' room off the main lobby of the Hotel La Grand. Allen was sitting on the sofa studying the map given him by the young man from the car rental agency. His finger was tracing the route from Argenteuil toward Rouen when his concentration was disturbed by the entrance of an almost attractive woman. She had bleached, brassy blond hair and far too much make-up. She looked to be about forty, maybe forty-five. The short evening dress she was wearing was black and had a very low-cut neck line. The upper half of her large breasts were bare and bulging. She looked as though she had poured herself into the dress and was now overflowing at the brim. In general, Allen observed, she had a sexy figure. The woman sat down on the other sofa which was facing him. She crossed her legs. "Not bad," he thought. Then she lit a cigarette. Allen tried not to stare but he couldn't take his eyes off of her. He felt like a school kid. Since his wife died, about six years ago, there were very few women in his life. Of course he dated but no one seriously. He had entrenched himself in his work, however there were times when work was no substitute for sex. He was definitely not celibate.

She knew he was staring at her and she gave him a smile of encouragement. He had never been with a hooker but he could see how one might be attracted to this one. He smiled back. She raised one eyebrow. It was a definite question. Was he interested? And then the idea hit him. Yes, he was very interested! He moved next to her on the sofa. She said, "Bon soir," with an even more generous smile. She was obviously pleased with her conquest.

"Bon soir, Madam. Do you speak English?"

"A little," she said. "Do you have a room here?"

"No, but we could take a drive somewhere."

She had a puzzled look, "With an auto?"

"Yes," he said. "But I must get rid of the lady I am with."

"Oh, you are with someone? Then perhaps another time."

"No. No!" Just then Ashley entered the lobby. When she saw the scene, she smiled knowingly. Allen continued before Ashley was close enough to hear, "Please wait. It will take a few minutes." She took a puff of her cigarette, blew the smoke away from Allen and nodded affirmatively. As Ashley approached them, the woman visually absorbed every square inch of her and couldn't understand why this man would want to change from such a beautiful partner. She was all the more pleased with herself. Allen got up and short-circuited Ashley. He took her by the arm back to their original sofa.

"Please don't let me interrupt, Allen," she said with a teasing intonation.

"Shut up and listen." She had never seen this side of Allen before. She had always liked him but thought of him as weak and indecisive. Her attitude changed instantly when she saw how serious he was. "Look," he continued. "Let's think this through logically. They know we're in here. They also know that we have to come out sooner or later." She nodded to indicate that she was following his line of logic. "Now, how the fucking hell are we going to get out of here and to the car without being seen or shot at or at least followed?" Ashley just stared at him. It was sinking in. It was so obvious she didn't know how she hadn't thought it.

"Of course, you're right. So we're stuck here?"

"No. That hooker is our ticket out."

"What?"

"Look. She takes your place and she and I walk out of here to the Citroen. She's about your height and blond. It's still dark enough that when they see me, they'll assume that it's you with me. You stay here. I let them follow me somewhere. They think that you're going to meet Marc. Surely by now they know he's not at the hospital. Hopefully, if Claude was clever enough, they have no idea where Marc is so logically they'll follow me in the hope of getting to you wherever that Citroen goes. Right?" She didn't answer immediately. She was tired and sleepy and not completely comprehending.

"Isn't that a bit convoluted?"

"Maybe but I think it will work. Ashley, it's our only chance out of here. Give me ten minutes after I leave. Then go to the rental agency and get another car. Do you have money?"

"Yes. The hospital gave me all of Marc's valuables. I have some cash and whatever is in Marc's wallet."

"Good. Here's the map." He pointed out the route for her. "Do you still have Claude's directions to the cottage?"

"Yes. In my purse."

"Great! Just go on to the cottage and I'll meet you there when I can."

"It's nice of that woman to help us."

"Ashley, I hate to tell you this but she hasn't the foggiest idea."

"Allen, what the hell are you doing! She doesn't know?"

"Trust me. She thinks I'm cute and that I'm dumping you for her."

"Oh, how sweet of you!" She understood, finally, and switched gears. "Do you really think it will work?"

"Yes," said Allen. "It has to! Now remember. Give me ten minutes. Oh, yes. Give me your coat."

"My coat?"

"Please, Ashley," he said showing that he was tired of explanations. "Trust me." She removed her coat and gave it to him. "Now look angry and slap me." She just stood there staring at him. "Ashley, for heaven's sake! Be angry and slap me!" She did. He thought she overdid it a bit, but the show did have to look real. Ashley played along and left the lobby pretending to be angry. Allen smiled and walked over to the woman. She had taken in the whole scene.

"The lady is very angry, yes?"

"Yes. My car is at the entrance. Will you please come with me? It is cold. You will need this coat."

"But I am comfortable without it."

"Please. For me." He wanted to make her look as much like Ashley as possible.

She knew men could be kinky, of course, but this was a new one on her. A coat fetish! She put on the coat as he helped her with it in a gentlemanly fashion.

"Merci, Monsieur."

They walked out the lobby entrance arm-in-arm. They headed toward the white Citroen. He opened the door for her and she got in. As he walked around to the driver's side he inconspicuously looked around. No sign of anyone except the sleepy doorman. Nevertheless he was certain they were watching him. He could almost feel it.

"Where are we going?" she asked.

"For a drive." She was getting more and more suspicious of him. In her profession there were many danger signals and one was going off now!

"Perhaps this is not a good idea. Please take me back to the hotel." Allen saw that she was frightened. And why not? His behavior must have seemed very strange to her. He drove another few blocks and made a sharp right turn into a dark alley. The hooker was ready to leap out and run.

He grabbed her arm and gently said, "Please, I mean you no harm." He handed her two one hundred dollar bills. He was running out of them fast. She took them and stayed reluctantly in the car, still prepared to make a dash for it. "I must explain," he said. "You are a very lovely woman and I am being unfair to you but this is a life and death matter." She was trying to understand him. There was a definite language barrier. He continued, using sign language as he spoke in the hope of helping her to understand. "There are bad men after us. They think you are the other lady at the hotel."

"Por qua?"

"Because you resemble her."

"Res-emb-ple?" She didn't understand the word.

"Resemble... look like her."

"Ah, oui! The coat." He was making progress.

"She must get away and meet her lover." That she understood.

"You are not her lover?"

"No. I am a good friend. I am trying to help. But I am placing you in danger. The bad men will follow us and try to hurt us so we must go away fast."

"No. I will leave now!" With that she opened the door, ran down the alley and quickly disappeared. He didn't try to stop her. Actually, he had accomplished what he needed. They would follow the Citroen. He would make sure to keep a good distance from them so as not to spoil the illusion that Ashley was with him in the car. He turned around, exited the alley, made a right turn again and headed south toward Orleans. The eastern sky showed the first sign of dawn. He looked into his rearview mirror. There were several cars behind him. He went faster. He looked again. This time Allen could see a dark colored car pass another and re-enter the caravan three cars behind him. Traffic was light so he could accelerate. He was doing about 120 kilometers/hour. The dark car could be seen more clearly with the growing early morning light. It was dark blue and was keeping a steady pace behind him. When he accelerated, it accelerated. When he slowed down, it slowed down. Now he was sure. They were following him.

"How long can I keep this up? Can I lose them?" he asked himself. He kept driving toward Orleans and the Loire Valley. Two hours had passed. He looked in the mirror and didn't see them. He couldn't have lost them, and they certainly didn't give up. He took the road to Tours, keeping a steady speed of about 110 or 120, always checking his mirror. He was alert but began to relax a little.

Then Allen began to think, "What the hell am I doing? How did I get into this? Sure, Marc needed me and I couldn't turn him down. He's always been a loyal friend. Okay! I helped him! How much more should I do for a friend? There is a limit. I'm risking my life! For Marc? For Ashley and Marc? No! for *Ashley*." He could never admit it before. It was all for Ashley. He felt like a traitor to Marc but he couldn't help how he felt. "No. This is stupid. She sees me only as a friend. Nothing more." He would never reveal his feelings. He'd never tell. Then what was he really doing now? Yes, it was for Ashley, but he knew he would never have her. Then why continue? Why not run to the nearest police station and spill it all and save himself? It was guilt. He was trying to make up for his forbidden feelings, trying to make it up to Marc, trying to justify this dangerous chase. "Okay," he thought. "Okay, I've admitted it. But now what? How the fuck do I save my ass?"

He found himself alone in the barren countryside. He saw a crossroad ahead. A car was waiting for him to pass. No! It was pulling out into his path! The God damn idiot! He slammed on the brakes. He skidded and finally recovered. It was only about 200 meters away now. He was praying for a miracle. God, it was the dark blue sedan! He could just, maybe, avoid the crash. He had only a split second to make the decision! Should he stop? In a pig's eye! No way! He was now only 100 meters away from collision. Allen floored the accelerator. The transmission instantly responded and he zoomed up to ninety kilometers per hour. He aimed for the blue sedan's right rear fender. It was the only chance. "Please, God!" He slammed into them. The force of the collision made the Citroen swerve to the right and off the shoulder of the road but Allen never stopped. As he accelerated again he looked over his shoulder and saw the sedan do a three sixty, flip, roll and finally come to rest on its driver's side. "A fucking, bloody miracle!" He had actually done it! He was doing 140 and didn't slow down until he reached Tours.

* * * * *

Ashley glanced at her watch. Allen had told her to wait ten minutes. Just to be safe she waited twenty. She walked through the lobby and out the doors into the chilled early morning air. She had no coat. She cursed Allen and then felt ashamed. He was doing his best and maybe his plan would work. Ashley walked around to the side entrance of the hotel.

She approached it cautiously. It had all happened here only a short time ago. It seemed safe enough now. She crossed the alley and went into the office of the auto rental agency. There was the same young clerk behind the desk who had come into the hotel to rent Allen the Citroen. He looked up and instantly recognized her. It had been only a few minutes ago. Ashley tried to appear at ease and very natural. She realized that the clerk was totally confused.

"Madam, is there a problem?"

"No, not at all. The gentleman had to leave first. He must make several stops and I must not be late. Can you rent me another car?"

"Oh, Madam, that will be very difficult." Ashley had had it and she blew.

"Okay! Cut out the crap and get me a car! There are no more stupid Americans here to give you one hundred dollar tips for what you should be doing anyway. Now! Tout de suite!" The young man didn't expect this from the quiet woman he had seen a few minutes before.

"Oui, Madam." He quickly drew up the contract for a Renault. She signed it and put it on one of her own credit cards. He was about to hand her the keys and changed his mind. "I shall be happy to bring it around for you. Only a moment."

"Merci." She was proud of herself. Five minutes later she was on the road to Argenteuil. In the early morning light she could see that no one was following her. Allen and the hooker must have been successful decoys. Ashley thought of Allen with the woman. She laughed out loud. It was so implausible. Someday it would make a great story at the dinner table.

Ashley glanced at the piece of paper in her hand and at the same time kept an eye on the road. It was Claude's map and instructions. She saw "a flashing yellow light." Yes, that had to be it. With each moment she would be a little closer to Marc. Now he was all she could think of. "Marc... Marc...!" Soon she would be in his arms. Soon she could give him the warmth of her body and heal him. Soon they would be safe. Soon they would be home.

Chapter 21

The sun shone through the east window of the cottage. The thickly wooded area filtered out much of the warmth, but not the soft morning light that shone into the bedroom where Marc slept. One beam crept slowly upward from Marc's chest to his face. He had been asleep for about four hours and the effects of the morphine injection were wearing off. As the single ray of sunlight fell across his swollen eyelids, he began to awaken. For a moment he was disoriented, but then he started to put it all together. He was in the cottage and Dumont had brought him here. The headache and facial pain made him remember that Allen had operated on him. He was supposed to remember something else... What was it?

Oh, yes. Claude was going to return in the evening and they were going to have a party... or something like that. Shit. He didn't feel much like partying. But there was something else... It was right there but he just couldn't get the thoughts to connect. Then he was distracted. He really had to take a leak... bad! He threw back the covers and sat up letting his feet hang over the side of the bed. Marc allowed the lightheadedness to pass before he tried to stand. He could feel the throbbing and swelling in his face. He understood it and expected it. He took a few steps holding on to the wall for support and was surprised at how much strength he had. It wasn't like before. He remembered the IVs and the blood transfusions. That explained it...

Where the hell was the bathroom? Slowly he made his way through the parlor and into the kitchen. He saw the door and opened it expecting to find the bathroom but instead he found himself outdoors and standing in his bare feet. Claude was great but didn't he think a guy would have to piss? Didn't French patients need to piss? He looked up and saw the outhouse a few meters straight ahead. No way! He turned toward a bush near by and finally relieved himself.

Although it was a clear sunny day the air was cold. He was wearing only a patient gown from the hospital. Claude had insisted on taking Marc directly from the recovery room. He had pushed the gurney through the basement and out the service entrance to his car. There was no way to get Marc's clothes and make an unnoticed exit from the hospital at the same time. Marc began to shiver in the raw wind. Slowly he went back inside where he found a pot of cold coffee sitting on the gas stove. Matches! There had to be matches. He found them on the wooden table. Soon the coffee was ready. It had never tasted so good before. He was getting stronger by the minute. Although the warm brew seemed to diffuse through his entire body, he couldn't stop shivering. Marc wasn't up to building a fire but at the same time he didn't want to return to bed. He'd had enough of bed during the past few days.

He returned to the bedroom only to pull the blankets off the bed and drag them to a fireside chair. That was better.

Sitting up felt good. He drew the blankets tightly about him and up to his chin. He reached for the coffee and began to sip it again. Much better. But there was something, some distressful thought that was trying to surface. It was something he had to remember. What was the last thing Claude had said? "When you wake up, Ashley will be here." That was it! Oh, God! He remembered, "Ashley... the guy was trying to choke her and I couldn't help her!" For a moment he was terrified. "But she must be all right. Claude said so." There were a few blanks but he recalled most of it now. Then where was Ashley? That thought spun round and round in his brain. He realized that he was exhausted and closed his eyes. Sleep came almost instantly.

* * * * *

Allen slowed down as he approached the outskirts of Tours. He found himself on the main commercial thoroughfare. It was nine o'clock in the morning and the street was already crowded with shoppers and people were going about their daily business. The days were short at this time of year in France and one had to get an early start to take advantage of the daylight. Parking was impossible. Allen drove around the side streets for at least twenty minutes before finding a parking space. He was starved. He hadn't eaten a thing since noon yesterday, before he went into surgery to operate on Marc.

As he got out of the Citroen he began to recall the events of the last twenty-four hours. It didn't seem real but when he saw his right front fender, crunched hood and enormous dent in the door, the reality was confirmed. If anyone had been sitting in the passenger seat, he would have been killed. Allen walked toward the main street and began to organize his thoughts. First, something to eat. Next, a call to Houston to check in with his office. He should call Marc's office too. Mrs. Warner needed to know that Marc was going to be delayed in returning home so that she could plan his schedule.

Then he recalled the telephone message informing Marc and Ashley of the death of Wertheim. Ashley was certain that it wasn't an accident. He remembered Wertheim well. They had worked together in the early days of silicone implant research. "Brilliant guy," he thought. "What a damn shame! Who sent the message?" Then he remembered that it was someone named Vicky. Everything was happening so fast that Ashley hadn't told him who Vicky was. He was having difficulty believing that all these happenings and close calls were originating from Alcott. Allen had always had a very warm relationship with the laboratory and all the executives.

It was only a few months ago that he had engineered the meeting between all the manufacturers' key people and the plastic surgery societies' representatives. He sat at the same table with J.T. Roswell when they pledged to support one another against the FDA's onslaught. It was a firm commitment to share scientific information. There was to be a union between the industry and the profession for the best that science could offer the patients, a union that would make history and serve as a glorious example of what could be achieved in a free society. What had happened to that fine objective, to that historic union? It was the God damn memo! Was it enough to kill for? Apparently, yes. He'd had first-hand experience. How could they?

Perhaps it was some kind of mistake. He had to get home to try to smooth it out. Could it be that Wertheim's death was an unfortunate accident? Was it possible that the attacks on Marc and Ashley were mere coincidence and the memo played no part, was only a red herring? Even though he didn't want to believe it, he knew that the probability of coincidence was about as likely as... as... his ever having Ashley. Ashley! Everything always came back to her. It was she who had given him the courage to pull off the escape from Paris. Even at a distance she influenced his life. He wondered if Marc realized how lucky he was.

Hunger took over his thoughts, and as he walked along the main thoroughfare he spotted a pastry shop. He ordered a cafe au lait and a croissant. That would hold him for a while. He glanced at his watch and counted back seven hours. It would be only about two o'clock in the morning in Houston. The phone calls would have to wait. The adrenaline had worn off and he was exhausted. Allen checked into a decent looking hotel. He had promised to meet Ashley at the cottage but first he had to rest. He flopped face down on the bed and instantly fell asleep.

* * * * *

Ashley made the final turn off the dirt road and parked near the grove of trees. She got out and walked anxiously toward the cottage. When she opened the door she saw Marc asleep in the chair. Quietly she entered, taking care not to awaken him. She stood there looking at him and saw that his face was more swollen than it had been. Then she remembered that Allen had told her to expect more swelling for a few days. They were together again and the thought made her smile. She loved to watch him when he was asleep. He looked so much like an innocent boy.

The cottage was cold. She had been cold all the way from Paris since she had no coat. Her next thought was to build a fire. She looked about and found the door off the kitchen and realized that it was the back door to the outside. Ashley found the woodshed. In two trips she brought in enough logs to last for several hours. As she arranged the logs in the fireplace, one rolled away from her and fell to the floor with a thud. Marc was awake. She went over to him. "Hi, Babe. How are you doing?" she asked gently.

"Better. I thought something happened to you. But you're here. You okay?" Ashley was relieved to hear his voice and to know that he was again cerebrating normally.

"I'm fine." With that she planted a lingering kiss on his forehead. "Let me get a fire going." He handed her the matches from the table beside him. After a few minutes, there was a crackling, warm fire. They sat there hypnotized by the orange flames leaping upward. They didn't speak for a few minutes.

Marc began, "This is more than I bargained for. I'm not willing to go on with it."

"What do you want to do, Marc?"

"God, I just want to go home and work something out there. Maybe I could talk with Chuck Walker and diffuse the whole thing."

"Honey, if Chuck were the friend you think he is, don't you think he should have warned you of the danger you were in?"

"Maybe he didn't know." Marc was trying to convince himself.

"Marc! He's Roswell's right-hand man! He knew what Alcott was doing to Wertheim for years. Did he lift a finger to stop it? Face it! He's a company man to the core." He knew that she was right.

"But there has got to be a solution and I won't find it here." Just then they heard a noise outside. Ashley went to the window and cautiously pulled the curtain aside. She stood there for a long moment. Nothing. She was about to give up. Finally she was relieved to see a deer dash into the grove of trees. "What?" asked Marc anxiously."

"Just a deer."

"Ashley, get that shotgun off the hearth and give it to me." She looked at him as if to ask why. Then she did as he had said. He checked to see if it was loaded. It wasn't. "Please look around for some cartridges. There must be some around." She searched about and finally found them in a kitchen cabinet.

"Here, I think this is what you want."

"Good." He loaded two cartridges and held the shotgun across his knees. "If there is a next time, I want to be ready."

* * * * *

It had taken Dr. Claude Dumont over two hours to get back to the hospital. He went directly to his office and placed a call to the police. "Homicide division, Inspector Raymond Moreau, please."

"This is Inspector Moreau."

"Good morning, Inspector. This is Dr. Dumont from the hospital."

"Good morning, Doctor. How are the patient and Mdsl. Barton today?"

"Well, that's it, Inspector. I don't know. They left the hospital without permission. No one seems to have seen them leave. It must have happened at about three o'clock this morning when the security guard took a break to use the toilet. No one realized they were gone until I made my morning rounds. Those foolish Americans! It is too soon after surgery to be safe. I thought I had best call you."

"You did right, Doctor. Have you any idea where they might have gone?"

"None, Inspector. But since he will probably get into trouble with infection or bleeding, you might check with the other hospitals in and around the city."

"Yes. That's a good idea. I'll do just that... The woman... she is beautiful... Don't you think, Doctor?"

"Yes. Very." It was obvious that Moreau was no fool.

"Doctor, if you should hear from them, you will let me know, won't you?"

"Of course, Inspector, immediately. Goodbye." Dumont knew Moreau suspected that he was involved. Now he, too, had to be careful.

Moreau hung up the phone, leaned back in his chair and began to pull at his mustache. It was obvious that Dumont was lying. But why? What was it all about? There was something he didn't know, a missing link. Why were the attacks made on the two Americans? Why did they run? They were guilty of no crime, or were they? The man at the hospital was killed in self defense. That much was obvious. The hospital guard confirmed the attempted kidnapping of the woman.

During these thoughts he became aware of an aching muscle spasm in his neck. He let go of his mustache to massage it. He had been at this game too long to ignore that signal. Why was the woman so evasive about answering his questions? Why didn't they seek help from the police? What was she hiding? What were they afraid to reveal? He sensed that the Americans were not yet out of danger. It was obvious that Dumont was helping them to escape from another possible attack, or from further questioning, or probably both. He resumed twisting the end of his mustache while trying to piece it all together. "Dumont was helping and he had lied. He might be the key... He is the key!" He sat up straight in his chair, picked up the phone and dialed.

"Leoncour here."

* * * * *

Dumont heard his name being paged. He picked up the phone to call the hospital operator. "This is Dr. Dumont. You have a message for me?"

"Yes, Doctor, extension 700, the nursing supervisor."

"Thank you." Eventually the supervisor came to the phone.

"Dr. Dumont, your patient is missing! Perras... He was last seen with you wheeling him out of recovery."

"I don't understand." He lied. "I took him straight to his room and he was fine... That woman looked very suspicious to me. I will call the police immediately." That seemed to satisfy the nurse. She had done her duty.

He placed one more call. It was to his brother. "Hello, Paul? Good morning."

"Good morning, Claude. To what do I owe this great honor?"

"Paul, I hope you don't mind. I'm letting a friend use the cottage for a few days.

"Thank you for letting me know! Claude, will you ever change?"

"Probably not. But thank you. It's for a good cause. I owe you one."

"One!" Mon Dieu!"

"Okay, several. Thank you. Goodbye."

Across the Seine, on the left bank, in an apartment building basement, the man took off his earphones and turned to his partner. "They're in some cottage that the doctor's brother owns. It shouldn't be too difficult to find out. Call Conners and tell him we've picked up the trail."

* * * * *

When Allen awoke, it was dark. He looked at his watch. It was only four o'clock in the afternoon. He had a five-hour drive to the cottage, six if traffic was heavy. He called his office in Houston. It was just past nine in the morning at home. He told his secretary only that he would be home on Monday as expected and he asked her to set up an appointment with J.T. Roswell a day or so later. Then he called Marc's office. Mrs. Warner answered the phone. He explained simply that Marc was in a little accident, not to worry and to postpone his surgeries and appointments for about two weeks. "Two weeks! Small accident! What..." He didn't give her a chance to finish.

"I'll be home on Monday. Send his patients over to my office, only the ones who must be seen. Just say he's been delayed due to flight schedules, a flu bug, or think of something but don't alarm them. I'll be glad to handle any problems until Dr. Hamilton returns. Thanks. I knew I could count on you."

"But..." He hung up. The less said, the better.

He was hungry again and thought he'd get something to eat before the long drive ahead of him. He found the hotel restaurant. It was much too early for dinner. However they accommodated him with a cheese plate and fresh mixed fruits. The vin de province went well with it. He had only one glass. He paid the bill, checked out at the desk, found his car and was on the road toward Orleans. It was already five o'clock. Traffic was heavy as he suspected it might be. He felt much better now. He had told Ashley he'd get there as soon as he could. He couldn't call the cottage. He didn't have a phone number. Probably there was no phone anyway. He hoped she wouldn't worry. Well, maybe just a little. After a while he approached a crossroad. Despite the darkness and traffic, he was certain that it was here he had slammed into the blue sedan. The road was clear now. No sign of the wreck. It was as though it had never happened.

* * * * *

Claude arrived at the cottage as promised. He was sure he hadn't been followed. Ashley greeted him at the door and gave him a favorable report on the patient. "He's been alert and his memory is improving," she said with a smile. It was nine o'clock in the evening and Ashley was starved. Even Marc was hungry. Claude had brought fruit juices, fresh bread, cheese, sausages, wine, everything he thought necessary for several days. He also brought medications and fresh dressings for Marc. He checked his patient and changed the dressings. He cleansed the suture lines under the right eyelid margin and in the scalp.

"How am I doing, Doc?" asked Marc with a swollen grin.

"Very well. You must have had a good surgeon."

Ashley was preparing the feast in the kitchen. Finally she called out, "Come and get it." Marc got to the kitchen table without assistance. During the meal Claude told them how he had lied to the police and to the nursing supervisor. They had a good laugh over it.

After a moment Marc asked, "Do you think they will look for us?"

"Why should they? You have done nothing," said Claude

Just then Ashley said, "Did you hear that? Outside. In front."

"No, what?" asked Claude.

"Quiet, she whispered!" They stopped talking. Marc got up from the table and, faster than he thought he could, got to the shotgun he had left beside the chair. Ashley and Claude sat at the table not daring to move. Ashley could hear her own heartbeat. There was a dead silence. Then it was broken by the sound of a creaking step. Claude said, "It might be Allen." Ashley called out in a tremulous, frightened voice, "Marc, it's one of them!" He ignored their words of caution. Marc had sensed earlier that something might go wrong. He was now functioning out of instinct, the primal instinct of self preservation. He was running on pure adrenaline. He raised the shotgun and aimed toward the door. Suddenly there was a knock. No one said a word.

"Hello, in there. This is Inspector Moreau." Marc lowered the shotgun. Claude turned pale. Ashley came to her senses and said,

"Come in, Inspector."

Chapter 22

Rockville, Maryland

October 6, 1989

Commissioner Wade Messerman was sitting at his desk. To an observer his office looked like a library that had been hit by a tornado. There were piles of books, enormous stacks of medical and legal journals, volumes of notes and depositions, which seemed to be carelessly strewn about the room. To the Commissioner this was perfectly organized chaos. He demanded that no one clean, touch or move a single scrap of paper. It was a maddening maze through which only he could maneuver. He could retrieve any book or article instantly. The Commissioner had been reading journals for hours. Finally he put down the material, took off his wire rimmed glasses, sat back and stretched. He was pleased with himself. He had covered every base. It was his move, and it was an unmistakable checkmate.

Implant

He pushed the intercom button. "Alice, get Cook and Watson in here."

"Commissioner, Watson just passed my desk. He said he was going for a coffee break."

"Stop him! Tell them to haul their asses in here. Now!"

"Yes, Sir." Within two minutes Cook and Watson stood before their boss.

Cook was a young attorney, only a few years out of school, who had started a solo law practice in Baltimore. Although John Cook had been at the top of his class he soon learned that it was sink or swim in the real world and he simply couldn't cut it. After struggling for two years and getting deeper in debt, he closed his office and was looking for a job. These were lean years for attorneys, even the best of them. The market was flooded and the competition was tough. The fact that he had no social skills didn't help the situation. Finally he found a job with the FDA through a head hunter. Messerman recognized his abilities and hired him. He needed no social skills there.

Gerald Watson had been with the Agency for about two years. He was thirty years old and had a background in advertising. He was open, superficially friendly and had a sixth sense for seeing through people. He and Cook complemented one another and together made a great team.

They stood at attention. Cook straightened his tie. Watson coughed nervously,

"Excuse me, sir." Although there were two chairs, Messerman didn't offer one to either man. He loved to see them respond to his wishes and to see that they knew he was in charge, in charge of their livelihood, in charge of their lives. Messerman got up from behind the desk. He slowly walked around the two men as though it was a military personal inspection. He reveled in his power over them.

"Cook, what's happening on the Hill since we circulated the summary?"

"Sir, I believe that your summary of the hearings is getting a lot of attention. Senator York and especially that woman Representative from Pennsylvania, what's her name... Stanley... Sandra Stanley... they're making a lot of noise about it. As you know, they're both very influential. York has the most clout with the Democrats up there. I overheard him talking to a group about checking into the silicone problem and they were all nodding in agreement. And Stanley, she's a women's libber who always hated the implants, always thought it 'diminished women, not augmented them.' I heard her make that comment."

Messerman turned to the anxious looking Watson. "Mr. Watson, I think we're ready."

"Yes, sir!"

"I want you to make up a news release for every major news syndicate and for television and radio networks. I want it on my desk by noon today. Cook, I want you to help him with it by giving him, in detail, what you know they're saying on the Hill. Call the Senator and Sandra Stanley now! Get their quotes. This is it, men! Get your asses in gear!" They had been waiting for this moment for months. Watson had the releases halfway prepared. They did an about face and excitedly left the room to do their chief's bidding. They were going into battle armed and ready. By two o'clock that afternoon the news syndicates had the release. This was hot!

> After four years of "in depth" study and research, an investigation so thorough that the conclusions are unmistakable, we have found that the silicone gel mammary implant does not fall within the guidelines of the FDA in proving *safety and efficacy*. We believe that the implant must be reclassified

from Class I, which required only limited ongoing research and allowed free use in the medical community, to a Class III. This is essentially a reclassification to an experimental device status. The Congress of the United States has given the Agency the power to do this for any device approved prior to 1976, which is found to be potentially harmful or dangerous.

We have found that the silicone gel has the capacity to diffuse through the system and migrate to other organs. We have further evidence that it may be involved in causing autoimmune disease, such as rheumatoid arthritis, scleraderma and lupus erythematosis. Our studies indicate that there is a possible link to breast cancer.

We are advising the public that those women who have silicone breast implants should consult with their doctors regarding future care, treatment or surgery. Women who have these implants should look for any unusual symptoms, such as chronic fatigue, unexplained temperature elevations, frequent respiratory infections, aching joints or chronic headaches.

Sometime in January, 1990, the silicone gel mammary implant will be withdrawn from use, except in very special cases such as breast reconstruction for cancer. We plead with the public not to panic. We are not here to alarm anyone. We are here to serve, inform and to protect.

The next day, October 7th, Messerman was flooded with phone calls, which of course he expected. The press had gone wild over the release. It made the front page of every major newspaper. The morning and evening news gobbled it up. Martha Foster of the *Eyes on America* show announced an exposé to be broadcast the following week. She would have experts to discuss the problem. She would have interviews with innocent patients who had been lured into the "diabolical operation." They would demonstrate the horrible deformities caused by the silicone implants. Even WWN news was planning a special report, *Beauty and the Breast.*

The Commissioner sat behind his desk. Messerman was "forced" into holding a press conference at one o'clock that afternoon to clarify the FDA's position. He stretched his arms and smiled. He had done it and he was proud of himself. Now everyone would know his name and respect him. Now he was really going places.

* * * * *

Vicky Lange had spent the night of October 6th with Dave. This was not an unusual event. They had spoken of marriage but Vicky would never make a commitment. It was frustrating as hell to Dave who never knew were he stood with her. He was ready for something stable in his life. Lately he had been wondering whether or not Vicky was to be the stabilizing influence. She had never told him about Marc's visit or about the memo. That was privileged information.

It was Dave's day off. He was sitting in his robe at the breakfast table and was enjoying his last cup of coffee. Vicky sat across from him. She was completely absorbed in reading the morning newspaper. There it was, finally. She had been waiting for about two weeks for this news to break ever since Marc's visit. But she wasn't idle. She had been preparing for half-page ads in the newspapers and in women's magazines. Vicky was making plans for a television ad and was seeking a public relations firm to represent her. What an opportunity. A once-in a-lifetime shot. Her work with battered women would now pay off. She would become their champion.

Dave was feeling ignored. "Hello," he said. She put down the paper. "Must be something very interesting."

"Yes, very," she said. "They say it's unofficial at this time, but the FDA is probably going to take the silicone breast implants off the market."

"No! That's Marc's major area of interest. He studied with Allen Greenberg during his residency."

"Who is Allen Greenberg?"

"Only the guy who invented them. This is going to be a real blow to Marc and, I guess, to just about every plastic surgeon in the country."

"Yes. Well, I had better get to the office," she said.

"Will I see you tonight?"

"I can't. I've got to prepare some briefs. Sorry. Maybe over the weekend."

"Vicky, we've got to resolve this..."

"Not now, Dave, please. I really have to go." She left him at the table, got into her little compact and was on her way. Soon she would have a real car, fine jewelry, a big house with acreage and horses. Yes. There definitely had to be horses. She was going to have them. She was going to have it all!

Chapter 23

Allen had been driving for hours. Traffic was heavy and his muscles ached from being tense at the wheel. He was happy to be near the end of his journey. It would be only a few more minutes, half an hour at the most. He was anxious to see that Ashley was safe. He couldn't get her out of his thoughts, and finally he admitted that he didn't want to. He didn't like feeling as though he were a traitor to Marc but he simply couldn't shut off his emotions. She was everything in a woman that he had ever dreamed about and never had. At the same time there was his concern about Marc whom he hadn't seen since surgery. Although he knew Claude could handle any unforeseen emergency, he couldn't help worrying about his former student and friend. He was anxious to get out of this entire mess and return home to see what was really going on with Alcott. He still had hopes of smoothing things over. Allen was physically and emotionally drained. He had never had a day like this last one.

* * * * *

At the cottage Inspector Moreau had told Leoncour to stand guard outside while he went in. Leoncour flattened his body against the far side of the woodshed. Here, where he was well concealed, he had a good vantage point to observe the front and back doors. Because of the firelight from the cottage window, he had enough view of the path leading from the road to see anyone approaching.

Moreau knocked and announced himself. There was absolute silence for a long moment. Then he heard a feminine voice, "Come in, Inspector." He cautiously entered. The first thing he saw was Marc with a shotgun. Ashley and Claude came into the parlor from the kitchen.

"Good evening," said the inspector. "It seems as though you were expecting an unwanted visitor," he said to Marc.

"What are you doing here?" asked Claude in a tone of surprise.

"When I spoke with you earlier today, Dr. Dumont, I had the distinct feeling that you were... having some difficulties." He wanted to say "lying" but thought he might get further by treading lightly, at least at first. "It seemed most unusual to me that you were missing a patient. That is unusual, isn't it, Doctor?"

"Yes, I see what you mean, Inspector," said a very embarrassed Claude.

"It took some inquiring here and there but it wasn't too difficult to determine where you and your guests... I mean patient, might be." Ashley was now standing beside Marc and Moreau turned toward them. "Young man, you look rather foolish with that weapon. Please put it down!" Marc did as he was told. The inspector continued, "Don't you think, in view of the trouble you have caused and the apparent danger you are in, that you owe me some explanation?"

Marc replied, "Sir, it is not we who have been the cause of the problems but yes, we are in danger and if we can trust in your confidentiality, we want to explain. The truth is that we need your protection and help."

"Finally, Dr. Hamilton, you are coming to your senses. As far as confidentiality is concerned, I make no promises until I hear the story. The entire story, that is." It gave the inspector a feeling of reassurance that his signals and suspicions were again correct. While waiting expectantly, he turned with his back to the hearth so that he could see all of the trio. The flickering fire caused their shadows to perform a morbid dance about the room. Marc began.

"... and so, because they think that I have the memo and might reveal its nature at the plastic surgery meeting here..."

"Stop!" Bang! Bang! He was interrupted by the shout and the sound of shots from outside.

"Huh?" said Marc. In the same instant Claude flinched. Ashley jumped up, startled.

Moreau shouted, "Hit the floor, everyone!" He withdrew his revolver and slid along the wall, out of the way of the windows, to the kitchen door. Slowly he opened it with his back against the wall, while being shielded by the door itself. He fell to the floor and listened... Nothing! "Leoncour, where the hell are you?" he thought. He slowly advanced on his belly into the doorway with the revolver held out in front of him. He knew he was exposed.

"Inspector!" Finally, thank the Lord, it was Leoncour running toward the kitchen door. "I got them, inspector!" he said excitedly. Moreau thought, as he stood up,

"He's a fool but a damn good shot!" Leoncour was breathless as he entered the kitchen.

"There were two of them... Must have parked far down the road... Didn't hear a car... Heard footsteps on the leaves... looked up... saw two men coming out from behind the trees... They lowered themselves into a crouched position... and made their way toward the cottage... I saw their weapons... I called out a warning... They were turning toward me with no intention of stopping. They couldn't see me by the woodshed. I shot twice and got them both... They're dead."

"Nice work, Leoncour. Very nice indeed," said Moreau. "Let's have a look." He called to the three on the parlor floor. "It's all right. All is in control. I'll be back in a moment."

Ashley helped Marc up. Claude collapsed onto the sofa. He cupped his hand about his forehead, "Mon Dieu! Qu'est-il arrive? Que s'est-il passe?"

Leoncour led the way. He pointed, "Over there, Inspector." Moreau saw the two bodies lying almost beside each other. He still held his revolver. Moreau cautiously bent down to look more closely. They could still be alive. "Never mind, sir. They're dead." Moreau double checked by feeling for pulses. When he found that neither had one, he holstered his revolver. One intruder was larger with dark hair. His face was blackened with grease. He wore a black leather jacket and black sneakers. Leoncour had hit him squarely in the chest. The other wore a ski mask and was much smaller. There was a similar chest wound. Moreau pulled off the mask. The long brown hair fell and mingled with the blood in the leaves. "A woman!" exclaimed Leoncour.

"Leoncour, they come in all shapes and sizes... Another attempt! It's difficult to believe such persistence but given the facts, there are understandable motives." He saw that Leoncour didn't understand. "I'll explain later." They both checked for any identification on the bodies. "Anything, Leoncour?"

"Nothing, sir."

"I can't find a thing either. These were no amateurs," said the inspector. "Go to the car and radio headquarters. I want a lab team out here immediately. I want a police photographer, fingerprints, hair and fiber samples and later, dental x-rays and blood samples if necessary. Then contact Interpol. Let's see if they have anything on these two. But, Leoncour, very quietly. No press. No media coverage. That's the last thing I want and the last thing they need," he said as he tilted his head toward the cottage.

"Very well, Inspector." Leoncour headed toward their unmarked car and Moreau returned to the cottage.

The trio were by the hearth where he had left them. "It was another attempt. Leoncour got both of them." Ashley clutched Marc's arm. Claude's mouth was slightly open. Moreau continued, "We'll see if we can identify them and find a connection between them and the one the hospital guard hit. I'll make some very discrete inquiries from Interpol. Surely someone knows who they are."

"And the media?" asked Marc.

"Dr. Hamilton, your story is true. You couldn't make that one up. I have no desire to make this an international issue. I like my job too well and I don't think my superiors would be very pleased. So no media and absolute discretion. Although I have no particular interest in this silicone controversy, I do have a responsibility to protect visitors to my country. I would not endanger your lives further with publicity."

"Thank you, Inspector, for being so understanding," said Marc.

"Now, I believe you have overstayed your welcome in France. Don't you?"

"Definitely," said Ashley.

Suddenly Moreau said, "Quiet!" in a whisper. They became silent. Then they all heard a car door slam. Its echo bounced only once. It was very near. Moreau drew out the revolver and aimed at the door. The rest of them stood immobile.

Allen parked beside three other cars. He knew that one must be Claude's and the other, Ashley's. But the third? Leoncour had heard the car approaching and hid in the trees. As Allen closed his car door and before he had a chance to think, Leoncour was beside him with a gun at his back. "Get your hands up!"

"Don't shoot!"

"Turn around slowly! Dr. Greenberg! You gave me a fright." Leoncour lowered the gun. "Relax, sir. We're all a bit tense. There's been a little excitement here." Allen recognized the inspector's assistant and breathed a sigh of relief. "Is she all right?" he nervously asked. "I mean, is everyone all right?"

"Yes, Doctor, all is well, except for those two." He pointed to the bodies in the fallen leaves.

"You mean they tried again? I can't believe it! May I go in to my friends?"

"Of course, Doctor. Go right ahead." Leoncour returned to finish with the radio calls in his car. Allen took a few steps and nearly fell over the bodies lying directly in his path. He stopped short as though he had approached the edge of a deep chasm. Allen became nauseated by the sight and turned away. Carefully he skirted the bodies and headed toward the cottage.

Inside they heard the brushing sound of footsteps crushing the dried leaves on the ground. Moreau was ready. Ashley called out, "Don't shoot! We're expecting Allen." The door flew open. It was Allen.

"Christ, don't shoot. Its me!" Moreau recognized him from the day before at the hospital. He holstered his weapon once again.

"Didn't Leoncour stop you?" asked Moreau.

"Yes, he certainly did. When he recognized me, he said I could come on in."

"But I could have killed you!" Moreau was furious. He ran out the door shouting, "Leoncour, where are you, you stupid sonofabitch!"

Chapter 24
October 7, 1989

Vicky Lange sat at her desk. The wall to her left contained a built-in cabinet with a small but adequate bar and a twenty-one inch TV. She was intently watching the noon news.

> *...And now to Rockville, Maryland and our man on the scene, Tom Derney...*
>
> DERNEY: Just behind me stands the headquarters of the FDA. Commissioner Wade Messerman has just made an announcement that will affect the lives of over two million women in the United States alone. Those women with silicone breast implants may be facing a life of pain, disease and disability. The studies conducted under the auspices of the FDA indicate a link between the

implanted silicone devices and breast cancer as well as autoimmune diseases such as rheumatoid arthritis. Deputy Director Gerald Watson has just informed us that the Commissioner will be... There he is, Commissioner Wade Messerman! Let's see if we can get him live on camera. Commissioner! Over here, please, sir! Commissioner, we understand that you have made a world-shocking statement regarding the dangers of silicone breast implants. Could you clarify that for our national viewing audience?

MESSERMAN: I have made a formal statement of our findings over a four-year period of exhaustive research. That report has gone to those in Congress who are involved with health legislation.

DERNEY: Sir, we understand that there is now a definitely known link between the implant and breast cancer as well as other diseases. This is devastating news to millions of women and their families. What advice do you have for them?

MESSERMAN: We recommend that they contact their implanting surgeons and family doctors regarding future care, treatment or surgery. The silicone implant has failed to fall within the FDA guidelines for proving *safety and efficacy*.

DERNEY: Does that mean that all women with the silicone breast implants are doomed to a life of disease, disability... or worse?

MESSERMAN: I will only say at this time that the device has been reclassified by the Agency to a Class III, which means it is now considered to be only experimental and will probably be withdrawn from use. We do not wish to cause alarm. The FDA is here to serve, inform and to protect the public. That's all now.

DERNEY: That was Commissioner Wade Messerman. For further details of this shocking exposé be sure to watch the News Special with Anita Ramirez at seven o'clock this evening, Eastern Standard Time. And now, back to you, Bob."

"YES!" said Vicky aloud as she pounded her fist on the desk. She turned off the TV with her remote control and dialed the number for the *Houston Daily Journal.* "Advertising department, please."

"Advertising and Classified, Sheila speaking."

"May I speak with Tim Rudley, please? This is Victoria Lange."

"I'll see if he's at his desk. I'll put you on hold."

"This is Tim Rudley, Ms. Lange."

"Hi, Tim. You know the ad I proofed the other day and told you to hold? Well, I'm ready to go with it."

"Great! Now, that was to be a half-page and to run daily in the evening edition in the Today's Highlights section and the same ad in the Health section on Sunday?"

"Right."

"Just as corrected? You went over the proofs?"

"Right."

"When do you want it to start running?"

"How about tomorrow?"

"Gosh! There is supposed to be a deadline at one o'clock today for tomorrow. Just a minute. Let me check... Okay! We can just make it."

"Terrific! Thanks, Tim. There's more to come."

* * * * *

Across the city in the Galleria, Anne Warner was having lunch in a sandwich shop with Marge O'Neal. Marge was Dr. Ben Crosby's office manager. Since Dr. Crosby, who specialized in obstetrics and gynecology, was one of Marc Hamilton's best referral sources, Anne and Marge spoke with each other on the phone almost daily. They had become good friends and often had their lunches together. This was one of those times. They often compared notes on the patients whom they had in common but strictly on a professional basis. There was a bit of gossiping too, however this was limited to other personnel in the building or to some juicy tidbit from "a very reliable source." They particularly enjoyed Stoney's Sandwich shop because they could watch the noon time news on the thirty-inch TV screen while talking and munching.

"Anne, did you see that Karen Blake's makeup? Why, it's positively disgusting! You could scrape it off with a knife. I don't know how poor old Dr. Gallagher puts up with it."

"He probably loves it. Maybe it's better than what he gets at home," said Anne with a smile. Marge was laughing with a mouthful of her sandwich.

"Anne! You're awful, just awful! You're going to make me choke to death!" She settled down. "You must be having it easy with Dr. Hamilton at the meeting and all."

"Marge, I wouldn't tell anyone else but I'm really getting worried. He's so good about checking in with me when he's away and now, not a word. You know Dr. Allen Greenberg…"

"You mean the boob guy… what?" Marge leaned a little closer to Anne. She didn't want to miss a word.

"Well, he called me from France… some town called Tours… and told me Dr. Hamilton would be detained and said he'd had a *slight accident*. He actually hung up before I could find out what he meant. Now why wouldn't Dr. Hamilton call me himself?"

"Probably having too much fun with Honey Bun." Marge began to laugh.

"Marge O'Neal! Now who's awful! Don't you say one ugly word about that sweet Ashley! They are so cute together! I just love to see two people..." Anne stopped in mid sentence when the TV caught her attention.

> WWN brings you a special report. And now to Rockville, Maryland, and our man on the scene, Tom Derney.
>
> DERNEY: Just behind me stands the headquarters of the FDA....

The women stopped eating and listened intently to the entire report. "My God!" said Anne. "I've got to get back to the office." She got up from the table abruptly and left Marge with her mouth hanging open.

When Anne walked into the office, all four lines were flashing. The answering service couldn't keep up with the calls. She expected this after the FDA announcement.

"Dr. Hamilton's Office, Mrs. Warner speaking."

"Is this Anne?" asked the anxious voice on the other end. "This is Mary Thomas. Did you see the noon news?"

"Hi Mary. Now don't worry. I'm sure there is some mixup. Are you having a problem with your implants?"

"Well, no, but..."

"Mary, I have to put you on hold. My other lines are ringing off the wall. If I lose you, I promise to call you back."

"Dr. Hamilton's Office, Mrs. Warner speaking."

"Mrs. Warner, this is Jo Beth Hanes. Dr. Hamilton did my breast augmentation about six months ago. I saw the news report and wanted to know..."

"Jo Beth, please excuse me. My phones are going crazy! I promise to answer all your questions but I'll have to put you on hold."

"Yes, Mrs. Finch. No, I'm sorry. He's out of town at a meeting."

"At a time like this!"

"Please hold..."

"Hi, Mr. Kern."

"Where is that goddamn sonofabitch Hamilton! I want to talk to him now! I'm gonna sue his ass if it's the last thing I do!"

And so it had begun. Mass hysteria, an epidemic of panic. Anne thought about Commissioner Wade Messerman's last words on the live TV interview...

> ...We do not wish to cause alarm. The FDA is here to serve, inform and protect the public.

"Serve, Inform and protect," she repeated to herself. "What utter bullshit!"

* * * * *

It was 10:00 AM in Seattle when Chuck Walker was on his coffee break. Everyone, including the girls from the steno pool, was huddled around the TV in the lounge. They were listening intently to the WWN news special:

> ...The silicone implant has failed to fall within the FDA guidelines for proving safety and efficacy...

Chuck was furious. "God damn Messerman! The sonofabitch has gone and done it! Really done it!" he said aloud to no one in particular. He spilled hot coffee on his hand and burned it. "God particular. He spilled hot coffee on his hand and burned it. "God damn! Shit!" He turned away from the surprised faces and ran down the hall toward J.T.'s office. They had never heard their senior vice president swear like that before. They were buzzing among themselves,

"What does it all mean?"

"Is it possible that the implants are really dangerous?"

"Do we have any personal liability as employees?"

"It's a damn lie! It's all politics!"

"No way! It's stock market motivated!"

"Yeah, maybe! But what about our jobs?"

"Yeah, our jobs!"

Chuck didn't wait to be announced. He threw the door open and marched into Roswell's office. Roswell calmly looked up from the papers on his desk and waited for Walker to say whatever was on his mind. "J.T., I just heard the news special..."

"Yes. Jack Gehman, from Sloan-Gehman in Akron, Ohio just called me. Unfortunate, but not unexpected," said Roswell in a very controlled and level voice."

"That bastard!" said Chuck under his breath.

"Now Chuck, surely you're not surprised. We all knew it was coming. Stop worrying. All is under control."

"But it's all coming apart. Everything!"

"Shut the door and sit down." Chuck did as commanded. "This is no time for hysteria. I told you all was under control. You know that Conners is doing his job so please, calm down."

"Yeah! Conners is doing his job! Wertheim! Hamilton! Even Ashley Barton!"

"Shut the fuck up! Are you nuts talking like that?" Chuck had reservations about the memo issue and the entire coverup ever since his meeting with Conners but then it was just talk and he chose not to hear it. He had looked away. He had deserted his friends. The guilt was unbearable, especially during the last week when he knew what was going on in Paris. The news special brought him back to the reality of it all.

"How the hell did this get out of hand? How could some fool's stupid research cost so many lives?" Chuck was fuming. "All because of a fucking memo? All because of the holy dollar? My friends! My career! J.T., I'm not going down the tubes with you! I'm sorry! You'll have my resignation on your desk within an hour."

"Sorry is right! You sorry yellow bastard! You're nothing more than a rat deserting a sinking ship!" Roswell's face was crimson. They had never had words like this between them. He calmed down. "Chuck, we can't let Messerman do this to us. We've been together too long. I depend on you. I need you." Walker wouldn't cool down.

"J.T., all you need is Conners. You don't need me."

"What are you going to do?"

"The right thing for once in my life! Maybe God will forgive me for not stopping it when I could have."

"What are you saying? You're going to spill it to the media? What? Walker, remember, I still have Conners."

"Is that a threat? I guess I'm not surprised. Now you listen, you fucking sonofabitch!" He was in Roswell's face. "Do you think I haven't learned to cover my ass around here? Get this because I'll say it only once. I have copies, notarized copies of everything; memo, data, coverup, murder plans, all of it. And I've left copies with two sources to release to the media, FDA, Federal Trade Commission and Justice Department if anything, ANYTHING happens to me. J.T... Just don't fuck with me! I Quit!"

Walker stomped out. He hadn't felt so good in years. He only hoped that Marc and Ashley, somehow, had avoided

Conners' far reaching arm. They had to be okay. He had to have their forgiveness.

Roswell fell into his desk chair. For the first time in his life, he was frightened. He hadn't planned on Walker turning tail. He was sweating profusely as he reached for the phone. "Conners, get in here now!" Within five minutes Conners was there. He couldn't get himself to tell Roswell of yet another failure in Paris. He was nervous, very nervous.

"Yes, boss?"

"Everything go well in Paris?"

"Sir, I told you not to worry. All's well." He was lying of course.

"Well, I guess the shit just hit the fan," said Roswell.

"So I hear."

"Conners, I want you to watch Walker. Don't do anything. Just watch him and let me know about any unusual activities." Conners was astonished.

"Our Walker? Chuck Walker?"

"He just resigned. He knows too much. He knows everything, the bastard."

"Yeah, I guess he would know everything."

"And one more thing. Dr. Allen Greenberg will be here tomorrow. He's probably nervous and upset."

Conners thought to himself, "Upset? I wonder why! Just because we almost got him?"

Roswell continued, "I'll talk with him and see how it goes. I'll give you instructions after I see him. If he's smart, he'll be reasonable. If not, you may have another job to do."

"I'll wait to hear from you, boss." Conners left. He had been preparing for this day. He remembered Roswell's words from last week... "I'm taking you down with me..." He had some phone calls to make and a few loose ends to tie up before his plans were finalized. He wasn't going down with anybody. By this time next week he'd be on easy street and all this would be nothing more than a memory.

Roswell was worried. He had plenty to worry about. He wasn't looking forward to tomorrow. He wasn't sure about how he was going to deal with Greenberg but he wasn't going to let Dr. Fucking Greenberg walk all over him! Not him! Not Jonathon Tyler Roswell!

Chapter 25
October 6, 1989

Leoncour was driving the white Citroen with Allen beside him. It was almost 11:00 AM when they took the turnoff to Charles De Gaul II Airport. Only two hours earlier at the cottage Inspector Moreau had obtained everyone's statement. Allen left nothing out. He went into detail about slamming into the blue sedan on the road to Tours. That was when he learned that the driver and his accomplice were killed instantly. Only once had Allen ever wanted to actually kill another human being. That was about ten years ago in Houston. While his wife, Susan, had gone into a supermarket to do the week's major shopping, he went next door to browse about the bookstore. After about half an hour, he heard a commotion outside and a woman's scream. It was definitely Susan's voice. He dropped the book and ran outside in time to see a man grab her purse and hit her in the face with his fist. Allen reacted instantly. He ran after the guy and eventually caught him without even stopping to think that the thief might have a gun or knife. He grabbed him by the collar, spun him around and didn't stop smashing his face until the police pulled him off. He had wanted to kill. There was no doubt. Even now as he remembered the incident, his hand formed a fist.

Allen realized that if not for his quick thinking at that moment on the road, he would probably be dead. This realization didn't help much. He had killed two men. The thought sickened him, and he knew it would haunt him for the rest of his life.

Allen's statement had cleared up a mystery for Moreau. As usual, the men in the sedan had no identification. Their fingerprints had been sent to Interpol. The latter, in checking with the FBI and other foreign secret service agencies, found that Rupert Hastings and Carl Myers were Americans with a long history of ties to organized crime and had been suspected of being the hit men on at least two other occasions.

The inspector told Allen that the incident was reported officially as a hit and run. Unofficially Allen had actually performed a service for the country. Moreau had explained, "Dr. Greenberg, I do not believe in men taking the law into their own hands. However, my years in this profession have taught me that although most men are honorable, some are capable of almost any crime, given the proper circumstances. While I consider myself a professional, I am also a realist. As there are no witnesses, no French court could hold you responsible. I will not make a ridiculous issue out of your act of self preservation. You will have to come to terms with what you have done. You will have to live with this. I see no purpose in holding you in France. Before I change my mind, I want Assistant Inspector Leoncour to drive you to the airport. You are to leave France immediately. Can I trust you to return if you should be required to give further statements in the unlikely event of any court hearings?"

While these thoughts and old memories were stirring in Allen's mind, Leoncour hadn't shut up for a second during the two-hour drive. He kept going on and on about the two intruders he had shot, how he had spent long days practicing to become an expert marksman and how proud and elated he was about this latest achievement. He was now one step closer to becoming a full inspector. Allen thanked him and praised him for saving the lives of his friends but wondered how much difference there was between the psyche of the intruders and their killer. Of course the motivation was the difference! Leoncour had acted in the name of the law and he was grateful, truly grateful to this man. But to Allen at this moment it was all the same, merely a difference in perspective.

His sobering thoughts were interrupted by Leoncour. "We are here, Doctor. Have a safe journey home." They shook hands.

"Thank you again... Inspector," said Allen as he stepped out of the car.

Leoncour noted the respectful title and smiled. "Au revoir, Doctor. Bon voyage."

Allen went directly to the Atlantic Airlines desk. He was too late for the morning flight to Houston. The next available flight was to Kennedy with a three-hour wait and then he would have to change terminals to catch a flight home. It was simply too much hassle. He chose to take the nonstop flight to Houston departing at 9:05 the next morning. He figured he could use the rest anyway and checked into the adjoining airport hotel. He stripped off his clothes and lay naked on the bed. It felt great! It was the first time he had been able to fully relax since all the incredible events had begun about forty-eight hours ago. It seemed as though it had been a week. He started organizing his thoughts again. Tomorrow he would be home. He wondered how he would respond when asked about how the meeting went. He had to check several patients, his and Marc's. He had promised Marc to call Vicky and let her know about everything. She was to do nothing before his return. He wondered about going to Seattle and confronting Roswell. Allen hoped that his secretary had arranged for the meeting on the next day after his arrival home. Roswell! How would the CEO of Alcott Laboratories receive him? It didn't matter, he decided. It had to be done!

* * * * *

At 7:30 AM it was still dark. The grounds about the cottage were bustling with police, photographers and forensic lab personnel. Inspector Moreau had ordered the area surrounding the bodies to be cordoned off. Everyone who came in direct contact with the bodies wore rubber gloves. This was routine. The photographer had captured every possible angle. Copious notes were taken describing in great detail the positions, the wounds and the clothing. Fiber samples were taken, bagged and marked in the hope that these would help the identification process. Before the bodies were removed to the morgue for the coroner's detailed organ and tissue studies, fingerprints were taken on the site.

Moreau was meticulously orchestrating the proceedings. It was one of his own men who had fired the fatal shots and he wanted no screwups because of shoddy techniques. After Leoncour had given his statement, Moreau had ordered him to surrender his weapon until the investigation was complete. And definitely there would be an investigation. Although the witnesses' stories corroborated with his and Leoncour's, there was to be absolutely no doubt that the killings were righteous. He wanted no blemish on his department. The inspector's work had just begun. There were pages of reports to file. There were going to be hours of interrogation for him and Leoncour. His head was throbbing just thinking about it. And then there still remained the positive identification of the bodies.

During the investigation outside, Leoncour had given his formal statement to the police stenographer. Following Allen's statement, Moreau had ordered Leoncour to take him "immediately" to the airport. The inspector was tiring of these Americans with their foolish problems. The death count had now totaled five and he had had quite enough! As long as they remained in France he felt responsible for their safety. Although he was sympathetic toward them, he wanted them out of France... and mostly, out of his life.

By 10:00 AM the initial work had been completed and the investigating team began to thin out. After Allen and Leoncour had left for the airport Ashley prepared breakfast for Marc, Claude and the inspector. She managed to put together a decent meal from the provisions that Claude had brought the evening before. Marc could now manage soft foods in addition to liquids. He hated watery eggs but it was another step closer to recovery.

During the meal they spoke of the events of the previous night. The inspector had finished his coffee. He sat back in his chair and began to twist the end of his mustache as the others chattered on. He was deeply engrossed with his thoughts. "True, Mademoiselle Barton, Dr. Hamilton and Dr. Dumont have given accurate accountings of the events of the previous evening... True, I can keep them for a few days in case there are any further questions regarding the reasons for the attempt on their lives... but the investigation could go on for months... True, it seems unnecessary to detain them longer and every moment they remain in France places them at greater risk... True, I can take responsibility for their safety for only a few more days at the most..."

"What do you think, Inspector? Do you think Alcott hired those men and sent them here? Inspector? Inspector..." said Claude trying to get Moreau's attention.

"Hmm? Oh! Yes, probably... Dr. Dumont, when do you think that Dr. Hamilton will be ready to make the journey home?"

"He is doing very well but this is too soon. I would really not want him to fly for about another two days and even that is early. The variations in cabin pressure could lead to sinus complications. Yes, two or three more days, I think."

"You will need to see Dr. Hamilton before his departure?" asked Moreau.

"Yes. I will want to cleanse the wounds, check for infection and change the dressings before he leaves." Marc nodded to indicate that this would be the proper course of care. He was to see Allen in a few days in Houston for suture removal and further followup.

The inspector continued addressing Dumont. "But you could manage to see him somewhere other than the hospital?"

"Yes, but what do you have in mind?" asked Claude with a hint of suspicion in his voice. The inspector was quiet for another moment. All eyes were upon him. What was he getting at?

"Dr. Dumont, when you are finished here, please go back to the hospital and tend to your affairs and kindly make yourself available during this investigation." Claude gazed down at his hands and looked insulted. "No, Doctor. You misunderstand. We are all most appreciative of all your efforts in behalf of Mademoiselle Barton and Dr. Hamilton."

"Claude, we can never hope to repay what you have done for us. You have endangered your career... your life!" said Ashley.

"Claude, you have gone far beyond..." Marc was interrupted by Claude.

"No. Please. I did what I wanted to do. It is very difficult to explain. Let me simply sat that what I did was for... me... and please let it go at that." Ashley saw his quick glance toward her and then she understood. He continued, "The inspector is quite right. I can only be in the way. Besides I have neglected my work at the hospital long enough," he said tactfully. As he rose to leave he extended his hand to Marc. "Good luck, mon ami. I hope to hear from you."

"Definitely, Claude. Remember, we have to celebrate in Houston when this is all over." Claude reached for Ashley's hand. She stood up and said,

"Come here, you!" She kissed him on the cheek and hugged him especially tightly. Claude felt her hot tears. He knew that she understood.

Moreau walked out with Claude and urged him again to make himself available during the investigation. As Claude stepped into his car he assured the inspector that he would cooperate in every manner possible. Moreau waited until the car disappeared into the wooded terrain and until he could no longer hear its engine. He got into his car and switched on his radio. "Hello, headquarters? This is Moreau."

"How is it going, Inspector?"

"Well, I think, but a few loose ends to clean up. Please get me Sergeant Lourmel."

"One moment, sir."

"This is Sergeant Lourmel," said a female voice.

"Nina, this is Raymond."

"Ahh! How nice of you to call, Inspector! How long has it been... two weeks?"

"Nina, I need a favor."

"How thoughtful of you to ask!" Moreau was glad he was only speaking to her on the phone and not in person. He had neglected her and Nina was not a woman to be neglected. He still had the scars from their last violent encounter nearly a year ago when he had forgotten that they had a dinner engagement. She was fond of throwing dishes and he hadn't ducked fast enough. It made a nasty gash on his forehead, which required that he stay away from the office for a few days. The people at headquarters knew Nina and her temper. He couldn't face dealing with their whispers and snickers. But it had been worth it. Making up was wonderful and every time he saw the scar it reminded him of those passionate nights.

"Nina, please. This is important."

"What is it?" She responded to his serious voice. She knew she would do anything for him.

"You know the case I'm on... well, the two Americans, the plastic surgeon and his lady need a safe place to stay for a day or two, just until he is well enough to travel home."

"Yes?" She wasn't going to make it easy.

"Well, can you put them up at your flat?"

"At my flat! What nerve you have, Raymond! After ignoring me so, you ask for favors."

"Nina, this is urgent! Their lives are in danger. They need protection. And... I may seem to have ignored you but you are always in my thoughts. You know how I feel."

"Then say it."

"Nina!"

"Say it!" He knew her. She was the most stubborn woman he had ever known and yet she meant everything to him. He swallowed and looked about to make sure no one could hear.

"Mon Petit Chou Chou, je vous aime." He had said it in almost a whisper. He felt his face flush, even though no one was there to see or hear.

"Louder!"

"Nina, for God's sake! This is serious." She knew she had stretched it as far as she could with him.

"Bring them to my place after four o'clock."

"Thank you. I shall arrange for a few days leave for you... and dinner next week at Cafe Greco?" It was her favorite.

"Ahh, Cafe Greco. Bon. But don't you dare forget!"

He knew she would do it. It was simply a matter of how subservient he had to be and she had reached his limit. She was really a good person and an outstanding policewoman. The best. They would be safe with Nina. He returned to the cottage to tell them.

Chapter 26

October 7, 1989

Atlantic Airline's flight #41 arrived about an hour late at Houston Intercontinental Airport. There had been turbulence all the way from Charles DeGaul II and the pilot had left the seatbelt sign on for nearly the entire nine-hour flight. Allen had tried to sleep but it was impossible. There were few things he hated more than flying. He was grateful to be home.

He had to claim his bag and clear immigration and customs. Fortunately he had only the one bag which Leoncour had been kind enough to let him pick up at his hotel in Paris when he had checked out. Even with that it was nearly noon by the time he got a taxi to his office in the medical center. He sat back in the cab trying to relax, but he couldn't. The cab driver had the radio blasting with hard rock. The beat made his entire body vibrate. He forced himself to think through it. There were so many things he had to do immediately. He ran through the sequence again:

office, see several of his patients and a few of Marc's as well, see Vicky and catch the late afternoon flight to Seattle... Impossible! He just realized that there was no way he could get back to Intercontinental and make the flight. How the hell had he ever thought he could make it? He'd simply have to go to Seattle in the morning and that was that! He wasn't looking forward to a confrontation with Roswell anyway but it had to be done. He still had difficulty believing that Alcott was responsible for Wertheim's death and the violent episodes in France. Maybe it was some crazy misunderstanding. Maybe Marc and Ashley were wrong... Maybe they... Suddenly his thoughts were interrupted by the radio...

> ...We interrupt this program for a special news bulletin from Rockville, Maryland...

Although, intellectually, he knew it was imminent, the report caught him completely off guard. He had always hoped that somehow, through diplomacy, through the pledge of an alliance between organized plastic surgery and the manufacturers, they could derail the FDA's determination to kill the implant, to kill his *baby*. Allen knew damn well that the implant held no health hazards. All the years of research that had proved absolute safety were going down the tubes. Thirty years of use hadn't revealed any ties to breast cancer or to autoimmune disease. When he offered to present his data at the FDA hearings, he was ignored. They thanked him and said his presence at the hearings would be "unnecessary." There was no one who knew more about the implant than he. How could they exclude him!

The FDA had put on the face of cooperation in the early days of the investigation when Phillip Purcell was the

Commissioner. Everything made sense then. The FDA was going to listen to what thirty years of research and experience had proved. There was hope, more than hope. He was sure that the issues could be resolved and that the quality of life for millions of women could be preserved. Then, when Purcell retired and Messerman took over, everything changed. Purcell's promises of cooperation were no more than dust in the wind. Allen learned one thing for sure. You can't trust a government agency! The personnel and policies are as changeable as the colors of a chameleon. The individuals with whom you have a working relationship today are gone tomorrow. They are quickly replaced by others who have no obligations to the previous administration and who quickly put in place their own agenda and personal priorities.

The plastic surgeons had been duped. Perhaps if they hadn't been so naive in those early days and had begun to scream the truth, Messerman could never have gotten this far. But how could they? They were *professionals,* not politicians. Besides, the FDA had promised! Allen thought, "Would the major industrial unions have stood for this kind of treatment? Was the cigarette industry sitting in silent acceptance? Hell, no! They're fighting. But we were too professional to make any noise. By the time we realized the truth, it was too late. Too late! That's the story of medicine! Always a dollar short and a day late! We are such an easy target. And now what? The FDA has unleashed panic among the millions of women who have implants and placed terror in the hearts of their families without a shred of scientific data to prove that they are at any significant risk. It's unconscionable!" Allen was angry, frustrated. The demise of the silicone gel implant was at hand.

The taxi pulled up to the Medical Arts Tower on Fannin Street where Allen had his office. He was making a concerted effort to calm down before seeing his patients. He entered his office through the back entrance. He saw that Liz, his office manager, was on the phone. She looked up at him and nodded. She didn't have her usual smile for him.

"Mrs. Riley, I still think it best that you discuss your concerns with Dr. Greenberg. Will Thursday at 3:15 work? Good. See you then." She hung up. All her lines were flashing.

"Hi, Liz."

"Dr. Greenberg, thank God you're home! Do you know what's going on?"

"I just heard. Bad?"

"Bad? Well, the phones haven't stopped since noon. Alice and I are going nuts trying to calm everyone down while trying to keep up with the calls. Betty couldn't handle it and went home. Bad? I guess you could call it that."

"I see the waiting room is packed," said Allen.

"Dr. Greenberg, I tried to keep it as light as possible, but some people were so upset that I just couldn't say no. And then there are six of Dr. Hamilton's patients... Say, what's going on with him?"

"Too long a story for now, Liz. Let me wash up and let's get started."

"Well, you'll have to see them yourself. There's not a person to spare with the phone going crazy. Oh, I almost forgot. I took the liberty of changing your Seattle reservations to tomorrow morning. I knew it would be impossible for you to make the afternoon flight. I have you on the 9:00 AM and I changed your appointment with Mr. Roswell to 1:00 PM. With the time difference you should have no problem in making it. I guess I should tell you that Mrs. Moore..." He had a puzzled look. "You know...

Mr. Roswell's secretary, Virginia Moore, well, she said Roswell was acting very strange since the FDA announcement, like he's somewhat out to lunch. I thought I'd better warn you."

"Thanks, Liz. Just one more thing, please. Find an attorney, Vicky or Victoria Lange. Tell her I'm a friend of Dr. Hamilton's and I must see her this evening. I have a message for her. It's really important, Liz. Don't take no for an answer. Any time after six."

"I'll let you know," she said.

Allen got to work. Most of the patients required only routine followup. The three on whom he had done breast augmentations, just before he left for the meeting, were in a terrible state. They had just heard the news. He had to spend most of his time calming them down and explaining that he didn't feel they had anything to worry about.

"But the report is from our government! It must be true!" said one patient.

"Now, Doris, we've been dealing with implants for about thirty years. Even the FDA hasn't said that they are dangerous, only that they feel more testing is needed."

"Well, Dr. Greenberg, I'm not a guinea pig! I trusted you." She broke down in tears. For Allen this was like pushing a two-ton boulder uphill.

"Doris, if you trusted me before, please trust me now. I'll follow you very closely and promise to keep you informed of what's going on."

"Will you have to remove my implants?" she asked between sobs.

"I don't think we're talking about anything that drastic." She was settling down.

"Oh, I hope not. I really love them. I never felt so good about myself."

"You just stop worrying and let me see you next week. Doris, I promise you, you're okay."

"If you say so, Dr. Greenberg. I know you're the best. See you next week." He knew he'd have to go all over it again with her. He felt so sorry for his patient. It was all so unnecessary.

"God damn the FDA and Messerman! Let *them* deal with these patients!" he thought.

Finally he had finished with Marc's last patient. Liz stuck her head in the door. "Victoria Lange, seven o'clock this evening, at her office, and I have the address for you."

"Thanks, Liz. What would I do without you?" She smiled.

"Probably try to organize everything yourself and screw it up." She saw how distressed he was. "Dr. Greenberg, it'll all be okay."

"I hope so, Liz. I truly hope so."

* * * * *

Since Vicky's secretary had left for the day, she kept the outer door to her office ajar so that she could hear Dr. Greenberg when he arrived. She was curious and anxious to meet the man who had created the silicone breast implant. Vicky had removed her high heeled pumps about an hour earlier after consulting with her last client of the day. She punched in the code for her telephone answering service. She didn't want to be disturbed during the meeting. Vicky glanced at her watch. Another twenty or thirty minutes. She thought for a moment, "Why not? Plenty time," and reached behind her to the mirrored cabinet which contained a well concealed and well stocked bar. It was primarily for special clients and on occasion for herself. She poured two fingers of straight vodka and plunked in two cubes of ice, put her feet up on the desk, leaned back, sipped and reflected. The day had gone well and she was thoroughly pleased with herself.

It would all begin tomorrow. She expected an enormous response from the ad in the *Houston Daily Journal* and had hired a temporary secretary to help in answering the second telephone line. "Ahh, life can be so sweet," she thought.

Briefly she wondered about Dave and how he would react to the ad. Would he accept her action and support her? "Stop kidding yourself, girl. He'll blow and bellow. Dr. David Stein, the pillar of ethics and morality, will end it as cleanly as a cut with his scalpel." She really cared for him but he was so naive, so squeaky clean that it would never work. "So what the hell! It's over!" She took another sip. Then she thought about the class action suit, the publicity, the money. She was performing a service for the women of the world. They had been injured, deceived, exploited and they needed a champion. They needed Victoria Lange. Her cause was just and she would march with her banner held high. She wiggled her toes and smiled. It was the smile of self satisfaction, as though she had put one over on the entire world. Well, maybe she had.

She heard the waiting room door close. Quickly, she hid the glass in the desk drawer, put on her shoes, straightened her skirt, glanced into the mirrored cabinet and gently pulled a curl in front of her ear. She was ready. Vicky stepped out into the waiting room. "Dr. Greenberg?"

"Yes. Ms. Lange?"

"Pleased to meet you," she said as she extended her hand. She had expected someone much older and *nerdy*. Actually she found him attractive. She held the door for him. "Let's go into my office." She followed him in. Vicky gestured toward a chair as she sat down behind her desk. She smiled broadly. "I've heard so much about you, Dr. Greenberg."

"It's good of you to see me on such short notice. As you know, I've just this afternoon returned from Paris."

"Yes, of course, the international meeting. How was it?" she asked.

"That's why I'm here. May as well get to the point. You left a message for Dr. Hamilton and unfortunately he was unable to respond. He has asked me to serve as his emissary, of a sort."

"Yes. I informed him of the death of... a friend and asked him to call me. Is something wrong? You said he couldn't call."

"Ms. Lange..."

"Please call me Vicky."

"Oh, thank you... Vicky. First, it wasn't simply the death of a friend. Second, it was the probable murder of Matthew Wertheim, a former colleague of mine."

"You are candid, Dr. Greenberg. May I call you Allen?"

"Yes I am, and of course you may." She liked his direct approach and was getting more interested by the second.

"The official report was hit and run," she said. There was something very familiar to Allen about that. Vicky continued very cautiously. She had no way of knowing how much Marc had told him. "But in view of certain facts, I believe it could have been more than that."

"You mean the memo. Right?"

"Well! On target again, Allen. Is there anything you don't know?"

"Not much... but there is plenty you don't know."

"For instance?"

"For instance, there were several attempts to kill Marc, Ashley and me." Vicky's jaw dropped. She hadn't expected anything like that but she certainly understood how that was possible.

"Someone tried to... kill you, Marc... and even Ashley? But who? Why?" She was still playing stupid.

"Vicky," said Allen. I had hoped you would be candid with me as well."

"Okay," she said. "The memo. You mean Alcott. But... in France?"

"I do indeed mean Alcott. They did everything in their power to get their hands on the memo. They were convinced Marc had it in his possession and would make it public at the international meeting. Of course he didn't have the memo."

"Of course not. I have it in safekeeping."

"I figured you did. May I see it?"

"No, you may not," she said. "That's privileged information strictly between client and attorney."

"I understand. Anyway, Marc was nearly beaten to death. I had to do emergency surgery on him a few days ago. Ashley was threatened and almost kidnapped so there was no opportunity for them to answer your message. And so the reason I am here."

"Yes?"

"Marc said for you to do nothing until he gets home. I assume he was referring to the memo. He should be home tomorrow or the next day."

"In view of the FDA announcement today, I don't see any difference," she said.

"Perhaps not, but Marc was very clear on that point and it's only another day or two. Besides I'm going to Seattle tomorrow to meet with Roswell. No need to rock the boat before that. I'd appreciate your holding to Marc's wishes. I may be able to use the memo in some way as leverage if it becomes necessary."

"I see," she said as she was thinking...

"The memo must get to the media. It will absolutely make the case for a class action on the basis of conspiracy to defraud. It has to come out. I guess a few days more won't matter. But leverage to hold it back... Never!"

She changed the subject. "How bad is Marc?" she asked with some concern.

"Mainly facial injuries and a punctured lung. We nearly lost him."

"My God! And Ashley?"

"Okay. She's okay. What a woman. What a fantastic woman!" Vicky felt envious.

"And you said they tried to get you too?"

"You see, I was trying to get Ashley to a safe place while Marc was recovering... Vicky, it's too long and complicated. Suffice it to say, they tried and I was successful in avoiding them. But make no mistake. They were serious. I had a lot of trouble accepting that. I've had such a good relationship with Alcott for nearly thirty years that it's hard to believe they were behind it all."

Vicky was curious. "But how in France?"

"Vicky, they have an enormous network of global security. As in any large industry, industrial espionage and sabotage require security and counter-espionage tactics. It's kind of like an industrial war. It's supposed to be limited to information gathering, stealing a few secrets here and there, spilling false information to mislead and so on. Alcott knows that the memo, especially with the recent FDA publicity, could destroy any attempts to successfully defend the lawsuits that are sure to follow."

Vicky thought, "You bet your ass it will kill their defense. I know. And you're right on target again, Buster."

Allen continued, "And now, as unbelievable as it may seem, it's *any* measure, no holds barred, to prevent exposure of the 1976 coverup."

"She said aloud, "You mean... like a hit team?"

"You got it!" he said. "Roswell hired Earl Conners some twenty years ago to organize the network and to orchestrate extreme situations such as this. I don't know exactly, but information I happened to get in France shows that Interpol can connect the people who were involved with the attempts on our lives with international organized crime. They were known hit men directly connected with Conners and so to Roswell, his boss. Alcott is in deep shit."

"No shit!" said Vicky. "So Earl Conners is the man directly behind all this."

Allen continued, "Well, any way you want to look at it, Conners, Roswell or Alcott, it's all the same; the *Holy Trinity*."

"My God!"

"I wanted to give you the message and explain why Marc and Ashley couldn't."

"You have no idea how much I appreciate this, Allen. I was really getting worried with Wertheim's death, the FDA announcement and all. Thanks."

"I guess I'd best be going." He glanced at his watch. "I have an early flight in the morning."

"Oh... Allen, have you had dinner?"

He thought for a moment, Why not? He looked into her eyes and said, "No, as a matter of fact. I haven't." He was pleased that she had asked.

"I know a quiet little place, sort of gourmet. Want to try it?" she asked.

"Sounds great."

They got a cab and Vicky said to the driver, "The Black Rose, please." She turned toward Allen. "So, I understand the silicone implant is your invention."

"You could say I was instrumental in its development."

"Oh, don't be coy with me! It was all your work."

He laughed. "Well, I guess so."

"I'm really interested," said Vicky. "Please tell me about it. How did you get the idea?" Allen saw that she was sincerely interested.

"In the early 50s cosmetic surgery was beginning to bloom. World War II and Korea had given us the knowledge through the reconstruction of injuries to apply those principles to cosmetic surgery. As more and more procedures were being performed, the demand became ever increasingly greater. Almost anything became possible in the cosmetic, or aesthetic, arena. Rhytidectomies and rhinoplasties, that is, facelifts and nasal surgery, were becoming commonplace. Even breast reductions were not infrequently performed but breast augmentation... now that was another matter.

" It was a challenge and I decided to pick up the gauntlet. I was only a plastic surgery resident then. Anyway, I tried fat grafts from the abdomen or the buttocks. Those failed because of infection, absorption or both. Human tissue didn't seem to be the answer. The theoretical ideal was a nonreactive synthetic material that was compatible with human tissues and would give a controlled, predictable and desired result aesthetically as well as functionally. Now, remember, that was the ideal. Well, we started with polyether sponge. It was nonreactive but allowed scar tissue to grow into it resulting in rock hard breasts. Several other synthetic materials were tried but all failed for one reason or another.

"Silicone products were first developed in the 40s as a possible substitute for rubber when latex and rubber were in short supply due to their demand for the war effort. It gradually became used as an industrial lubricant. In animal experiments silicone seemed to be nonreactive with tissues. In the gel state it was soft, pliable and inert. So I thought... what would happen with the gel enclosed in a thin silicone shell, shaped like a breast and implanted subcutaneously?" In animals first, it was perfect. Later in cooperation with the FDA we were able to have human volunteers. Of course they were closely monitored. But it worked!

IMPLANT

Consistently, it worked. Now the breast could easily be augmented to almost any reasonable size, usually dictated by the individual's overall body proportions. This could be done with safety through a relatively brief surgical procedure. Often the operation could be performed with local anesthesia and a mild sedative. It seemed to be a miracle. To be sure, there were some risks, as with any surgery but most patients were more than willing to accept these."

"Such as what risks?" Vicky asked.

"The major problem that we faced was the development, in some women, of a thick scar tissue layer that encased the implant. Why that occurred in some patients and not in others is still not entirely clear. When it did occur, the breast would become more firm, sometimes hard. The frustrating part of it was that the hardness was unpredictable. There was no way to tell, no test prior to surgery to show who might be the person who would develop the thickened scar tissue. Most, fortunately, remained soft."

"What happens with those women who develop the thick scar?" she asked.

"Many simply lived with it. It is usually painless and they're happy just to be larger. Others choose to have the plastic surgeon try to remove the scar tissue and replace with fresh implants. Usually this is successful. In the late 80s the manufacturers developed textured surface implants. That seemed to be a big step in reducing the scar tissue problem."

Vicky was still questioning. "And other risks?"

"The usual. As with any surgical procedure, postoperative bleeding, anesthetic reactions and, rarely, infection may occur. For the most part it is one of the safest and most satisfying operations, not only because of the physical changes which are obvious but also because of the amazing psychological changes that frequently occur. Small-breasted women who seem to be shy and retiring begin to bloom after augmentation. They somehow feel more complete, more feminine. Naturally the surgery isn't for everyone. Nothing in plastic surgery is for everyone. It remains for the surgeon to screen patients who are poor candidates for the operation, either for physical or emotional problems or because of their unrealistic expectations. There are many women who are completely satisfied with what they have and more power to them. But many suffer the torments that come with living in a society where there is a strong sexual and social focus on the female breast. These become the patients for whom breast augmentation improves the quality of life."

"That's fascinating, Allen. I never thought of it that way. I had always believed it to be self indulgent and only for weak women."

"Oh no," said Allen. "Quite the contrary. It takes strength to admit that one has a problem and greater strength to resolve it. It takes a great deal of courage and determination to have the operation and to be willing to accept the risks."

"Or to learn to live with it. Maybe that's stronger," Vicky persisted.

"Or to go ahead and have the surgery, if the woman is certain that this is a solution for her, despite the criticism of others and various religious interpretations. Perhaps that's the strongest woman," said Allen.

"I can't really disagree," she said. "Ahh... we have arrived."

The cab pulled up to the curb in front of the Black Rose. They had no trouble getting a table. Vicky ordered a vodka on the rocks and Allen had a single malt scotch, neat. She continued to gather information. "So what is this controversy all about?"

"Not an easy question to answer." He sipped his scotch and thought about how to explain. "The FDA was given the power by Congress to review medical devices that the agency had

Implant

approved prior to 1976. The silicone implant was subject to that law, but the law did not require that all devices approved in that period had to be reviewed. Which devices were to be reviewed was solely determined by the FDA. Despite the fact that the past thirty years has proved the silicone implant to be safe and to have no known relationship to any disease, it has become a political issue.

Commissioner Messerman has his own personal agenda. What group was easier to target? We plastic surgeons are few in numbers, divisive among ourselves, turf conscious and disgustingly complacent. You wouldn't believe how adult men can gossip and quibble among themselves. Sometimes a meeting is more like an old ladies' sewing circle than an instrument for the exchange of scientific ideas. Believe me. I have attended enough of them. I may be exaggerating but I am certain we could have prevented this mess by showing strength and unity early on. No industry would roll over and play dead for a mere government agency. You can bet on that! And then there's Alcott, the primary manufacturer of the silicone gel. Look at how they have handled it: misinformation instead of truth, hiding their heads in the sand instead of coming forward with facts. This could have been diffused long ago with honesty, science, and integrity. Messerman wouldn't have stood a chance."

"Well, I think there's been talk about silicone migration to distant organs. What about that?" she asked. Finally the waiter took their orders. Allen continued.

"We've known about microscopic migration for years. They've been calling it *leaking implants*. Kind of makes it sound like a garden hose with holes in it. The truth is that we all have silicone in our systems. Even I do."

"You do?"

"Certainly. Tablets of medication are coated with silicone to make them easier to swallow. Many antacids have silicone as a major ingredient. Then there are toothpastes, body lotions and cosmetics, just to name a few. Even the needles and syringes for injections are siliconized. Bottom line... there is absolutely no *scientific* evidence, to date, that indicates this migration to be harmful."

"What about reading x-rays?"

"Boy, you sure are grilling me!" He was getting tired of this.

"Oh, I'm sorry. I didn't mean to impose. I'm just fascinated with the entire subject."

Allen thought, "Maybe a little too fascinated." Dinner came and between bites Allen answered her last question hoping that would end the interrogation. "An experienced radiologist can, with certain standard techniques, usually distinguish between tumor and implant, or scar tissue, or free gel. It's another acceptable risk which is minimized with regularly scheduled mammograms and diligent clinical followup... Now that's enough."

Indeed, it was enough. Vicky was now fully armed. Allen was exhausted. He'd been talking constantly for over an hour and the jet lag was rapidly catching up with him.

"Just one more question?"

"Vicky..." He was getting thoroughly disgusted.

"Please, just one more. Promise!" She raised her right hand. Allen put down his fork and looked at her. She was pouting like a spoiled child. He gave in

"Okay... One more, and that's it!"

"Okay," she said again self satisfied that she had won. "Can they prove, the FDA, I mean... Can they prove that the implant isn't safe?"

"No way! Not scientifically. I have thirty years of data from the laboratory and clinical studies that absolutely will prove the safety of the implant. If science prevails and not politics, the implant will survive. Vicky, I'm determined to make them listen to science! To truth! Maybe we can still win this battle." That frightened her. He was too determined. She let it go for now. She had enough to run with anyway.

"Poor baby," she said as she saw him sinking into complete fatigue. "Let me take you home."

"Your home or mine?" he teased.

"Yours tonight... and alone... but tomorrow's another day." He saw that she wasn't joking.

"Hmm... interesting, very interesting," he thought. But he knew it was impossible tonight. "Okay... how about next week, Saturday?"

"Call me," she said.

"Don't think I won't."

Vicky insisted on paying the check and Allen was too tired to care. She had the waiter call a cab. They went first to his high rise in the Galleria area. "Allen, it was great to meet you." She gave him a bit more than a peck on his lips. "Now get some rest and call me when you get back."

"Yes, Ma'am." He gave her a mock salute. "Good night."

He didn't bother to undress. He took off his shoes and tie and called his wakeup service. He had to catch the 9:00 AM flight to Seattle. Then he crashed.

On the way home in the cab Vicky was thinking and analyzing. She had taken mental notes of everything Allen had said. The words were spinning in her head and forming into concrete ideas and strategies. *Safety, migration, free silicone, science, politics...* but the last thing he had said still bothered her... "I can absolutely prove the safety of the implant..." The cab pulled up to her garden apartment. She would have to take a cab to her office in the morning. Vicky hadn't wanted either of them to drive this evening. A cab seemed so much more intimate and she wanted Allen to feel comfortable and at ease. Apparently it had worked. Vicky was confident that she had everything she needed. As she walked into her apartment, she began to sing softly to herself, *Tomorrow, Tomorrow...*

She was wired. She couldn't sleep. There was too much to absorb. She was on overload. If only she could shut it off and get some rest! No use. Her mind was racing. She stared at the night shadows on the ceiling... and then she thought, "Yes, just one more thing... I'll call tomorrow."

Chapter 27
October 8, 1989

Earl Conners was in his apartment packing a suitcase. He kept thinking about J.T.'s words last week, "I'll take you down with me." It was repeating in his mind like a broken record. He had led J. T. to believe that the attacks on Hamilton and on Ashley were successful. It didn't matter. He wasn't going to be here when it hit the fan. His thoughts were interrupted by the phone for the second time this morning.

"Yes. Fine. I'll take care of it." He hung up and resumed packing. "God, it will be a pleasure to stop taking orders," he thought.

* * * * *

Before boarding the plane for Seattle, Allen bought a copy of the *Houston Daily Journal*. He folded it and tucked it under his arm during the boarding process. As the plane took off he leaned back, closed his eyes and tried to visualize various scenarios when he would come face to face with Roswell. He decided to be direct, get Roswell to admit everything and take it from there. Allen was still exhausted from yesterday. The effects of the jet lag alone would have been enough. He really should have excused himself and not have accepted Vicky's invitation to dinner, but he was very interested in her and simply couldn't turn down the opportunity. The future held great promise on that score. But he was no fool. He knew he was being used and pumped for information. He went along with it anyway. He didn't see the harm. Besides, she was Marc's attorney and Allen wanted her to understand all the intricacies of the situation.

Allen was almost asleep when the attendant offered him coffee. He accepted it gratefully. Perhaps it would help him to wake up. While sipping his coffee, he opened the newspaper. There it was. He wasn't surprised that it had made the headline:

SILICONE BREAST IMPLANTS
ARE HEALTH HAZARD

The article was basically a condensed version of Messerman's announcement from yesterday with a definite, subtle slant which led the reader to assume that the implant "...could be a major factor in causing breast cancer and autoimmune disease." That pissed him off! "Anything to sell newspapers," he thought with disgust. He sipped his coffee and turned the page angrily. He was browsing through the various sections when he came to *Today's Highlights*. He scanned the first page which told the success story of a poor farm boy who had become a

Implant

Houston billionaire in the banking industry. He turned the page and folded the paper in half. It hit Allen right between the eyes! An entire half-page ad :

> IF YOU HAVE SILICONE BREAST
> IMPLANTS DID YOU KNOW THAT
>
> 1. They may cause breast cancer or such diseases as rheumatoid arthritis, or Lupus?
> 2. You have probably been given false and deceptive information regarding the risks of silicone breast implants?
> 3. The implants leak and free silicone can travel in your body to other organs?
> 4. You may have been injured and are ill at this moment because of silicone in your body?
> 5. The FDA has now made silicone implants an EXPERIMENTAL DEVICE?
> 6. YOU DESERVE TO BE COMPENSATED FOR THIS PERSONAL INJURY?
>
> For more information about silicone implants and your rights
>
> CALL
>
> VICTORIA LANGE and ASSOCIATES
> ATTORNEYS AT LAW
>
> (555)-IMPLANT

Allen couldn't believe it. She had to have planned the advertising campaign weeks ago. At least he had been no party to that. Still he felt as though he had been raped. Only last night she had flattered him, flirted with him, sucked up to him just to pump him for information she could use as ammunition. The little bitch! She was in control. She had the memo. She would give it to the media when it would be most advantageous for her. He had to warn Marc. Sonofabitch! Who could you trust anymore?

He was offered breakfast but refused it. Allen was too upset to eat. He tried to sleep but he was too angry. The frustrating part of it was that there was nothing, absolutely nothing, he could do about it! Finally, close to landing, he tried to come to grips with it. He wondered if truth was a strong enough weapon against Vicky and the media's bullshit.

Allen arrived in Seattle at about 10:00 AM. His appointment with Roswell was for 1:00 PM so he had a couple hours to kill. He had skipped the meal on the plane. No great loss, but now he was hungry. He remembered Barney's Deli. He could get a great breakfast there at this hour and get several cups of coffee under his belt. Allen definitely needed the caffeine jolt. He wanted to be as sharp as possible for the meeting with J.T.

He had already put the Vicky issue on the back burner. First things first. He'd deal with her in Houston!

Virginia Moore met him at the reception desk. She looked worried and had been crying. "Hi, Virginia. What's wrong?" He saw that she was on the verge of tears again. She had been loyal to J.T. for over twenty-one years. When she interviewed for the position at Alcott, Virginia was a young widow with a teenage son. The insurance money was nearly gone and things were very tight. It had taken almost all of her reserves to go to business school. Her secretarial skills were only average but J.T. saw her ambition and motivation to succeed. He gave her the job, and time had proved that he had made the right decision. She was an outstanding organizer. During the first two years of her employment, he had learned to depend on her judgment. She had become his other right hand. J.T. was kind to her. He had helped her to buy a house and put her son through college.

Their relationship had remained strictly professional. Not that Virginia was unattractive in the least, nor that J.T. was some sort of saint. Far from it. He admired and respected her and to Virginia, Jonathon Tyler Roswell could do no wrong. Despite her close relationship with J.T. and the members of the board, she knew nothing of Earl Conners' real activities. That information was tightly controlled. Only Conners himself, J.T., Burns and Chuck Walker knew the truth. When the FDA announcement broke, she grieved for J.T. and cried until her eyes were red and puffy. Of course she never let on about her feelings and maintained a perfectly professional facade. That is, until she saw Allen Greenberg. After all he was like one of the family at Alcott.

"Oh, Dr. Greenberg, it's terrible. He doesn't deserve this. Please help him. He's on a tear, screaming at me, at everyone. I'm really afraid he... he..." She couldn't control it anymore. Allen felt so sorry for her. He knew how she felt about J.T. He hugged her gently.

"Now, now, Virginia. Stop your worrying. It will all work out." He tried his best to console her. "May I see J.T.?"

"Of course. He's expecting you. Please, try to help him, Dr. Greenberg."

"I'll try, Virginia."

She opened the door for him and whispered, "Just go on in." She closed the door behind him and returned to her desk.

J.T. had his back to the door and was gazing out the window at the park below. He didn't bother to turn around. "J.T.... J.T? J.T.!" Allen tried to get his attention and finally got a response.

"Oh, Greenberg, come in. Sit down." He still hadn't turned around. "Ah... how was the meeting?"

"J.T., are you shit'n me?" Roswell faced Allen for the first time. He seemed composed but distant. His eyes revealed exhaustion. He hadn't slept in days.

"Oh, of course. I was sorry to hear about Dr. Hamilton and Ms. Barton."

"So you heard?" Roswell had trapped himself and he knew it. "What did you hear, J.T.?"

"Oh, some mishap. I'm sorry."

"Sorry! You sonofabitch! Sorry! You nearly had them killed and you're sorry!"

Conners had led him to believe that the hits had been successful. He latched on to one word Allen had just said, "nearly." Roswell still had his wits about him and didn't show his shock at their still being alive. At that moment he could have strangled Conners with his bare hands. Allen continued to tear into him. "J.T., how could you? All for the fucking memo?"

"What are you talking about, Greenberg? What do you mean nearly killed? I heard they had an automobile accident."

"Automobile accident? No, that was me! Accident? I wouldn't exactly call it that!" Allen couldn't ever remember being so angry. "All for that goddamn memo!"

"What memo? What are you talking about?"

"So that's how you're going to play it!" said Allen close to shouting.

"I don't know what you're talking about," J.T. repeated.

"You goddamn sonofabitch! You're actually going to stand there and deny this whole thing? I thought there might be some explanation, some mistake. I came here hoping to find another answer but now I can see what I'm dealing with; a fucking, lying, murdering bastard!" Roswell was turning crimson.

"Hey, Greenberg, watch your mouth. Nobody talks to me like that. Nobody! Why, if not for me and my support, where would you and your precious implant be?"

"As I recall, J.T., you've made billions because of me and my *precious implant*, as you call it. So who owes whom?" Allen wasn't giving an inch. "Why don't you come clean, J.T. and tell it like it is?"

"I don't know what you're talking about," he persisted. Allen saw that he was getting nowhere. He realized that there was no place to go anyway except to the police.

"Okay," said Allen with resignation. "You can play your game now, but when Marc and Ashley get home, you'll have to answer to them and the police. You'll have to explain about Matthew Wertheim and the memo. What will you say then, J.T.? Are you still going to say you don't know? Fuck you, Roswell!" Allen turned, stormed out and slammed the door behind him. "Sorry, Virginia. I tried my best."

Roswell was going nuts in his office. Virginia heard the thuds and crashing. He threw the water pitcher to the floor. He threw his glass Baccarat paper weight against the door. Thousands of shattered pieces of glass lay about the room. He threw his desk chair against the window. More glass shattered. Virginia was afraid to go in. She sat at her desk with her hands covering her ears. She didn't want to hear. She didn't want to believe. Suddenly she heard his voice over the intercom. "Virginia! Virginia! Get me Conners! Now!"

Timidly she said, "Yes sir, immediately."

It was a bright, sunny afternoon with a nip of coolness that greeted Allen as he left Alcott Laboratories. He was searching for a taxi to take him back to the airport. He'd be early but he chose to wait there rather than at Alcott. He had a glimmer of hope when he arrived, but it soon faded when he collided with Roswell's brick-wall attitude. His hope had faded and then burst into an inferno of anger. This trip had been a complete waste. Allen now wondered what he had hoped to gain. It was all so futile. The only hope now lay in the hands of the lawyers and the courts, lawyers like Vicky... and maybe science. But he couldn't fool himself any longer. He knew that justice was whatever a lawyer could make a judge and jury believe.

Allen was trying to calm down as he looked for a cab. Usually they were plentiful here, so he remained near the entrance to Alcott. He began nervously pacing up and down. There was no cab in sight. "What else can go wrong?" he asked himself. He had been marching in front of the entrance for almost ten minutes. He thought about going back in and having Virginia call a cab for him. No. He couldn't go back. He'd never go back! He continued to pace and search, pace and search. Sooner or later one had to come. Across the street was The West Coast Insurance Company, a twenty-four-story highrise. He thought about someone calling a cab for him from there. "Just be patient and calm down," he said to himself. He decided to wait. If things went the same as they had so far today, no sooner would he cross the street than a taxi would come along. He paced and searched, paced and...

No one noticed the eleventh floor window with the missing glass. Nor did anyone see the barrel of the rifle extend just beyond the window's edge. Allen's forehead was centered in the cross hairs of the telescopic lens. It was a clear shot... NOW! Allen was slammed backward against the wall of Alcott Laboratories. His body slowly slid downward along the green granite wall until it came to rest in a sitting position with legs outstretched. The wall and sidewalk were red with blood. Dr. Allen Greenberg was dead.

Implant

A few passersby heard the single shot and ducked for cover. A few paid no attention, believing the sound to be the backfire of a truck. A few people saw the blood and saw the man collapse. They stopped in their tracks not knowing what to do. A woman screamed. A man turned aside and vomited. This was not only treachery and the untimely death of a man. It was the signal of the death of an era.

Chapter 28
Paris, October 8, 1989

Ashley and Marc had been staying with Nina for the past two days. She was like a mother hen and never let them out of her sight. Although they were absolutely confined to her apartment, she made it as pleasant as possible for them. She asked no questions. It was enough for Nina to know that Raymond wanted it this way. She knew that he would not have made this request of her if it had not been urgent and she would do anything for him anyway. Nina had grown fond of the young couple and took pleasure in seeing them so deeply in love. She saw how attentive Ashley was to Marc. Nina would smile, turn away and pretend not to see their tender gestures toward each other. It made her think of her relationship with Raymond. Of course they were much older but there was more spice, more fire, she thought.

Nina was small but muscular. She was about forty-five and looked a bit older. Her work was demanding. She was as good as any of the men at headquarters and had earned their respect. Her hair was dyed carrot red and she wore it up in a severely tight twist. Although her exterior was tough, she could be as soft and feminine as any woman. She prepared all the meals even though Ashley offered to help. They exchanged favorite recipes, talked about the latest fashions and hair styles. Marc would become thoroughly bored with their conversations and say with mock disgust, "Women!" And Nina would say,

"Fool, what would you do without us?" They laughed and made jokes. Even in these lighter moments Nina always had a revolver on her person in the pocket of her apron or under her bulky sweater. Marc and Ashley never knew it was there.

Marc was doing well. Claude came by twice to check him, clean the wounds and just visit. In more relaxed moments he told them of his boyhood adventures in New England. "So you have been in the States," said Ashley. Why didn't you tell us?"

"And when was there time to talk of such things?" answered Claude. He told them of his American mother and how she would never let him forget he was half American. Now they better understood why this man, a stranger, felt such a bond with them. He told them of his desire to visit America again someday. Of course they told him he had an open invitation.

It was during one of Claude's visits that Nina received a phone call.

"Hello? Oui... Oui... No. Dr. Dumont, it is for you." He went to the phone.

"This is Dr. Dumont... Much improved... I believe so, yes... To Dr. Hamilton? One moment..." He turned toward Marc and nodded. "For you this time. It is the inspector."

Marc said, "Good evening, Inspector... Tomorrow? Yes, we'll be ready... Right. No one! Six o'clock tomorrow morning. Thank you. Goodnight." He hung up the phone. "We're leaving in the morning for the airport with a police escort," he announced. They were finally leaving, leaving behind all that had happened during the last few days. It was hard for Marc to believe that it had been only a few days, less than a week. It was enough for a lifetime. "It's so strange, "said Marc. "I should be happy. I'm going home. What's wrong with me?"

"It's just that so much has happened. You haven't had the time to catch up with it all," said Ashley reassuringly.

"When it is all cleared up, you will be fine," said Claude. "I'm afraid you still have unfinished business at home, mon ami." Neither Marc nor Ashley slept that night.

It was still dark when Nina knocked on the guest room door at 5:00 AM. By 5:45 Marc and Ashley had showered and dressed. They had never dared to return to the Hotel Splendid to retrieve their belongings. They had packed the night before and there were only the few clothes that Nina had bought for them. They hastily downed the cafe au lait and croissants with preserves, which Nina had prepared herself. There was a knock at the door. It was Raymond. "Bon jour," he said and gave Nina a peck on the lips. "Are you ready, Doctor? We must leave."

"Yes Inspector," answered Marc.

"Nina, how can we thank you?" said Ashley. They hugged.

"Doctor, take care of this good woman," said Nina to Marc as she hugged him and gave him a gentle kiss on the cheek.

Ashley and Marc sat in the back seat of the unmarked police car. Moreau sat in front next to the officer driving. Both were in plain clothes. At the last moment the inspector had decided against the motorcycle escort. It would have been too obvious. Moreau was taking no chances. Although he found the young couple charming and had done all he could within reason, he now wanted them safely out of France and out of his hair. He had arranged for the plane reservations and the tickets, which

Marc had put on a credit card. "You have the tickets and your passports?" asked Moreau.

"Yes sir," said Marc.

Ashley and Marc were talking in the back seat. Moreau could only catch a word here and there but enough to get the drift of the conversation. "...to Alcott? When? Are you sure that's wise?"

"...has to get resolved! Wertheim... memo from Vicky."

"Doctor Hamilton, I strongly advise that you contact your lawyer as soon as you arrive in Houston and seek advice before you go running to that company. Is it *Alcott*? You have had quite enough to deal with, I would think. Let your police handle this. What can you possibly achieve by going there? You will have a tiger by the tail. Not an enviable position. If what you believe is true your police will be involved already. Please do not get in deeper than where you are now. I have made a formal report explaining your unfortunate encounters here, in France, and have filed your statements. This will go to the American Embassy and then to your State Department. The embassy will have received the report after your departure. We and they have all the information needed but I am familiar with... what you call... red tape? I see no purpose in your being detained further, especially since you are still very much at risk. Frankly I do not need any more problems. Be prepared for the State Department's contacting you at home. Tread gently, Doctor. You are not yet out of trouble!"

"Understood, Inspector. Thank you for your help," said Marc.

"Listen to him Marc. It's enough!" said Ashley.

They arrived at the airport two hours prior to flight time. Moreau didn't leave them for a second. The inspector knew that security was very heavy at the international departure gates and was anxious to get them there. He went just ahead of them to the security check point, flashed his badge and whispered something to the security guard who apparently knew the inspector, at least by name. He then motioned for Marc and Ashley to come ahead and bypass immigration. When they were nearly at the gate he said to them, "You will be safe here, but please be careful. I wish you well. Bon voyage." He smiled and shook hands with both of them. Before he left, Moreau pointed at Marc and smiled. "Keep him in line, Ms. Barton."

"I will, Inspector. I promise. Thank you for everything."

There was still another hour before Atlantic Airlines flight #41, the direct flight to Houston, was to be boarding. Near the gate was a coffee shop. Marc suggested that they kill a few minutes over another coffee. He was beginning to feel like himself again. The total rest imposed upon them by Nina and the inspector had encouraged the healing process. Although the edema was still apparent, he was able to conceal most of the bruises with the large dark glasses he wore. They ordered *cafe American*. It wasn't even a reasonable facsimile, but they drank it anyway.

"Now Marc, I'm not going to have an argument about this! You're not going back to the office for another week!"

"But..."

"No, you're not! Besides, Allen told Mrs. Warner to change your schedule and that he would see any of your patients who needed attention. There is absolutely no reason..." The television screen caught their attention. It was in English, WNN News:

> *... report from the FDA regarding the dangers of the silicone breast implant has created panic...*

They put down their coffee and listened intently. When it was over, Marc said, "I guess that's it. As much as I hate Alcott, and they deserve whatever they get, I really feel sorry for all those women and their families. All this for nothing! It's simply showtime for Messerman. I really thought Allen and I could make a difference."

"You have made a difference. You know the truth."

"And just where do you think that will get me? Killed, maybe?"

"Look, we'll get the memo from Vicky. What's to stop us now from getting it into the hands of the media? We're not in danger once the coverup is exposed."

"You're right but remember what Vicky said about the class action suits. I don't care about Alcott, but the plastic surgeons are going to be sued too. That coverup is going to bounce right up our asses. God damn! It's going to look like we were in bed with them all the while!"

"But you're the one who is going to tell the truth, the truth about the coverup, the truth about implant safety." She tied to reason with him.

Marc stared into his coffee cup for a long moment. "Ashley, I wish I had the same confidence about the truth. There is pure truth, what you're talking about... and then there is the truth that a judge and jury are made to believe. They are not necessarily the same. Can't you understand that?"

"Yes, of course I do. But sued is better than dead!" He had no argument for that. They heard the call for boarding.

By the time the fourth hour in flight had passed it seemed as though Paris had been a bad dream. Changes in cabin pressure made Marc pretty uncomfortable throughout the entire flight, but at last the plane landed. They got their bags, cleared U.S. immigration and customs and got a cab.

The taxi drove through the Memorial area, took the turn onto their street and stopped in the circular driveway of their house. Marc paid the driver who helped them place their bags next to the front door. It was wonderful to be home. October was a beautiful month in Houston. The sky was clear and the cool breeze from the west was tempered by the influence of the Gulf. Ashley took a deep breath and relaxed for the first time in a week.

Marc was always having trouble with the lock on the door. "I'll get that fixed first thing tomorrow," he thought. Finally he opened the door. "Go on in," he said. "I'll get the bags." Ashley went ahead. Marc turned and got the two bags. He kicked the door. It opened wider but he didn't see Ashley. He put the bags down. Marc fought to get the damn key out of the lock. It was stuck. He gave up for the moment. He called from the foyer, "Hey, where are you?" No answer. Not a sound. He figured she was in the bathroom. He picked up the bags again. Marc headed toward the bedroom through the library.

"Why are women always in the bathroom. Every time we..." He didn't have a chance to finish the thought. Just as he turned the corner into the library he saw her and was gripped with horror. A man had his hand over her mouth. and he held her immobilized. In his right hand was a gun which he had jabbed into Ashley's ribs. She was pressed tightly against the man's body. A second man held a revolver aimed at Marc. He dropped the bags and yelled, "Leave her alone! Please don't hurt her. What do you want?"

"Get your hands up! Doc, haven't you had enough? We don't want to get tough. Just be cooperative and we'll let her go," said the short man in jeans. He aimed the gun directly at Marc's chest.

"You're from Alcott, aren't you? What will it take for you to believe that we don't have the memo!"

"Just stay cool, Doc! We know that... Now, we're all going to take a little drive." Marc's heart was pounding. His eyes moved from Ashley to the gun and back again. There was no way!

"Look," he said with his voice trembling, "I'll cooperate. Just tell me what you want." Ashley was squirming, trying to get free of the strangle hold the larger man had on her.

"Keep her still," said the man in jeans. "Knock her out if you have to."

"No! Please, don't hurt her!" pleaded Marc again. "Ashley, be still," he said to her firmly. "It'll be okay." She stopped. Her eyes were wide with terror.

"Now that was smart, Doc. See, we just want cooperation. Let's go to the garage. Give me your car keys, Doc, and we'll..." He was interrupted by the front doorbell. "Okay, nobody move! Don't make a sound! Doc, you expecting someone?" asked the man holding the gun on Marc.

"No," said Marc. "No one."

"Doc, you and I are going to the door... slowly." The man with the gun was in complete control and as cool as steel in winter. "No funny stuff or she gets it here." The other gunman shoved the weapon harder into her side. Ashley didn't move. "Open the door real casual and get rid of whoever it is. I'm gonna be behind the door so remember..." he said as he indicated his possession of the gun again. Then he tilted his head toward Ashley. "And lady, not a squeak out of you! Hear?" Ashley was able to nod indicating that she understood.

Marc slowly walked through the library and into the foyer with the man behind him. He put his hand on the doorknob. There was another doorbell ring. Marc jumped at the sound. The gunman remained calm. He positioned himself behind the door in such a manner that he would be concealed from view and he would be able to see out through the opening of the door at the hinges. He could observe every move Marc made. Marc waited for the signal. He slowly opened the front door. A man stood there. He was dressed in tan slacks and a white shirt which was open at the collar. He had a young appearance but the forehead furrows and lines about the eyes indicated that he was somewhere in his late forties.

"Hi. Dr. Hamilton?"

"Yes," said Marc as evenly as he could. "Can I help you?" He had never seen the man before.

"Well, I'm Jim Sloan, your neighbor. We moved in while you were away. The postman left a special delivery letter for you." He extended his hand. The gunman saw and contracted his index finger slightly on the trigger. He had a good shot if it became necessary but he hoped he wouldn't have to shoot and alarm the entire neighborhood. Marc slowly took the letter without so much as a glance at it.

"Thank you." It was a bit curt. The young man looked embarrassed. Marc tried desperately to think of a way to show some signal, a sign of impending disaster.

"Ah... actually I wanted to meet you. We're new in town and..."

"This is a very bad time," said Marc. "We just walked in and..." The gunman tightened his grip a fraction more. "...and we're exhausted. You know, jet lag and all. Otherwise, I'd invite you in." He saw that it was impossible. He couldn't risk it. Jim Sloan looked disappointed.

"Perhaps another time... unless, just for a minute..."

"No!" Marc almost shouted. "Sorry. I'm very tired. Another time... of course... another time."

"Oh, by the way, here is your door key," said Sloan. It was stuck in the lock." He handed the key to Marc. He hesitated for a fraction of a second as if waiting for Marc to change his mind. The trigger finger was less than a millimeter from firing.

"Thanks... ah... See you next time," said Marc.

"Well, bye. See ya." Sloan turned and walked down the steps. Marc closed the door. He was about to turn when the gunman motioned for him to stand still as he moved to the side of the curtain covering the window by the door. He pulled the curtain aside very slightly. He could barely see Sloan because of the large live oak trees obstructing his view. When he was satisfied that he was gone, he said to Marc,

"I'm proud of you, Doc. You done real good. Now let's move slowly back and join the lady." They went back into the library. Nothing had changed.

"Alcott's going to win this hand," thought Marc. He was resigned to compliance. For the man holding Ashley, Marc held such hatred as he had never known before. There was nothing he could do! He was utterly frustrated. He wanted to kill and he couldn't!

"Okay, the car keys, Doc." Marc reached into his pocked for his key ring. "Uh... Very slow! Now, easy... Toss it over." The gunman grabbed the keys in midair with his left hand. The gun never moved off of Marc. "Okay, now..." It was the doorbell again. "Sonofabitch! I don't believe it! That asshole is back?"

"What the fuck's goin' on?" Those were the first words spoken by the other man, who was obviously getting very nervous. "Open the door and waste him! Then we'll do these two and be out of here!"

"Shut the fuck up, dumbass! I'll handle this!" It became clear to Marc that the men meant to kill them, preferably elsewhere, but here if necessary! But why? They said they knew that neither he nor Ashley had the memo. What could Alcott gain by killing them?

"Okay. Everybody cool. Doc, we're gonna have to do it again. Same game." The doorbell rang again.

"Christ! What nerve!" thought Marc. He saw there was no way that Jim Sloan could help. The jerk was going to get them all killed. He waited for the signal as before. He opened the door and was ready to verbally rip into.... But no one was there!

Chapter 29
October 8, 1989

David Stein awoke three minutes before his alarm clock went off. He was so accustomed to being awake at 5:30 AM that his biological clock was usually sufficient. He took advantage of the extra three and remained in bed to organize his thoughts. During residency training he had learned to be fully awake instantly, even from a deep sleep. He had a 7:30 bowel resection. It would be a long case, probably adinocarinoma, probably a colostomy. He wanted to see Mr. Jamison before they gave him his pre-op injection so that he could give him some reassurance and he absolutely had to talk with Mrs. Jamison, who was a basket case. He shut off the alarm before it went off, did twenty pushups, twenty deep knee bends and ran in place for ten minutes. No sweat! He was still in great shape. He hit the shower for ten minutes, shaved, and dressed for the day.

Implant

At 7:00 AM he entered the doctors' lounge at the hospital and changed into his scrubs. The lounge was packed with surgeons who were about to start their first cases for the day. Generally they were a congenial group. They teased one another a bit and told the latest jokes, which would bring roars of raucous laughter, usually. As Dave approached the coffee machine everyone fell silent. He looked about and heads turned away. "That's strange," he thought. He looked down at his pants. "That's stupid! If I had pissed myself they'd be laughing." Dr. Wells, the orthopedist and one of Dave's best buddies walked in. "Hey, Tom!" said Dave. He got back a cool, "Hi." What the hell was going on? He was being treated like a leper. He took his coffee and sat down on a bench next to Bill Morris, a plastic surgeon and a good one. They were friends even though it was a known fact that Dave referred all his cases to Marc Hamilton. Bill had his face buried in the morning paper. "Morning, Bill."

"Morning," said Bill as he continued reading. Dave had had enough.

"Okay guys, what's going on?" One surgeon was staring at the floor. Another walked out. Bill didn't respond. Dave was about to give up and go to his o.r. when over the intercom came, "Dr. Morris, Dr. Morris, your patient is ready in room sixteen." Bill folded the paper, pitched it at Dave and walked out. The others in the lounge followed suit. Dave looked at the paper. No! It wasn't possible! She couldn't! But there it was, half a page! She had never said a word. So that was it. The guys thought he knew. Bill thought he knew! Shit! The sneaky bitch! It was over! He'd call her after the case. He sat there for another moment to calm down. He had to put it out of his mind. He had surgery to do. There would be plenty of time later to deal with Ms. Victoria Lange, Bitch at Law.

Vicky had gone into a partnership arrangement with two personal injury attorneys. She was the organizer and had insisted on the name for the firm, *Victoria Lange and Associates*. They had agreed since, she argued, it was her idea and her money for the ad. It was going to be a 40-30-30 split. Vicky was to get the 40. She was not an expert in personal injury and knew she would need help with the implant suits. They were more than willing. This was going to be a bonanza and they were going to be the first in Texas!

The three of them were sitting in Vicky's conference room. They had previously had several meetings and were about ready to go. All they needed were clients. It was early, 8:15 AM. They were having coffee and were waiting for the calls from the ad to start. The secretary, Nancy, wouldn't be in for another fifteen minutes. Vicky had asked her to start early today. She had hired a temp from an agency to get the second line. While they were waiting Robert Thornton began. "Vicky, I still think we're going to have to name the plastic surgeons as parties in the suits."

"I agree," said Melony Hodges. If you want to keep these cases in State Court, you have to have a party to the suits in Texas."

"On what grounds can we do that?" asked Vicky.

"Are you joking?" asked Thornton. "That's a piece of cake. We simply say that the plastic surgeons intentionally and knowingly misrepresented the characteristics and the properties of the implants in order to mislead and induce patients into undergoing implantation. And that, my dear Vicky, spells malpractice."

"And who knows, when the well runs dry at Alcott and the other manufacturers we can move on to the plastic surgeons. They carry huge malpractice insurance policies. It's *insurance* for us to name them as parties," said Hodges.

"Okay. You've convinced me. We go after them!" said Vicky.

The secretary came in and took the phones off service. It didn't take three minutes when it began:

"I just read the ad in the paper and I'd like some information..."

"May I speak with Ms. Lange? I'm mad as hell about my silicone implants... Why, I was never told that...!"

"I'm not actually having a problem but how much can I sue for?"

"...and every morning I wake up with a backache since I had those horrible implants..."

"...I never had colds so often, but since..."

"...I'm so scared! I don't want to die! I know I'm going to have huge doctor bills... and I'm broke! Please, tell her to see me! She has to help me! I don't know where else to turn!"

Vicky stood over the secretary as she was about to pick up the phone. "How's it going, Nancy?"

"Ms. Lange, we're booked solid for the next three weeks. It's only been three hours. What do you want to do?"

"Start filling in Saturdays too. After that, refer them to Thornton or to Hodges," said Vicky. She went back into the conference room with a bottle of champagne. "Guys, here's to us... and God bless silicone!" They drank. Vicky downed her glass in one giant gulp. "I think it's time to release the memo," she said. They toasted themselves again.

After the celebration Thornton and Hodges returned to their offices. The calls continued to pour in. By 2:00 PM the three attorneys were booked solid with appointments for six weeks ahead. Vicky was very pleased with herself. She was about to go out for a late lunch when Nancy stopped her. "Ms. Lange, it's Dr. Stein."

"Oh, okay. I'll take it in my office." She returned to her office and closed the door behind her. Vicky knew what was coming. She took a deep breath and braced herself. "Hello, Dave."

"Thanks, Vicky! Nice piece of work!"

"So you've seen the ad."

"How could I miss it! Vicky, how could you do this? Marc is my best friend. Do you think he'll believe that I didn't know about it?"

"If he's such a good friend I would think he'd believe you," she said.

"I thought you were friends with Ashley. What kind of friend are you, Vicky?"

"Don't get self righteous with me, Dave! I did what I had to do."

"Had to? Bullshit!"

"Look, Dave, I'm sorry you're so pissed off but an opportunity like this comes along once in a lifetime if you're lucky. I'm on the merry-go-round and I want that brass ring. Nothing is going to stop me! You can come along if you want to."

"A brass ring! I was fool enough to want to give you a gold ring. God, what a jackass I am! I guess I never really knew you, Vicky."

"Well, what you see is what you get," she said contemptuously.

"Thanks. I think I'll do business elsewhere. Oh, and Vicky... go fuck yourself!" She had known it was over before the call. No surprise.

"Oh well," she thought. "Soon I'll be able to get whatever and whomever I want. Too bad, Dave. It would have been a kick." She had no trouble eating a hardy lunch.

* * * * *

Marc looked to the right and left. He saw no one at the door. He stood there for a moment trying to understand. Finally the nervous gunman whispered, "Who is it? That preppy again?"

"No. No one," said Marc. The gunman was getting suspicious and worried.

"Shut the door, Doc, and..." Crash! Before he had a chance to finish the sentence two police officers had forced their way through the rear sliding glass doors and were in the library in a flash with their forty-fives. Ashley squirmed and kicked when she saw them. She managed to free herself partially from the man's grasp in the same instant that he was distracted by the officers.

"Drop the gun and let her go!" said the officer who was nearest. "I said..." The attacker pushed Ashley toward the officer. That move caught the cop off guard and obstructed his aim. The gunman took advantage of the moment and shot the cop in the chest. He died instantly. The dead policeman's partner, who was a mere pace behind, got off a shot. The killer stumbled and fell to the floor. In the very same moment that the rear glass door shattered the gunman at the front entry dropped into a protective crouched position behind the table in the foyer. Marc was shoved aside by two more cops who emerged from the shrubs on either side of the front entry. One took cover behind the door and the other fell to the floor of the foyer. Marc barely missed being shot by the crouching gunman. Ashley was screaming. She thought Marc might have been shot. The officer in the library ignored her and started toward the foyer. The surviving gunman was trapped.

The cop on the floor yelled, "Drop it!" The gunman panicked. When he saw the other cop coming toward him from the opposite direction, he spun around toward him with his weapon aimed to fire. Before he could pull the trigger the cop on the floor got him in the back of the neck. The gunman, wide eyed, dropped his weapon, clutched his throat and fell to his knees. His hands were covered with blood. The second shot from the cop on the floor found its mark at the back of the head and finished the job. It had all taken only seconds, barely enough time for Marc to realize what had occurred. His first thought was of Ashley. Was she shot? He ran into the library.

"Marc!" she yelled. He caught her running into his arms. She was sobbing and totally out of control.

"Ashley, Baby! It's okay. It's okay." She couldn't stop. "Honey, we're all right! It's over."

The library walls and floors ran with blood. One cop bent over the downed officer in the library and checked for a pulse. He was dead. "Bobby! Bobby!" shouted the officer frantically. He shook his partner as though he could shake him back to life. When he realized it was futile, he sat on the floor beside the body and cradled the head on his arm. He cried softly as he rocked back and forth. His partner of five years was gone. His lips moved in disbelief, "God, no! Not Bobby!" Somehow he'd have to tell Jenny. The other officer cautiously approached the two gunmen on the floor, kicked away their weapons and checked to make certain that they were dead. Then he took notice of Marc and Ashley. "Are you two okay?" Ashley couldn't stop her paroxysms of sobs. Marc nodded affirmatively.

"We'll be fine, officer." Marc held Ashley tightly. Then the policeman walked over to his buddy who was on the floor aimlessly rocking Bobby.

"Chuck, come on! Get up!" All Chuck could say was,

"It's Bobby, Fred! It's Bobby!"

Fred went to the telephone in the library and dialed headquarters. "Officer down! Yeah, we got 'em both. No... We had no choice. They were warned and wouldn't drop their weapons... Bobby Riggs bought it. Yeah, the couple's okay but Chuck's in pretty bad shape. No... Bobby was his partner... Right." He hung up. "Okay folks. It's all over. Let's go into the living room." He left Chuck with Bobby.

"Ma'am, can I get you a glass of water or something?"

"Thanks officer," said Marc. The kitchen's to the left." When he returned, Ashley took a swallow and started to come to herself. She and Marc sat on the sofa. He wouldn't leave her side. Finally Ashley spoke.

"Marc, how did they know? We just got home."

"I don't know but I'm damn glad they're here." He turned to the officer and said,

"Thank you. Thank you, officer. I thought we'd had it! But how did you know?"

"The chief got a call from Paris this morning... a police inspector, Morell, Morvel, or something like that."

"Moreau," said Marc with a smile as he turned toward Ashley.

"He seemed to be certain that this was going to happen and the chief believed him after a few minutes of explanation. You two are lucky we got here in time."

"I'm so sorry about the officer," said Ashley. Fred just turned away and walked toward the window.

They heard the sirens. Two ambulances and two police cars pulled up into the circular driveway. By this time a large crowd had gathered on the walk in front of the house. Jim Sloan emerged from the first car. He walked into the living room. "Everything under control, Fred?"

"Yes, Lieutenant." Sloan introduced himself to Ashley and Marc.

"Dr. Hamilton, I'm sorry to have frightened you but when I saw you, I knew you were in trouble. I had to try to get in or at least get an idea of what was going on. Thankfully, you kept your cool."

Marc said, "I wanted to give you some kind of signal but I knew he could shoot both of us."

"You did exactly right," said Sloan. "If you had tried anything at all, I'm certain at least one of us would be dead. I know this is a terrible time but would you and the lady please come downtown with us? We have some questions and a few points to clear up."

"Do I need my lawyer?" asked Marc. Sloan smiled.

"No, sir. We know you're both okay. Let's go to the station first. If you want your lawyer there will be no problem."

The paramedics brought in three body bags. "What a waste. What a damn waste," said Marc. He and Ashley walked out with Fred. They had to push through the crowd.

"Okay, folks. It's all over. You can go home. Please make some room for these people to get by," said Fred.

"What happened, Doc?" asked a neighbor. Marc didn't answer. They got in the back seat of the first car. As they looked back toward the house, they saw two officers supporting Chuck.

"Poor guy," said Ashley. "It was his partner. He gave his life for us, Marc." She began to cry again softly but this time gentle, mournful tears.

"Who were those two guys?" asked Marc.

"We don't know yet. There was no identification on either one," said Fred. "Hopefully the lab will come up with something."

They arrived at the station. Ashley and Marc followed Lieutenant Sloan to his office. He called in a stenographer. The interrogation by Sloan was tactful and sympathetic. He knew what they had been through. Over a two-hour period Marc and Ashley unraveled the story: the memo, Wertheim, Roswell, Alcott, Paris, the whole thing.

"Sounds like Mr. J.T. Roswell has a lot of explaining to do. Doctor, do you know a guy by the name of Earl Conners?"

"No," said Marc. "I don't know him but I've heard that he's the head of security for Alcott."

"Inspector Moreau mentioned that Interpol had Conners connected with organized crime in the U.S. and abroad," said Sloan. "I'm willing to bet that Roswell used him for all his dirty work. We'll have to get the Seattle Police Department's cooperation. I think we'll have Mr. Roswell and Mr. Conners behind bars very soon. Doc, I got a couple more questions."

"Shoot," said Marc.

"Why would Alcott keep trying to get you and Ms. Barton if, as you say, they know that you don't have the memo?"

"I think they realized that we know all the facts in the memo and could implicate them in the death of Matthew Wertheim. Remember, we met the man and he was terrified that something might happen to him, especially since he believed that the FDA was about to stir everything up."

"I see," said the Lieutenant. "Just one more, Doc. Off the record, are those implants really safe?" Marc turned toward Ashley. Would she allow him to tell the lieutenant? She nodded affirmatively.

"Lieutenant, do you think I'd let my future wife have the surgery if I had any doubts? I did my training in plastic surgery with the man who invented the implants, Dr. Allen Greenberg. He has spent the last thirty years proving, scientifically, the safety of the silicone prosthesis. I know his work. Then there is my own research as well. There is no question in my mind or in Dr. Greenberg's about the safety record of the implant. We know the facts! Dr. Greenberg and I will make public our data and hopefully, we'll be able to reverse the FDA's decision. But that won't be easy, Lieutenant. Nor will it be easy to change public opinion."

"I hear ya! But what about the FDA? Why would they make such a report if it's false?"

"Lieutenant Sloan, surely you have a good understanding of politics and power struggles. I'm certain they exist in your profession."

"You bet your ass... sorry, Ma'am... we do! The captain is under the thumb of the commissioner of police and he's sucking up to the mayor and the mayor... Well, I understand... By the way, I didn't say any of that, right?"

"I didn't hear a thing," said Marc. "So, Lieutenant, what happens now?"

"You are free to leave. I'm sure that after we contact Seattle the DA will want your stories again. There will be a trial if Roswell and Conners are indicted by the Grand Jury for the murder of Wertheim and the attempts on your lives. I'm not sure, but since this crosses state lines and national borders it may become a federal case. One way or another, they'll pay. I'll get a car to take you home so that you can pack some clothes and necessary personal articles. I'm sorry but since the forensic personnel are at your house, you'll have to stay elsewhere for a day or two."

It was about 5:30 PM when Ashley and Marc, accompanied by an officer, walked in and saw the mess in the foyer and library. Both rooms were cordoned off for the investigation. Again they experienced the photographers and police laboratory personnel. It was like deja vu, France all over again. "Marc, I couldn't stay here anyway. This has to be cleaned up first!"

"As soon as they let us, I'll get a cleaning crew to come in," said Marc. The phone rang. It was Liz, Allen Greenberg's office manager.

"Dr. Hamilton, I've been trying to get you all afternoon! It's horrible! Please, please come! I don't know what to do... I can't get his son... I don't know what to do... I called your office and Anne is on the way over... I don't know what to do..." The rest of her words were unintelligible.

"What happened, Liz? For heaven's sake, tell me!"

"Just come! Come now!" Marc turned to Ashley.

"That was Liz, from Allen's office. She's always been such a level-headed woman but now she's near hysteria. Something terrible must have happened. I've got to get there now."

"I'm coming with you," said Ashley. "Didn't Allen say he was going to try to straighten things out in Seattle?"

"God! I hope I'm wrong about what I'm thinking. Let's go!"

They walked into Allen's office. Liz was lying on a sofa and Anne Warner was trying to comfort her. When Anne saw Marc her eyes searched him from head to toe. Her voice quivered. "Dr. Hamilton... are you all right? He called from France and said that you were in an accident."

"Who called?"

"Dr. Greenberg... just the other day. Are you okay?"

"I'm fine now, Anne." He assured her. "What the hell's going on?"

"It's Dr. Greenberg..."

When Liz saw Marc, she sat up and grasped his hand. Her eyes were red and swollen and the tears were flowing. "He's dead, Dr. Hamilton! He's dead! Dr. Greenberg was... was... shot down like a dog... in Seattle."

"Oh no! Not Allen too!"

"No! Not Allen! No!" said Ashley. The three women were crying.

"What happened, Liz? For God's sake, tell me!" he said louder than he meant to, in an effort to get through to Liz.

"He went to Seattle to meet with Roswell face to face. Virginia called me and said they had a terrible argument and Dr.

Greenberg stormed out of the office. Mr. Roswell went berserk! I... I... can't..."

"Go on, Liz. You're doing fine. Tell me," said Marc more gently.

"He went out, probably to get a cab Virginia said, and just before he could get one, the police said someone shot him from the building across the street."

"Shit!" said Marc. "I can't believe it... Allen dead. I can't believe it!" Marc realized that even with all his concerns, even with his own life in danger, Allen had taken the time to call. He wanted to cry but wouldn't let himself. Someone had to remain strong. They needed to lean on him. "Do they think it was Roswell?"

"No," said Liz. "Not directly anyway."

"What do you mean?" asked Marc.

"Well... she said that after Dr. Greenberg left..." She started crying again.

"Please, Liz. Easy now. I know how you... feel. Marc was choking down his emotions. "Just tell me the rest of it."

"I'll try, Dr. Hamilton." She made an effort to compose herself. "After Dr. Greenberg left, Mr. Roswell went crazy. He was throwing things and yelling and he asked Virginia to call Mr. Conners. Virginia said that Mr. Conners is head of security at Alcott. She put him through and they spoke for only a few seconds. Of course she doesn't know what was said, but about fifteen minutes later Dr. Greenberg was... killed. The police came and took Mr. Roswell in for questioning or to jail, I guess. I don't know about Mr. Conners."

"That bastard! The no good...! Have you called Dr. Greenberg's son?" asked Marc.

"I've tried. He must be out."

"What's his number?" He dialed. Todd Greenberg answered. By the tone of his voice Marc realized that he knew. "Todd, this is Marc Hamilton..."

"I know, Dr. Hamilton... The police found me a few minutes ago. My father's dead. My Mom, and now my Dad." Todd was sobbing.

"Todd! Todd! Listen! What arrangements are you making? What can I do?"

"The police said it was a coroner's case and they won't release the body until tomorrow afternoon. An autopsy is required by law..." There was a long pause. "I'm sorry. I'm trying to get my thoughts together. It's so hard, Dr. Hamilton. I know you loved him too."

"Yes, I did, Todd. He was my teacher and friend."

"I called Temple Beth Shalom and I think the funeral will be Thursday. Would you please be a pallbearer?"

"I'd be honored, Todd." Marc's eyes were tearing. Ashley took the phone. They knew Todd only slightly. They saw him rarely. Allen and Todd had drifted apart after Susan's death. He was a fine young man and something of a computer genius.

"Can we call some people for you, Todd?" she asked.

"Yes, please. I'm contacting the family but you'd know better than I about the doctors who would want to know. Please. That would be a big help."

"Of course we will. Do you want Marc to help you with anything else?"

"No," he said. I have to do this myself."

"I understand," said Ashley. "But we're here if you want us... for anything."

"Thanks, Ashley... Ms. Barton. Thanks." He hung up.

Ashley said, "Marc, we need to call Ben Crosby, Dave... oh, and Vicky. I nearly forgot! We need to see her."

Anne Warner called Marc aside. "Dr. Hamilton, this isn't the best time..."

"I'm okay, Anne. What is it?"

She began again. "I know this isn't the best time but have you seen this?" She handed him the morning paper with Vicky's ad. "I think you need to see this." Marc's eyes widened and his jaw dropped in disbelief. He handed the paper to Ashley. She couldn't say a word. She sat down in a chair, thought for a moment and then threw the paper to the floor.

"What else? What else!" she said. Marc sat beside her.

"That two-faced, lying, treacherous..." He was fuming. How could he call her now? As far as the memo was concerned, it didn't matter anymore anyway. In fact it made no sense to keep it under wraps. The damage had already been done. He was afraid of what he might do if he saw Vicky now. He wouldn't call. "Dave!" he thought. "No! He couldn't! Not Dave. He couldn't have known."

* * * * *

"Yis-gad-dal v'yis-kad-dash sh'meh rab-bo..." The cantor was chanting in Hebrew the prayer for the dead, for Allen Greenberg. On that Thursday afternoon in Houston the temperature had dropped into the 50s. It was the first norther of the fall. The wind and the somber mood made it feel much colder at the graveside service. Marc looked about. It was a huge crowd. Dr. Allen Greenberg was a man well loved. Almost every department of the Medical Center was represented. Doctors, nurses, secretaries and even patients were there to pay their last respects. After the mournful chanting the rabbi gave the eulogy. Marc wasn't listening. What could the rabbi say about Allen that he didn't already know?

Although Vicky was inconspicuous in the crowd, Ashley noticed her. When everyone else bowed his head in reverence, Vicky held hers high and looked straight ahead. Ashley nudged Marc and nodded toward Vicky. "What nerve to show up here!" she said. Ashley made eye contact with Vicky and wouldn't break the visual lock. Vicky's expression was flat and her eyes were as cold as the gravestones. She looked away first. She got the message.

Dave stood beside Marc and Ashley. Yesterday he tried to explain that he had known nothing of Vicky's plans until he saw the ad. Marc stopped him and said that no explanation was necessary. He knew Dave too well.

After the rabbi concluded the service the pallbearers placed their carnations on the coffin, which was then slowly lowered. Todd, whose grief was evident, was the first to take a shovelful of earth. He turned the shovel and let the earth slowly fall on the lowered coffin. Dust to dust. Dave followed, then Marc, then Ashley and all the rest. Each shovelful made a hollow sound as it hit the coffin. It was the sound of death, itself. It penetrated to the very soul and echoed the emptiness left by Allen Greenberg's death.

They were returning to the car when someone touched Marc on the shoulder. Marc turned and couldn't believe his eyes. It was Chuck Walker. "Marc, we have to talk." It took Marc a moment to recover from this totally unexpected encounter. He never thought that Chuck Walker would have the guts to show up here. It had become clear some time ago that Chuck knew everything, knew every plan made by Roswell and implemented by Conners.

"You want to talk with me, Chuck? Why?"

"Well, I don't think you understand," he said.

"Chuck, I understand everything! You knew and you didn't raise a finger to stop it. You knew it was our lives at stake, Ashley's and mine. And you did nothing! Absolutely nothing! I don't want to talk with you. I don't ever want to see you again.

Get out of my sight!" Walker didn't say another word. He turned and walked away.

* * * * *

Walker's attorney had warned him that he could expect a Grand Jury indictment at any moment. Roswell was in the same position. He had tried to shift the blame onto Conners, but Conners couldn't be found. He had disappeared as if by magic. Despite all police efforts, there was no trace of Earl Conners. Warren Burns had turned state's evidence and fingered Roswell and Conners for Wertheim's murder and the Paris incidents. Through a plea bargain, he got ten to twenty years for his involvement in the conspiracy to murder Wertheim. Roswell continued to deny everything, including the attempt to kill Marc and Ashley in their own home. There wasn't a doubt that he would be indicted for first-degree murder.

Roswell knew what was in store for him. He became more despondent with each day that came closer to his incarceration. Virginia stood by him. She was the only one who did. It was three days before the hearing when Virginia walked into J.T.'s office. He was standing at the window and was looking at the park below. This was all he had done for days. He wouldn't eat, even with Virginia's coaxing, and he couldn't sleep. He lived at the office and wouldn't go home. He refused to see his wife or children. He no longer looked like a proud patrician. He had three days' growth of beard and his silvery hair looked wild and unkempt.

"Mr. Roswell, you have to eat something," she pleaded. "Let me go out and get..."

"Virginia, you know I'm not a bad person."

"Of course I know that, Mr. Roswell."

"Haven't I run this company well?"

"Yes sir, you have... And now, how about some...?"

"Why are they trying to get me, Virginia? I was only trying to save this company from disaster. Now that the memo is out, all because of that gutless fool Wertheim, Alcott doesn't stand a chance. I only tried to stop that false lab data from distorting the truth. Why the hell didn't I shred it while I had the chance? So much for hindsight!" he said with bitterness. "You understand, don't you, Virginia?"

"Yes sir, I do... Now..."

"Yes, please. Get me a... a club sandwich."

She smiled. "Oh, you'll feel so much better with some food in you. I'll be back in a couple minutes."

Roswell heard the outer door close as Virginia left. He went to his desk and pulled out the bottom drawer on the right. He took the thirty-eight out of its holster and checked to make certain that it was fully loaded. He walked over to the window and looked down at the children playing in the park. He looked up at the gray layers of cloudy sky. It would be the last thing he would ever see. He placed the gun barrel in his mouth and pulled the trigger. Jonathon Tyler Roswell's judgment would now come from a higher court.

Chapter 30
January 16, 1990

Marc and Ashley were married in December. It was a small wedding. The reception for fifty people was at Armando's. Claude came as he had promised. It was a wonderful reunion. After the wedding Claude went to Milbridge, Maine. Nothing was as he had remembered. There were no magical fall colors nor the fresh scent of pine. It was winter, cold and dreary, with enormous snow drifts swept high by the gales off the Atlantic. The old house that he remembered so fondly from his youth had new owners who had modernized. The lovely verandah was gone. The Victorian gingerbread trimmings were gone. The clapboard exterior had been replaced with aluminum siding. And of course the Browns were gone. Claude didn't stay in Milbridge long. He went on to visit Montreal and Quebec City. He realized that it was true. You can never go back.

Almost every day Marc received notices of lawsuits against him. The same was true for all the other plastic surgeons in Houston, throughout Texas and in many other areas of the nation. The class action suits were gathering momentum with the memo exposed. Vicky's firm was the unquestioned leader in the development of the suits. She had expanded to eight members in order to handle the load more efficiently. Their first case was set for trial in August 1991 in Harris County, Texas.

The emotional toll on Marc was enormous. The self-doubt was overwhelming. Had he really harmed those patients? Had he done something wrong? Would he lose the malpractice cases against him? His life's work, his most precious possession, was in question. Only Ashley meant more to him. He could neither eat nor sleep. He had no interest in anything. He went to the office and worked like a robot, without emotion. The lawsuits were tearing him apart. Ashley tried her best to pull him out of his personal snake pit but it wasn't enough.

"Marc, you can't do this to yourself. You can't do this to us!"

"Maybe I really did something wrong, Ashley," he said flatly.

"Stop! You know you didn't do anything wrong! And even if you had, aren't you human? You're not God!"

"They're out to get me, Ashley." His ego was destroyed and Ashley couldn't bear it. The practice was suffering. No one trusted plastic surgeons anymore. The patients' confidence had been demolished and was replaced with hate and vengeance. Two plastic surgeons in Texas had declared bankruptcy. The pressure was unbearable for many. One plastic surgeon in California had committed suicide. Ashley wasn't going to let this continue. She had to bring him back.

"Marc, can't you see that these lawsuits are not really directed at you, personally? It's not for anything you did or failed to do. It's fear and greed. Marc, it's not you, Darling."

"Fear and greed... Fear and greed," he kept repeating.

It went on for months. Sometimes he canceled what little surgery he had and stayed at home. Anne Warner was going mad trying to keep up with the demand by attorneys to find and copy medical records of breast implant patients. It was unbelievable what fear and greed had unleashed. Ashley was afraid to leave Marc alone for a single moment. Then, finally, she had an idea. She phoned Todd Greenberg. It had been nearly five months since the funeral.

"Todd, this is Ashley Hamilton."

"How are you?" asked Todd, somewhat surprised by the sudden call.

"I'm fine but these lawsuits are killing Marc."

"I know. It's a real mess. They're even suing my father's estate! I'm sorry Dr. Hamilton is taking it so hard."

"Todd, I have an idea. If you'll help, it just might work."

"Sure. I know how much Dad cared about both of you. What can I do?"

"He's going to the office early tomorrow and should be home at about two o'clock. Come over and have lunch with me, say about noon, and I'll explain then."

"I'll be there," said Todd.

Marc got home at 2:15 PM. Ashley met him at the door. "Honey, I have a surprise for you. Todd Greenberg is here to visit with us," she said.

"No! Please! I don't want to see anyone. You know..." He didn't have a chance to finish.

"Hi, Dr. Hamilton," said Todd. I hadn't heard from you and came by just to say hello."

"Oh, hi, Todd. I'm sorry but this isn't..." He was again interrupted by Todd.

"So... how are things going?"

"Lousy, Todd. They hate me. They're out to get me. If Alcott couldn't, my own patients will. My practice has turned to shit... And you ask..."

"So, Dr. Hamilton, what the hell are you doing about it? Crying in your beer?"

"Why you stupid..." started Marc.

"Why don't you get up off your ass and fight?"

"Fight? Ha! That must be some joke," said Marc sarcastically.

"No joke, Dr. Hamilton. No sir, it's no joke at all. What do you think my father would have done? I'll tell you. He would have fought like hell! He would have pissed on the FDA and the lawyers. He knew he was right and he knew who he was. He's dead but you're not! You can change public opinion. You have the power to do almost anything you want. Dr. Hamilton, if you let my father's murder have no meaning, then that will be your crime!" Todd was angry for real. "And believe me, I'll never let you forget it!"

There was dead silence. Marc sat down and stared at the floor. Ashley was watching his every action. Todd started for the door. She held her breath.

"No! Wait!" said Marc. "Todd, I'm sorry. You're right... Just give me a few days to think this through... You and Ashley are right. I won't let them get away with destroying me. And Todd, there was never a man I respected more than your father. I promise you, I won't let them destroy everything he worked for. I'm not going to let them forget Allen Greenberg. I swear it!"

It worked! He got busy. He started making plans and he became more involved again with his practice. His new exuberance became infectious. Slowly patients returned, and when they asked about the silicone implant he spent time with them, explained and told the truth. That was what Allen would have done. He stopped thinking of the suits as personal attacks.

They weren't. It was the product of frightened and angry patients being exploited by greedy lawyers.

Gradually his confidence in himself returned. He started making plans for a new research project, a new implant, one without the silicone gel, without the stigma that the FDA and media had created. Ashley saw his revitalization. She saw the old Marc being reconstructed before her eyes. She had saved him from himself and Marc knew it. From this adversity their love for one another matured into something more, an indestructible bond that would last a lifetime.

* * * * *

Early in 1996 the Global Settlement was still up in the air. Although the suits continued, at last Marc could take it in stride. Now he had better things to think about.

It was the annual meeting of the National Plastic Surgery Society in Los Angeles. Marc was presenting a paper based on five years of research. The title of the paper was *The Breast Implant of the Future*. He was at the podium and Ashley was sitting proudly in the audience.

> ... and in conclusion, the implant of the future will be nonreactive with human tissues, more durable, more transparent to x-rays and will thus avoid masking the possibility of breast tumors. It will be aesthetically the most perfect breast implant yet created. The new silicon *shell with a* triglyceride *filler will be one of the major advances of this decade. As we enter the twenty-first century the breast implant will have a rebirth, free of any stigma and ready to meet aesthetic*

and reconstructive challenges and the demands of women the world over. Augmentation mammaplasty will continue its role in the improvement of the quality of life.

Epilogue

Vicky's firm had their first big win against Alcott Laboratories with the 1991 case. The fifty-eight year old plaintiff who complained of having developed rheumatoid arthritis following augmentation mammaplasties with silicone breast implants won the unheard of sum of $7,000,000 with the punitive damages. It was a tough fight. Vicky's firm was good. They were able to get expert witnesses who were willing to testify to anything for money. Actually it was the exposure of the memo that was the major factor in the loss for Alcott. "...kill the rats and don't tell the doctors..." was a phrase repeated over and over again until it echoed in the mind of every juror.

Now Vicky was no longer afraid of scientific data destroying her cases. Allen Greenberg was dead. His voice could have been a genuine threat. His student and protégé, Marc Hamilton, had the knowledge to hurt her but he was emotionally shattered. Even if he recovered, she knew that she could rebut any testimony he might give. She had proved that she could hire doctors who would prostitute themselves and say whatever she wanted. She had caught the brass ring. It was perfect... almost perfect.

In March 1996, an attorney for one of the largest malpractice insurance companies made a connection with a United States Senator. Through him, he learned that Roland Massad, the infamous consumer advocate, had been having discussions with Commissioner Wade Messerman regarding the current silicone implant controversy. Massad had been personally responsible for the destruction of several industries and had been a real pain in the ass for many major Washington lobbyists. He was thoroughly in favor of the FDA's position in the silicone issue. Of course he denied that his wife's being a prominent trial lawyer had any influence in his complete support of the agency.

The senator said that Massad's apparent involvement had "a rotten odor" and that Capitol Hill was buzzing about a conflict of interests. Further, he said that Messerman didn't have "a chance in hell" of being appointed Surgeon General. He had antagonized too many influential people. Messerman's association with Massad proved to be a major blunder. "Washington isn't having any of that crap, and I seriously doubt that Mr. Messerman will be able to continue as Commissioner of the FDA," said the senator.

It was April 1996. Vicky was working on the closing argument for one of her biggest cases when her secretary, Nancy, interrupted her. "Ms. Lange, it's an overseas call."

"Overseas? Who is it?"

"He wouldn't say. He insisted on speaking with you personally. Do you want to take it?"

"Hmm... okay. Thanks." She picked up the phone. "Hello?"

"Well, hello, Ms. Lange. It's been a long time." Her eyes opened wide with fear.

"Who is this?"

"Come on, Ms. Lange. You couldn't have forgotten my voice. We spoke together often enough a few years ago." Her face was flushed with anger as she tightened her grip on the phone. Through her clenched teeth she said,

"I told you never to call me! How dare you!"

"Now, now, Ms. Lange. Temper, temper."

"What do you want?" she asked with hostility.

"Congratulations on the Robinson case. Seven million sounds very impressive."

"Thanks! So?"

"Well, I think you'll agree that I was instrumental in achieving that for you. I thought you wouldn't mind sharing some of it... say two million?"

"You fucking sonofabitch! We had a deal! You got two hundred thousand and that's it!"

"Let's say I feel that I deserve a bonus."

"Piss on you!"

"Vicky, please. This is only business. Don't take it so personally."

"If you think I'm giving you another dime, you're crazy!"

"Vicky, be reasonable. I did Greenberg for you so he couldn't refute your witnesses."

"Yeah! And you fucked up with Hamilton and sweet Ashley!"

"Vicky, it's not fair of you to blame me for that. I sent my two best men to their home. It was going to be clean as a whistle! How was I to know that the fucking French police would warn the Houston cops? I'd call it an unfortunate turn of events. But it doesn't look as though you suffered any because of that."

"That "unfortunate turn of events," as you call it, means that those two still have factual knowledge..."

"Well, it seems that it made no difference in the Robinson case. I think you owe me! I think you owe me big!"

"And if I say NO?"

"That would be very stupid and I know that you're much too smart for that. Do you think that I haven't protected myself? Listen... this is my insurance..." He held the receiver to the tape recorder... *Vicky, be reasonable. I did Greenberg for you...*

"God damn you! You're recording this! You stupid sonofabitch, don't you realize that you're putting yourself in jeopardy?"

"I don't think so, my dear. Write this down. Wire the funds to account #17106-14-B-18, Banko do Brazil, Rio de Janeiro. I'm in no great rush. Ten days will be fine. By the way, I'm married now to a beautiful Brazilian citizen. I guess you know that makes me a citizen of Brazil too... Vicky, I can't be extradited from Brazil! Besides there's no way anyone could find me, just in case you have any of your usual ideas." There was silence at the Houston end. "Vicky, are you still there?"

"Okay, ten days but never again! Do you hear me? Never!"

"Well, as I see it we're going to have a long and profitable relationship. You don't have to worry about me, Vicky. I'll always be reasonable... as long as you play fair with me. Well, again, congratulations. Keep up the good work."

Earl Conners laughed as he hung up the phone. He knew he had her. She had no way out!

About the Author

Donald Raymond Klein, M.D., F.A.C.S., retired from his thirty-year Plastic and Reconstructive Surgery practice in Dallas, Texas, in 1995. He is a member of numerous professional organizations and founding member of the American Society for Aesthetic Plastic Surgery, Inc.

His educational background includes a B.S. degree from Western Reserve University in Cleveland, Ohio; an M.D. degree from the Ohio State University College of Medicine, where he was a member of Phi Society; and internship at St. Luke's Hospital in Cleveland, Ohio. He has served residencies in general and plastic surgery at Baylor University Medical Center in Dallas.

He served in the U.S. Navy as a Lt. Commander in the Department of Plastic and Reconstructive Surgery at St. Albans Naval Hospital, Long Island, New York.

Dr. Klein has published many professional articles and papers on various topics of plastic surgery. *Implant* is his first novel.